The Archivist

"Martha Cooley has given us something valuable and rare — a thoughtful and well-written first novel, suffused with intellectual and moral integrity. . . . Cooley is an accomplished stylist — there's scarcely a graceless or unintelligent sentence in the book — and a subtle chronicler of the inner life. . . . *The Archivist* treats serious questions in a humane and passionate manner, and leaves one thinking about these questions long after one has read the last page."
                                  — Brian Morton, *New York Times Book Review*

"*The Archivist* is many things: a speculative academic mystery; a meditation on obsession; a study of madness; a soliloquy to solitude. Cooley weaves all these genres together with nary a dropped stitch."
                                  — Miranda Schwartz, *Hungry Mind Review*

"An engrossing, ambitious debut about love, art, and insanity. . . . Cooley brilliantly employs Eliot's poetry and troubled biography as a window into Matt's tragic past."   — Megan Harlan, *Entertainment Weekly*

"A solid accomplishment. . . . Martha Cooley has looked back in time with a steady, penetrating gaze. . . . Fans of literary fiction will want to make the acquaintance of the talented Ms. Cooley."
                                  — Adam Begley, *New York Observer*

"Sublime . . . supremely satisfying. . . . As Cooley's characters relate to Eliot's verse, it comes alive, igniting their passion and touching their troubled souls."   — Stephanie Barna, *Charleston City Paper*

"An imaginative and compassionate novel . . . that probes complex questions — about love, religious faith, and the conflict between a writer's desire for privacy and the reader's hunger for revelations."
                                  — Merle Rubin, *Christian Science Monitor*

The Archivist

A NOVEL

MARTHA COOLEY

LITTLE, BROWN AND COMPANY

Boston   New York   London

Originally published in hardcover by Little, Brown and Company, 1998
First Back Bay paperback edition, 1999

This story is a work of fiction. The characters are all fictitious except for the poet T. S. Eliot, his first wife, and his friend Emily Hale. In real life, Hale and Eliot wrote one another many letters, and Hale bequeathed Eliot's side of their correspondence to Princeton University, where it is currently sequestered. Any resemblance by any other characters in this story to actual persons, living or dead, is entirely coincidental. The other characters, locations, events, and dialogue are all the product of the author's imagination.

The author is indebted to Lyndall Gordon for her masterful two-volume biography of T. S. Eliot.

Acknowledgments of permission to reprint previously copyrighted material appear on page 327.

Library of Congress Cataloging-in-Publication Data
Cooley, Martha.
    The archivist : a novel / Martha Cooley. — 1st ed.
        p.   cm.
    ISBN 0-316-15872-0 (hc)   0-316-15846-1 (pb)
    I. Title.
PS3553.05646A87   1998
813'.54 — dc21   97-38385

10 9 8 7 6 5 4 3 2 1

MV-NY

PRINTED IN THE UNITED STATES OF AMERICA

In memory of my grandmother,

ELEANOR STROTHER COOLEY

(1886–1986),

who read me poems

I keep my countenance,
I remain self-possessed
Except when a street piano, mechanical and tired
Reiterates some worn-out common song
With the smell of hyacinths across the garden
Recalling things that other people have desired.
Are these ideas right or wrong?

T. S. ELIOT
"Portrait of a Lady"

One

WITH A LITTLE EFFORT, anything can be shown to connect with anything else: existence is infinitely cross-referenced. And everything has more than one definition. A cat is a mammal, a narcissist, a companion, a riddle.

I've been reading T. S. Eliot again, the nice hardback edition of his poems that Roberta gave me before she left. I'd almost forgotten how heady Eliot is, how much thinking he crowds into "Four Quartets":

> The knowledge imposes a pattern, and falsifies,
> For the pattern is new in every moment

I cannot imagine what Vivienne Eliot must've thought when she read those lines. Locked away in Northumberland House, listening to German bombs dropping on London, waiting in vain for her husband to take her home.

Hearing his poems in her head. Alone, listening, forced to reconsider everything.

> What is that sound high in the air

> London Bridge is falling down falling down falling down

Roberta, too, will reconsider. She'll be stunned, of course, when she hears the news about the Hale bequest. But after she mulls it over, the whole thing won't seem so astonishing. I think she'll appreciate my motives even if she can't condone them.

I picture her in her kitchen, the new poems spread out on her table. By now she's probably learned them all by heart — or the best parts, anyway. I wonder what they'll prompt. More of her own, I trust; else why read Eliot — or anyone else?

We shall see.

ALTHOUGH I'VE ALWAYS BEEN CALLED MATT, my first name isn't Matthew but Matthias: after the disciple who replaced Judas Iscariot. By the time I was four, I knew a great deal about my namesake. More than once my mother read to me, from the New Testament, the story of how Matthias had been chosen by lot to take the place of dreadful Judas. Listening, I felt a large and frightened sympathy for my predecessor. No doubt a dark aura hung over Judas's chair — something like the pervasive, bitter odor of Pall Malls in my father's corner of the sofa.

As far as my mother was concerned, the lot of Matthias was the unquestionable outcome of an activity that seemed capricious to me: a stone-toss by the disciples. I tried with difficulty to picture a dozen men dressed in dust-colored robes and sandals, playing a child's game. One of the Twelve had to carry on, my mother explained, after Judas had perpetrated his evil. The seat couldn't be left empty. Hence Matthias: the Lord's servants had pitched their stones, and his had traveled the farthest.

So much for names. To the first-year students at the university where I work, I am merely Mr. Lane, the grey-mustached warden of the obscure Mason Room. But to graduate students I am something like a god, indispensable and unavoidable, keeper of countless objects of desire. And in reality? — in reality I'm the

5

archivist at one of America's most prestigious institutions of higher learning, where I oversee a collection of rare books and manuscripts, the notes and letters of dead writers and other *prominenti*, and boxes of miscellany donated by eccentric graduates. This archive, housed in a quiet wing of the main library, is among the finest anywhere; and I am its guardian.

I assumed my post in 1965, the year T. S. Eliot and my wife Judith died, and since then I've inhabited a secure realm. Of course, there have been the predictable encroachments of microfiche, computers, fax machines . . . I make use of these things, in fact I find them entertaining; but they have nothing to do with the life of the mind. The genuine scholars, those for whom books are nearly everything, pay little attention to the junior librarians with their keyboard fixations. The real scholars come to me. In this part of the library, I alone know where everything is. I have memorized the stacks and shelves and drawers, I could find books in the dark: by their broken spines, their covers' textures, their heft in my hand.

My work has always satisfied me. When scholars ask me about an unusual book that I haven't seen before, I experience an almost physical pleasure. It's as if I'm a boy again, scavenger-hunting. When I'm on the trail alone, sure of my ability to find what I'm looking for, I experience my rewards.

Naturally there are frustrations, when things are misplaced or my time is wasted. I'm rough on pseudo-scholars, but I like assisting anyone who's serious — even novices who can barely use the card catalogue. I look for the sign of real intention, that hunger which comes over a person's face when he really needs to find something in print. Except for a few of the oldest and most fragile manuscripts, I allow the collection to be read and used by anyone who passes my inspection. I don't hoard the treasure.

Materials not open to the public, however, are another story. Now and then some unscrupulous researcher will ask for a "quick look" at items that remain under lock and key until a specified date. This pushiness instantly annoys me, though it no longer surprises me. With such researchers I assume a weary, antagonized look as I explain that certain bequests arrive with clear restrictions on accessibility. Violating those limits is a form of grave-robbing. Yes: the images that come to me are those of exhumation, the unearthing of something meant to lie fallow — something that will appear waxy and lifeless if brought to light too soon.

Of course I don't put it in just those terms. But the message gets across to anyone who thinks I'll pick up the shovel and dig for him.

I was set on edge, then, when last spring a young woman approached me about some letters of T. S. Eliot.

I want, said this woman in a tone neither loud nor soft but direct, to read the Emily Hale letters.

Had I not looked straight at her, I'm sure nothing would've ensued. But I stared at this woman, and in her eyes, which were large and curiously colored — a moss-grey shade, lustrous — I could see the genuine intention I've never been able to ignore.

There was something else. Her eyes summoned for me that strangely evocative line from Eliot's poem "Usk": *Where the grey light meets the green air.* And Judith, whom I'd buried two decades earlier. Since my wife's death I had encountered no one who reminded me of her in any way.

Glance aside — I heard the poem now as if it were being read to me — *do not spell old enchantments. Let them sleep.*

The young woman stood very still, waiting, her face a question.

The answer, I said aloud to her, is no.

7

M Y WORK IS WHATEVER I WANT IT TO BE, and I report to no one regularly. The head librarian — the man in charge of the University's entire collection — is a figurehead, well-to-do and poorly read, with whom I have only perfunctory contact. His deputy is Edith Bearden, who supervises several junior librarians. Once a week, over lunch, Edith and I trade news or solicit one another's advice on technical matters. We've always gotten along, and after all these years we know each other reasonably well. When I'm withdrawn, which I suppose I often am, she doesn't pull at me. But when she needs my help or wants my company (for libraries can be lonely), she's not afraid to break into one of my unresponsive moods. Hers is the only lasting friendship I've known, and I'm grateful for it.

Each month I supply the library's Board with a brief summary of the activities in my wing. I prepare these reports in my office, which adjoins the Mason Room. Normally I leave the connecting door open so I can see who comes in and out. On busy days the receptionist admits around twenty people; on quiet days we have only a handful of visitors, and peace reigns.

During those calm days I become a literal bookkeeper. First I return calls and answer correspondence from other archivists, and then I catalogue new acquisitions. After that, I check the drawers containing oversized materials and generally see that everything is as it should be. I need those hours of silent physical labor, when I am alone with the collection and can experience it in its entirety. It's become almost a living thing for me. The bound books and loose-leaf manuscripts and files of letters and photos are a many-voiced convocation I attend as a kind of permanent host. Whenever I can, I read. Familiarity with the collection is my first obligation.

When I was a child, I had dozens of books. My father built me a bookcase for my tenth birthday. It ran the length of one of my bedroom walls, and I prized it almost as much as the books I arranged neatly on its three shelves. I employed a very simple cataloguing method — alphabetization of titles, which meant that my Bible sat between *Babar* and *Boats Under Bridges,* a story about the difficult life of a New York harbor tugboat operator. I remember my mother expressing dismay at this arrangement. As a devout Presbyterian, she felt that the sacred Book should not be tossed in with profane paperbacks, and she urged me to keep my Bible next to my bed. It was her desire that I read it nightly and attend church each week with her, duties I fought then and have never undertaken since.

My mother was an unhappy woman, and unhealthy too — terribly overweight and easily agitated by small things. She entered marriage with few established friendships, and as my father discouraged the formation of new ones, she became something of a recluse. Gradually, as I was growing up, she isolated herself from the people in our neighborhood in Washington Heights who might have helped her. Eunice Carey, who had an antique toy train set I coveted, and Betty Keep, a cheery widow I used to accompany on long rambles through the Cloisters — these were women who wished my mother well and who felt sorry for me; I was, after all, the only child of an irascible accountant and a housewife who quoted the Bible a little too frequently. By the time I was twelve, my mother had ceased even the pretext of a social life for the family. And as both sets of grandparents were long dead and neither of my parents had siblings, I was effectively cut off from a community of adults.

Each Friday night my father satisfied his own needs for company by going to a bar around the corner from his office near Herald Square. There he would drink for a few hours with other dissatisfied husbands, finally wending his way home at around eight o'clock, smelling of smoke and scotch. My mother and I would watch him descend from the heights of his drink-induced good humor to the foul mood that typically enshrouded him. He would bark orders at my mother, who lumbered anxiously from table to kitchen to fetch him extra water or more salt, and in my direction he would level a barrage of questions about my performance at school that week.

Fortunately I was a good student. Books were my refuge; I made friends, but often they interested me less than books. And at home, in the face of my mother's perpetual anxiety and my father's cantankerousness, I retreated into my small bedroom, where my books awaited me, reliably patient and tolerant. Now and then my father would engage me in conversation about a story I was reading, or my mother would read aloud a poem by Wordsworth or Blake. Those interludes I remember with intense clarity. Everything else from that time feels like a bruise feels when pressed: painful in a dull, unmemorable way.

Judith used to say I became an archivist to spite my parents. I suppose that's partly true. I knew my father wanted me to go into a more lucrative line of work, and my mother was eager for me to become a teacher or (better yet) a pastor — neither of which I had any intention of doing. But the truth of my choice ran deeper. Having so few emotional resources to spare after wasting them on a soured marriage, my parents could make no hard claims on my future. That it should include higher education was perhaps the only point on which we three were in unspoken agreement. Even on this issue, though, there was friction. My father was proud of my academic competence but uneasy about my lack of interest in business, and my mother was concerned about my spiritual life, unsupported as it was by any church. Neurotic and awkward and ailing, she still managed to convince herself of the necessity of a spiritual community, and she went to church each week until she became bedridden. She could never accept my solitariness, though I'd learned it from her.

On the day I entered college, I realized in a bitter flash that I owed my parents nothing. I believed, however, that I owed something to books, which had kept me going throughout my least happy stretches, and this belief eventually outweighed all other considerations. After a half-dozen years of work in bookstores, I enrolled in graduate school and began the study of library science.

I saw myself then, and still do, as inheritor of a rich tradition, one that straddles the line between mind and spirit. The great librarians have all been religious men — monks, priests, rabbis — and the stewardship of books is an act of homage and faith. Even Thomas Jefferson, that most rational and ingenious of librarians, revered what he called the Infinite Power. It's impossible to be a keeper of books and not feel a gratitude that extends to something beyond the intellects that created them — to a greater Mind, beneficent and lively and inconceivably large, which urges reading and writing. Judith used to complain that libraries are full of too many false, banal books — and she was right, of course, though it's never bothered me. A library is meant to be orderly, not pure.

In 1939, when I was twenty-one, my father and I made our first and only trip together. We took the train down to Washington. My mother was quite ill, and my father (normally no traveler) wanted to get away from the apartment. He proposed that my college graduation present be a visit to the capital. I had been there

11

on a school trip and had no interest in the sights, but I accepted the invitation eagerly. I wanted to explore the Library of Congress.

As I'd anticipated, my father quickly tired of sight-seeing. By the time we reached Capitol Hill he was bored, and he left to seek out a bar on Pennsylvania Avenue. Alone and happy, I entered the library's cool foyer. At college I'd read many descriptions of the vast collection, but I was unprepared for the beauty of the building itself — its vaulted ceilings and marble floors, its magnificent circular reading room fitted with mahogany benches, rows of soft reading lamps, and heavy brass-trimmed doors that kept out all noise. I walked around the upper gallery, reading the inscriptions that ring the second-story walls just below the ceiling, and I knew then that eventually I would claim such a place as my home.

My mother died that year, my father four years later, in 1943. A few months after his death, I went back to Washington to see the library again. This time I took color photographs, explored the stacks, and talked at length with the librarians. I also wrote each of the wall inscriptions on note cards. When I returned to New York, I bought a leather binder and made myself a scrapbook of the photos and cards.

Judith knew as no one else did what libraries meant to me. The scrapbook was among the first of my possessions I showed her, not long after we met. My memory holds an indelible image of Judith turning that book's pages, reading the inscriptions aloud. Literate as she was, she identified most of the authors. Then she read her favorite inscription: *The True Shekinah Is Man.* It came, she said, from the Kabbalah — the writings of Jewish mystics.

I asked her to explain the concept of *shekinah*. As she spoke about the Trees of Life and Death, I watched her full, mobile mouth, her long-fingered hands and slender arms, the shadows at her collarbones. Her entire body was suddenly an astonishing surprise to me. I can clearly remember how she looked up from the book's pages, her gaze locking with mine. I knew unconsciously, as one senses a cry before hearing it, that my life was going to be changed.

Crossing the room, I circled her shoulders with my arms. Her hands tightened at my back as we held each other for the first time, swaying back and forth, our lips skimming each other's cheeks and then meeting, lightly at first, my teeth on her tongue gently pulling and being pulled. I had experienced nothing so urgent and terrifying as the sound of my pulse at that instant, the blood-driven beat of my heart.

J UDITH WAS TALL — nearly as tall as I am: six feet —
and slender, with elegant hands, short dark hair, a long
waist and narrow hips, a beautifully shaped backside,
prominent collarbones and kneecaps, broad feet. Her face was
slightly olive in tone, its skin supple and shiny. Her eyes were
grey-green, almond-shaped, and widely set beneath thin dark
brows. She moved with a fluid, graceful ease that attracted notice.

We used to read T. S. Eliot aloud. For utterly different reasons, we were among his admirers. *Time the destroyer is time the
preserver* — we loved those impressive contradictions of Eliot's,
that authoritative way he had of stating a paradox. Perhaps too
tidy, too controlled? Yet he did know something about destroying
and preserving; and about time.

Judith said she read Eliot because he understood how the sacred resides in time, *is* time. For me, reading his work is like trying to intercept a butterfly. It comes so close you can see its
markings, the luminous wings, and then as you extend a hand it's
gone — hidden among other flickering objects of consciousness.
There's a pleasure in this approximation, I suppose, and even in
the failure to apprehend. I don't mind the obscurity of Eliot's
verse. (What good, after all, is an insect pinned on velvet, gor-
geous but dead?)

In the thirties and forties, living in London, Eliot wrote about a thousand letters to a woman named Emily Hale, an American he had known since adolescence. But after his wife Vivienne died in 1947 and he was freed from the nightmare of his failed marriage, he repudiated Emily Hale. He felt, he wrote her, as if something in him had frozen and couldn't be revived.

Vivienne Eliot had spent the final decade of her life locked up in a sanitorium in London — a high-walled institution from which she made several desperate but unsuccessful attempts to flee. Eliot chose never to visit her there. Perhaps she wrote to him, pleading, though that is doubtful. She must have suspected his role in having her committed, but she didn't cease loving him, directing toward him the same intense, narcissistic heat that had driven him away. She was unbalanced but extremely perceptive, as people on the borders of sanity tend to be, and she knew things about Eliot — things he could communicate to no one, things transmitted obliquely in his poems, the objects of guesswork for his readers. Not acts but rather emotional capacities — dark, angry, punishing tendencies that the rising star of modernist verse couldn't afford to expose.

Beneath the mask of the penitent, Eliot was a hugely ambitious man. He knew that with her madness, his wife could decimate all his possibilities. Although he figured out how to protect himself from her, the stain of their relationship lingered, ineradicable. He and she were too intimately bound up in each other's terrors to disengage, even with the help of forced separation. ("As to Tom's *mind*," Vivienne wrote to a friend shortly before her lockup, "I am his mind.")

From such possession he sought exorcism — and achieved it. But it had to be paid for, and Emily Hale was sacrificed along the way. After Vivienne's death, Eliot pulled back. He visited Emily only a few more times, and his letters were infrequent and perfunctory. She never understood, never got over the shock of repudiation. Like Eliot she was a master concealer; she didn't reveal the extent of the damage she had sustained. There was a brief hospitalization, in the fifties, for "nervous exhaustion," but no other visible evidence. She resigned herself to the unfathomable. In the place within her where rage might have been, there was a desolation she could not share even with old friends. (In one letter to a woman she'd known for years, she referred to a "miscarriage" — and not a physical one — which was as close as she could come to the truth of her aborted relations with Eliot.)

Vivienne the hysteric had tried, even at the end, to break out. Emily, more stable and less imaginative, chose convention: the silence of the spinster, the relief of her acting and teaching careers, the solace of memory. But Emily was not without her own implacable sense of what must be done. In 1957, she took it upon herself to amass all her letters from him and deposit them — with strict instructions that they were to be sequestered until 2020 — in the library of a major American university. Eliot, furious, cut off all communication. In 1963, she wrote him a short, impressively honest letter pointing out the necessity of her action and reminding him of the future — not theirs but that of his work. Scholars would want to read her letters to him as well as his to her, she said; their twenty-year correspondence chronicled important events, ideas, feelings. Wouldn't it make sense for him to give her letters to the same institution that had received her bequest?

Eliot did not approve, would not respond. But Emily had already made her move. His side of the correspondence had arrived at the library, I later learned, in five identical grey cardboard boxes tightly bound with white string. My predecessor — by all accounts a highly disorganized man — evidently failed to decide what to do with this gift from Miss Hale. He simply dumped the lot into one large carton, where they lay jumbled for eight years. When I arrived on the scene, I made it my business to provide order where there was none.

JUDITH AND I WERE MARRIED in Manhattan on V-E Day. We were giddy with excitement, convinced that the confetti on the sidewalks had been strewn around as much for us as for the war's end. We were each twenty-seven years old and had known one another for twelve weeks. I'd escaped military service because of a lower-back condition; Judith had spent the war years in a West Side walk-up, writing poetry and working as a secretary. We'd met in a bar.

Twelve weeks. It now seems such a short stretch of time — dangerously short, really. Yet in my memory those weeks are like a honeycomb in a jar: the clustered days, suspended in an amber sweetness, drenched and happy . . .

What did I notice about her? Judith resembled no one else I knew. My first impression was of quickness. She had a wonderfully agile, skeptical intelligence, and a certain aggressiveness — that of someone eager to engage new ideas and willing to be unsettled. Judith was less interested in Truth than in truths, and she trusted a good argument to flush them out. Right away I felt, in her company, the relief that comes when caution is unnecessary: when it is not merely possible but desirable to expose what one thinks.

She was my only genuine partner in amusement. My father had a dry, vinegary laugh; my mother's was a nervous trill, unpleasant and sad. In college my acquaintances were amusing in the wry, detached manner of our generation. Judith was the only person who could make me laugh hard at literally nothing. She had a way of becoming suddenly, ferociously funny, and sometimes giddy and out of control, like a small child.

She loved Manhattan, and she knew it well. Among my strongest memories are our long walks, hand in hand, up and down and across the city. She liked to eat while walking — ice cream in summer, hot chestnuts in winter, apples in autumn and spring. The scent of apple on her fingertips . . .

Our long strides were evenly matched. Judith walked with purpose, deftly circumnavigating stragglers, maneuvering us through Fifth Avenue crowds, jaywalking across busy intersections. Sometimes she put her arm around my waist as we walked, and this gesture felt protective as well as affectionate, as if she were assuming responsibility for my well-being.

I doubt she knew then how much I needed to feel safe, or how deeply this need disturbed me.

Their fear of fear and frenzy, their fear of possession, of belonging to another . . . Eliot wrote of the terrors of old men, but they were mine also.

In her lovemaking Judith was candid and unpredictable. With other women I'd revealed only a self I could risk showing, polite and restrained; Judith elicited from me other selves, more demanding but also more giving. She loved me hard, without any false promising; wordlessly she urged me to learn how to please not only her but myself. Though I couldn't admit it, the force of our intimacy frightened me. I struggled to stay open, waiting for something in me to give way, to allow me to love my wife unhesitatingly.

There were hints of trouble. Now and then, while we were talking, Judith would grow quiet and still. She wasn't daydreaming; she would sit for a minute in a state of tense vigilance, as if awaiting news that might be disturbing. Then, just as suddenly, she'd become animated again. I remember once coming home in mid-afternoon to find her curled up in my bed. Her eyes were red-rimmed; she'd obviously been crying. When I asked her what was wrong, she shrugged at first. Then she picked up a magazine that lay on my bedside table — one of those small-circulation literary journals that feature the work of young poets. She opened it to a poem by LeRoi Jones, a Beat writer.

I sat next to her on the bed and asked if she'd mind reading some of the poem aloud. Judith stared at the page, and I assumed she was trying to decide which lines to share with me.

No light under my fingers, she read, so softly I could barely hear her. Then she stopped.

I picked up the journal and read the poem to myself. It was called "The Death of Nick Charles," and it was long. I can't remember all of it, but a few lines return to me:

> *Emotion. Words.*
> *Waste. No clear delight.*
> *No light under my fingers. The room, The*
> *walls, silent & deadly. Not*
> *Music.*

The poem had a strange starkness, at once alienating and enthralling. I'd never read anything like it. I looked over at Judith, whose eyes were closed. Her eyelids' skin was purplish-pink, the color of vulnerability. I had no idea what to do. The experience reminded me eerily of times when my mother had cried, recounting her nightmares to me, and I could not console her.

Judith said nothing more. Uncomprehending and shaken, I climbed into the bed and held her — conscious of the silence that gripped us both, but incapable of breaking its embrace.

*   *   *

Why, I sometimes wonder, did Judith and I marry so quickly? Marriage wasn't a state either of us had sought. We'd both had a few brief romances, more friendly than ardent, in our early twenties, along with a handful of purely physical liaisons. Yet none of these experiences had left either of us feeling the need for a permanent companion. In our basic natures, we were reclusive.

Judith did have acquaintances she saw occasionally, and a few closer friends — women she'd known in college, all of whom had moved out of the city. She seldom communicated with them. Like me, she allowed intimacy only a small entrance; she knew how to bar intrusions. But Judith didn't like to be alone quite as much as I did.

In her casual dealings with people, she impressed me. Though she didn't have what could be called an arresting presence, she was a woman one noticed, whose attractiveness moved steadily into focus. People listened to her. She liked fierce literary or political discussion, and she would argue with someone she barely knew if the issue mattered to her. Yet considering her quick-wittedness, Judith was at times oddly insensitive to irony. She claimed to be bored by it. Once she cited Kierkegaard's argument that irony ends up destroying itself, but I think her rejection of it had deeper roots — in an instinctive ethic of engagement, in some deeply felt obligation not to step to one side of important questions.

Right from the start I knew that I understood my wife incompletely, partially. Yet there was no reason, I told myself, to be afraid of what eluded me. Gradually I would discover more of Judith, and she of me.

This much I would've said, had I been asked. Yet there were things I couldn't acknowledge. Her brief withdrawals, the vacancy that sometimes glazed her expression — these disturbed

21

me profoundly, and I had no words for my disturbance. I consigned it to the realm of silence.

On our wedding night Judith and I lay on our bed, feet on the footpost, drinking champagne and reading Mallarmé poems aloud in awful French until finally we both passed out. I remember awaking the next morning, groggy, to discover that Judith had already risen. She was in the kitchen in her robe, fixing us breakfast. As I watched her bend over the skillet, whisking eggs, I saw that my existence was bounded by that of another person; and I was full of awe, and something like dread.

We were together for fourteen years, and apart for six; and then she was gone.

What would she be like now? If she had overcome her demons, would I really have managed to vanquish mine?

Thoughts of a dry brain, said Eliot, *in a dry season.*

Judith's been gone for so long. She began leaving many years before her death, in fact. And I had a hand in her departure. I shouldn't have tried to take her God from her — the passionate, demanding God of the Old Testament, the God who spoke to the desert tribes as if they were his children or his lovers, capable of wounding him as much as he could hurt them. I found this God unacceptably proximate. The One I had known all my life was believable in direct proportion to the distance He took from all the particulars of my life; His force as well as my faith lay in this remove. But Judith had tried to set up her Jewish faith like a home, and over time I chipped away at it until finally there was no place for her to go.

The doctors at Hayden may have erred about the details of her condition. They need their labels, their certainties. What are depression and psychosis, after all, but lapses from realism? And what's that? But the doctors were right about the general crisis.

An insufficient God is better than no God at all.

T HE YOUNG WOMAN'S NAME was Roberta Spire. I discovered her identity when she returned, a few days after our initial encounter, to speak with me again. Immersed in cataloguing some new acquisitions for the main library, I was startled to look up and find her in front of me.

"Hello," she said.

It took me a moment to place her. She wore her hair, which had been loose around her shoulders when I first met her, in a tight knot that accented her jawline and gave her the air of someone older. I'd put her in her mid-twenties, but she now looked closer to thirty.

"Hello," I returned.

"I would like to see any letters written by T. S. Eliot to his family or friends during the period from 1911 to 1914," she said. She had a nicely modulated voice and fine enunciation. Clear speech is compelling, and I noticed hers.

"Which part of that period are you more interested in — his time in Paris or the return to Cambridge?" I asked.

"Both," she said.

"Why?" I said.

"A number of good reasons," she shot back, cleanly. There was no hint of a whine in her voice. A decent volley, I thought, but I'd make her run for the next one.

"Who was he corresponding with during that time?" I asked. I knew, and I suspected she knew I did, but I wanted to see her reaction.

"Apart from his mother Charlotte and a few other relations, he wrote fairly often to Conrad Aiken and possibly to Van Wyck Brooks. His Harvard friends. Undoubtedly to others I'm not aware of," she answered.

"Ah," I said, nodding. Then I stood, reaching into my trouser pocket for my keys. She'd done well, displaying both erudition and modesty — a winning combination, yet one she hadn't over-done.

"Your library card," I said. She produced the card quickly. It bore a photo in which her hair was once again loose. Her university code listed her as a graduate student in English literature.

"Roberta Spire," I said. "What sort of name is Spire?"

"It's from Spier," she said. "German. My parents changed it."

"I see," I said, and paused before launching into my caution-ary speech. She watched me closely as I talked.

"Your ability to enter the library will be permanently compro-mised if you break any rules," I said. "I'm taking you into a spe-cial archive. Only a few scholars are admitted there. You understand me?"

"Yes, I do," she said, without a touch of either obsequious-ness or sarcasm. I was expecting one or the other, and the well-maintained evenness of her tone surprised me. I put her card in my breast pocket.

As we walked down the quiet hallway, I could feel a battle of wills take form. She had passed the first test, but I still didn't trust her. I knew she wasn't after any letters to Conrad Aiken. Her high-heeled shoes and my old crepe-soled ones alternated in a loud-soft dialogue that might have been an argument, and though I led the way, I could see her determined walk as clearly as if I stood to one side of us both, watching a clash in the making.

At the door of the Mason Room I stopped abruptly, but she had kept her distance and didn't pile awkwardly into me, as hovering students sometimes do. She stood to one side as I produced my keys and opened both locks on the door.

"The receptionist is at lunch," I said. "Ordinarily she lets people in after I've approved their research requests. Come in. Shut the door hard behind you."

The battle took a turn at this point. It entered a lull. Roberta's object was clearly to throw me off, to fool me into thinking that she would perhaps settle for less than her initial request. We looked together at about a dozen of Eliot's letters — a few written from Paris to Aiken, the rest sent from Harvard to his mother and brother in the Midwest. I was struck by Eliot's descriptions of Paris, the wet dark streets at night, whores in doorways gesturing at him. We read in silence.

Roberta seemed restless. She tapped her heels lightly on the Mason Room's parquet floor. I decided to complicate things. Opening one of the combination-locked cabinets, I produced a surprise, a set of galleys for "The Waste Land." In them Eliot's markings mingled with the printer's in a delightful mash of the poetic and the technical. Leafing through, I pointed to where "extra leading" was scrawled in a rough hand after the ominous "Consider Phlebas." Eliot had edited the line in careful pencil, adding that necessary "once": "Consider Phlebas, who was once handsome and tall as you."

Without taking her eyes off the galleys, Roberta nodded. She smiled now and then as she turned the fragile pages with what I had to admit was real dexterity. Clearly she knew something about old manuscripts. Partway through, she paused and pointed, careful not to touch the print.

"'Those are pearls,'" she read, "'that were his eyes. Look! Here is Belladonna, the Lady of the Rocks, the lady of situations.'"

She turned and gazed at me.

"Do you know what 'Belladonna' means?" she asked. Her voice had lowered slightly.

I am unused to having students quiz me, and her question threw me off.

"Of course," I said. Immediately I regretted my defensive tone.

"Literally it means 'beautiful lady,'" she said, as if I hadn't answered. "Also it's the name of a poisonous plant. Curious, no?"

She was still staring at me, and I knew the time had come to draw the line.

"Listen," I said, "just what do you want? I've shown you some priceless portions of our Eliot collection. You are extremely lucky to have seen these things. I'm sure your work will be better for it."

Her gaze didn't flicker, and I thought I saw the beginnings of a smile at the corners of her mouth.

"I want," she said, "to read the Emily Hale letters."

Thus was our battle formally joined, after diversionary skirmishes.

"Sit down," I said, pointing at the large table in the center of the room. We both sat — on opposite sides, our arms on the smooth surface, our hands crossed in what might have looked to an observer like prayer.

JUDITH AND I SPENT the first few years of our marriage in what I would now call poverty, though at the time I didn't perceive it as such. Our furniture was shabby, but each of us had a desk. Mine, the larger of the two, also served as our dining table. I'd never been a hearty eater; a bowl of soup at lunch and an omelette in the evening was enough for me, and Judith never complained. She did most of the cooking, and she could stretch a small chicken into several meals.

I was attending graduate school in library science, paid for by a small inheritance I'd received upon my father's death. Neither of my parents would have approved of a librarian's degree, but I'd made up my mind, and they weren't around to dissuade me.

Judith worked as a legal secretary for a small midtown firm. My inheritance covered my tuition, and books and food for us both. Judith's salary covered rent. She used her lunch hour as writing time, and sometimes she stayed late to type her poems on the high-quality second sheets of her firm's letterhead. I could always tell when her day had been too busy for a proper lunchbreak: she would come home, find a pen and a pad of paper, and immediately lock herself in our bedroom for an hour, to make up for her lost time.

Judith shared her poems with me reluctantly, and by an unspoken agreement we kept our discussions of them to a minimum. I sensed that she found my comments distracting even when they were praising. Perhaps — no: in all likelihood — she knew what I really thought of her poems. The truth was that while I found them very well crafted, I was unnerved by them.

Many of her poems drew on Old Testament stories and situations. One of them dealt with the seduction and murder of the general of Nebuchadnezzar's army by the biblical Judith. After reading it, I wanted to know why Judith — my Judith — had written a poem about her namesake.

She said she'd wanted to imagine what it would be like to serve God in an extreme way, without any withholding.

For such a risk, God hadn't promised Judith very much in return, I said.

Flesh-and-blood Judith laughed and said my Christianity was showing. But I could tell I'd wounded her. Not long after this incident — which wasn't long after we were married — she told me that I seemed scornful of Judaism. We began arguing.

I don't think I'm scornful, I said. But why is it that for Jews, faith is always so questionable? I can understand doubt, but doesn't Judaism take doubt too far?

Christianity takes grace too far, Judith said. Like it's guaranteed — which it isn't. We're here for the repair of our breach, to restore grace. That's our job. It's pretty natural to have doubts in the face of such a job, isn't it?

It all sounds complicated, I said. Too complicated.

Our argument culminated in an uncomfortable silence. Later, in bed, it was resolved in tenderness. But I knew we were both shaken by it.

When Eliot's "Four Quartets" came out, after the war, Judith devoured it. She would sweep the apartment's splintery floors while reciting her favorite verses aloud: *History may be servitude, his-*

tory may be freedom. I remember reading to her from the fourth quartet:

> *You are not here to verify,*
> *Instruct yourself, or inform curiosity*
> *Or carry report. You are here to kneel*
> *Where prayer has been valid.*

Neither of us read aloud the question and answer that spoke most directly to our condition: *Who then devised the torment?* *Love.*

Perhaps Judith read them later to herself, as I did, and despaired.

S EVERAL LONG MOMENTS PASSED before either Roberta Spire or I spoke. During that time I kept my eyes on the table, to avoid being dragged into a visual tug-of-war with a student whose persistence was beginning to baffle me. Finally I broke the silence.

"Why those letters?"

Her mouth and jaw lost a certain tightness that had constrained them since our meeting, and she sat back in her chair in the attitude of one who has decided that at last some real business can be done. I noticed that she had the same sloping nose and thin brows that had set Judith's face apart from those of the women of my early childhood — my mother, Eunice Carey, Betty Keep. This woman was attractive in an unexpected way, as Judith had been. But unlike my wife, who had always dressed conservatively, Roberta wore a tight-fitting black sweater accented by a red and purple scarf; her pants, too, were black, as were the noisy heels I had heard earlier. Black was a color Judith had never worn, though I had pushed her to; she claimed it washed out her complexion. On a woman, black has a certain undeniable elegance — even when worn aggressively, as Roberta wore it.

"I'm fairly sure those letters will show that Eliot was feeling remorse for the way he treated his first wife, Vivienne. He walked out on her. All his friends kept her away from him, and eventually she was committed to a mental institution."

"I'm acquainted with the facts of Eliot's life," I said.

"Good," she said. "Then I'll cut it short. I want to read the letters because Emily Hale was probably the only person Eliot honestly confided in. With others he equivocated about his feelings for Vivienne. Nobody else really knew the workings of the marriage. But I figure Eliot told Emily the truth."

The quiet room in which we sat seemed to attend to us, as if all its books were appraising this exchange.

"Well," I said, "even assuming your curious theory is correct, what makes you think you have a right to letters that other scholars must wait for decades to see?"

"Because I'm not a scholar. I'm not doing this for a class or a book. I'm not interested in getting something from the letters — some personal gain, acclaim for a brilliant thesis, all that stuff. I'm a poet. I just want to know, for myself, what really went on between Eliot and Hale. What she wanted him to think about, to consider —"

"— to reassess?"

She looked somewhat startled by my interruption. Pausing, she stared at me for a moment; then she continued.

"Yes. I suspect Emily wanted him to rethink why Vivienne went crazy on him. He'd told all his other friends that it was Vivienne's nerves, her crankiness, her interminable complaints that made him leave her. I think it was something much simpler. He hated having to fuck her."

"Excuse me?" I said.

She leaned forward. "Having to fuck her," she repeated evenly. "He felt unclean. Having sex got in the way of having Christ, and Vivienne *was* sex to him, all the physical and emotional mess of it. Emily was a different matter; she was the safe

31

one. Never mind that *she* might have wanted *him* — he told himself that he didn't have to want her, since she wasn't his wife or a mistress, just his very great friend. That meant he could talk openly with her. But you know all this, don't you?"

"Do I?" I asked.

"Yes," she said. "Because you've read the letters."

I became quite unsure of how to proceed. There was a brief silence between us; then Roberta spoke again.

"I can tell," she said. "But I won't. Tell anyone else, I mean."

I raised my brows. "How good of you," I said. "And how can you tell?"

"Your use of the word 'reassess.' It's too precise for you not to have read the letters."

"You're assuming," I said, standing, "that your fantasy about Eliot and Hale is true. Moreover you're allowing your imagination to fuel some rather odd notions about me. I'd say that this conversation has outlived its usefulness. Shall we go?"

She said nothing, though her heels tapped out their stubborn rhythm as I escorted her back to the main library. There I handed her card to her.

"Silence," I began, but she finished the phrase for me.

"The better part of virtue," she said, and was gone.

THE FIRST TIME JUDITH LEFT was in the autumn of the third year of our marriage. I arrived home from an evening class to find a note telling me that she'd gone to Boston to stay with a friend. She would be there indefinitely; I could write her but was not to call. She was sorry, but she felt as if she were coming apart, and she didn't want me to watch.

I was stunned. She might as well have told me that she was going to Antarctica. I sat at my desk, staring at the note and struggling to make sense of it. I remember feeling a peculiar detachment — as if I were someone else, trying to unravel a mystery that was captivating but in which I wasn't personally implicated.

I tried to conjure images of my wife, to reconstruct her behavior over the last few months. Were there clues I'd been blind to, hints of unhappiness or turmoil? All I could think of was her fatigue. She had often seemed tired. The law firm where she worked had been especially busy of late. Yet for the most part she'd maintained her writing schedule, and we'd been leading our usual life: a walk after work, a bottle of wine at supper; reading, listening to the NBC Symphony on the radio. On weekends we would visit a couple of museums or galleries and take a long stroll across Central Park.

There had been two small breaches in the calm of our life together. Judith had wanted me to go with her to a local synagogue for Yom Kippur services, and I had refused. The holiday had fallen on a Thursday, and I felt I couldn't afford to miss my classes. I'd never before accompanied her, and I saw no reason to begin doing so. I assumed she attended holiday services out of habit, as she never went at other times of the year.

She was clearly disappointed, but we didn't speak of my refusal. Several weeks later she expressed a similar disappointment in my indifference to a new British-instigated cease-fire in Palestine. I was cynical about all the antagonists in that part of the world — the Egyptians and other Arabs, the Jews, and especially the British — but she wanted the Jews to prevail, and my lack of heat distressed her. She called me complacent. I tried joking with her, but she wouldn't back off.

Don't you see how important it is to have an actual home? she asked.

Yes, I said, but when different people claim the same place, who can say who's right?

It's obscene that Jews have to fight now for a homeland, she said. This should not be going on. Not after what's already happened.

I didn't give these incidents their due. And although Judith's note disturbed me, I told myself she was overtired and needed to get away for a little while. I read Eliot while awaiting her return — for I was certain she'd come back, and all in one piece. The end of "Little Gidding," in "Four Quartets," seemed to be making a personal promise of redemption, my own and that of my marriage: *All shall be well . . .*

I couldn't acknowledge the fear that stalked me. At the core of my wife's love for me lay a single searing question: *Are you going to show me who you are?* She didn't accuse; the question was a plea. And I had no reply. Love required speech, and beyond a certain point, speech could only be dangerous. Unconsciously I had begun a migration into the realm of silence, and Judith knew — as I did not — what its consequences might be.

She returned the next weekend. She looked haggard, and we spoke little about her departure or her stay in Boston. I told her I was glad to see her, and I took her out for a good dinner — surprised at how glad I really was. I'd thought I was angry, but instead I found that I was shaken. Suddenly I realized that what I'd most wanted, during her week away, was to be left alone, and I had come perilously close to having my wish granted.

ROBERTA CAUGHT UP WITH ME in a hallway near the Mason Room early one morning; on her face was the look of one who'd snagged her prey. After we exchanged perfunctory greetings, she invited me to have breakfast with her. This time I hid my surprise and suggested the cafeteria in the library's basement.

She didn't like that idea. "No. Neutral territory," she said. "Off campus."

Something in her seriousness made me give in. We walked outside and followed a brick path to the campus gates, where she paused before pointing up the street.

"I know a good place a few blocks north," she said.

"Fine," I said. "It's your breakfast. I don't eat this early in the morning."

We entered a small coffee shop after a brisk walk during which neither of us spoke. The place smelled of bacon fat and burnt toast, two of my favorite scents, but I wasn't in the least hungry. Roberta clearly was. She tucked into a sizeable portion of fried eggs and sausage while I sipped coffee. Her table manners left a certain amount to be desired, but her speech was as eloquent as it had been during our first encounter. She started off cleverly, on a pacific note.

"It occurred to me," she said, crumpling one egg-stained napkin into a tight wad and helping herself to another from an adjacent table, "that you might want to know a little more about my motives. About why I'm so interested in the letters. Or in Eliot and Hale, for that matter."

"How keen of you," I said, smiling at her.

She picked up a piece of toast and eyed it carefully, then trimmed off its burnt edges before consuming it in three rapid bites.

"As I told you, I'm a poet. In my second year of the graduate writing program. This year I'm supposed to prepare a chapbook-size manuscript of my own work and to write two long papers, each on a poet of my choice. I've written one paper and outlined the second, but neither has really engaged me. They're just academic requirements as far as I'm concerned. I read lots of different poets, but I don't enjoy holding forth on them in a scholarly way."

I nodded, and she drank some coffee before continuing. I signaled a waitress to give her some more.

"I'm very interested in the experience of conversion — all kinds, but especially religious. When my parents were in their twenties, they converted to Christianity. They were Jews before that, in Berlin — not serious Jews, they came from assimilated families — but after their escape from Germany and their emigration to America, they converted. To the Dutch Reformed Church. They raised me as a Christian; I didn't find out until a few years ago that they used to be Jewish. Their name was Spier but they changed it to Spire — you know, like the thing on top of a church. Clever, huh?"

Again I nodded.

"To make a long story short, I'm now in the midst of figuring out my — how should I put it? — my affiliations. My parents'

37

revelation created a fair bit of tension between us. I can't understand any religious conversion. I've always thought, where this stuff is concerned, people respond to the symbols of their childhood. It's like a reflex. You know — play a little organ or recite some Latin or Hebrew, and the convert is right back in the thrill or terror of that first spiritual impulse. Conversion strikes me as something done out of desperation — an attempt to deny something you're stuck with — something that can't be changed by an act of will. But I clearly hold a minority view," she finished. "I mean, people do convert all the time, and nobody thinks they're strange because of it. So I must be missing something."

"And how does this relate to Eliot?" I asked.

"Ah," she said. "You know that Eliot converted to what is sometimes called Anglo-Catholicism, to the Anglican Church. It's up there next to Catholicism in terms of rite and liturgy. I want to know what that conversion cost him. There are clues in his work, of course, but I'm sure he wrote about it in detail to Emily Hale. Also about Vivienne's role in his conversion. It happened when his marriage was falling apart. I think he was driven from the arms of his neurotic wife into those of a neurotic church, and I find that an interesting swap."

I began laughing, and Roberta stared at me without expression.

"Listen." I wanted to take her down a peg. "You're talking about a very complex process. A swap? I doubt it. I'm sure Eliot undertook both the ending of his marriage and his pledge to the Church in all seriousness. He wasn't a frivolous man."

She pursed her lips. "I don't deny his seriousness," she said. "But I'm not interested in that." She pushed some spilled sugar into little hills on the tabletop. "Eliot knew he was in a completely untenable situation, and he had to get out of it. Vivienne was making him feel like a man in prison — it's all there in 'The Waste Land'! — and there was the Church, beckoning . . ."

She cupped her chin in her hands and looked away from me. Her eyes, more green than grey in the morning light, were fringed with dense, dark lashes.

"Do you remember those lines in 'Four Quartets'?" she asked. "'From wrong to wrong the exasperated spirit / Proceeds, unless restored by that refining fire . . .'?"

She recited well, without pomposity. I could tell she knew the work.

"He wrote so often about fire," she went on, turning once more toward me. "He saw so many things in terms of burning. Imagine a life in which fire is the governing symbol! 'The only hope, or else despair . . .'"

"'To be redeemed from fire by fire,'" I finished.

This time she nodded at me, and neither of us spoke for a moment.

"It offered something good," I suggested. "Something necessary."

"Yes," she continued. "From one fire — that crude sexual desire he hated in himself — to another — the love of Christ. There's the swap. He wanted what he called a condition of complete simplicity, and he got it. One fire for another — redemption for suffering . . . But you know the verse that follows after that bit about simplicity?"

"'Costing not less than everything,'" I answered. "But he put that line in parentheses, as if to downplay it."

This time she laughed.

"Oh, come on," she said. "You aren't fooled, are you? It's the most important line in the poem!"

I didn't know where Roberta was headed. My thoughts were like cotton, impossible to organize. I wanted more than anything to leave the coffee shop and return to the library. My companion was not, however, of similar feeling, and I didn't have my way without some final words between us.

"Well," I said, "it's not the most important line to me. Shall we go? This has been illuminating, but I have work to do."

"Hold on," she said. "The letters. We need to discuss the letters."

"What is there to discuss?" I said, as coolly as possible, though I could feel a growing pressure at my temples.

"Don't you see? Those letters are the part of the picture that's missing." Her tone was urgent, and she fastened her eyes on mine. I couldn't stand up, though I felt I must; my left hand lay unmoving on the wallet that I'd placed on the table.

"I need to know what it cost Eliot, mentally and emotionally, to convert," she said. "I need to find out what he gave up. You don't get something for nothing! 'Four Quartets,' 'Ash Wednesday' — they make clear what he felt he'd gained. But I'm convinced that only Emily knew what he lost. Only she knew how desperate he really was. Remember? — 'the greater torment of love satisfied'? Everyone thinks he's talking about Vivienne there, and of course he is, on one level. But beneath that? The screwed-up marriage was the sign of a deeper problem. And Emily Hale was the logical person for him to confide in about that."

"Why?" I asked, unable to restrain myself.

"She was the first woman he loved. After his mother, of course. To such a person one tends to spill everything."

I saw my opening. Standing, I pulled ten dollars from my wallet and handed the money to an approaching waitress.

"You have a charming notion of first love," I said to Roberta, easing my voice carefully through a narrow passage between condescension and flattery. I was by this time somewhat restored in confidence, but I had to press my advantage.

"Perhaps," Roberta said, obviously on guard.

I opened my palm to receive the change from our waitress and handed back a generous tip. The action achieved the desired effect. Roberta grew suddenly flustered.

"Wait. You just paid for breakfast — you weren't supposed to!"

"A small thing," I said. "Shall we?" I motioned toward the door.

She was struggling toward graciousness. "Thank you," she said at last, proceeding ahead of me. "Especially since I did all the eating."

"I hope you feel" — I searched for the right word as I held the door for her — "replete."

On the sidewalk she turned to me. "Yes," she said. "But unsatisfied." She waved as she stepped away from me. "I'm going this way. I'll see you."

I watched her walk off. The sight of her filled me with distress and longing such as I hadn't felt in years.

JUDITH'S PAST had something layered about it. Beneath the gauze of ordinariness that covered its surface were different textures — things I came to sense about her experience, not see directly. When I first met and fell in love with her, I could see nothing directly. I wondered at nothing but my good fortune at having found her. The discomforting sensation of boundedness that I felt the morning after we were married did visit me occasionally, but I dismissed it as a residue of my solitary years.

As time passed, I began sensing in Judith a deep seriousness — something more than mere soberness, or the quietude of an energetic mind. Very gradually, I began to see how much inner effort her outer equipoise required. Judith lived with a continual tension, obscured by good-naturedness but always there. To myself I described it as a kind of shadow: the underside of an earnestness I'd always found attractive in her. And I wondered, sometimes, where it came from.

Certainly not from Len and Carol Rubin, the uncle and aunt who'd raised her. They were entirely unserious people. Judith's natural parents had died in a car accident when she was a baby. Len, the only sibling of Judith's mother, and his wife had taken in their niece as their own child. They had none of their own; Carol was infertile, and in a sense Judith was the answer to their prayers.

Yet that puts it too strongly. Neither Len nor Carol were much given to importuning. They had no large unmet needs. Together they skimmed the surface of things, helping themselves to what they found — lighthearted fun, mostly — without bothering about what might have been or could be. Judith used to say that Len and Carol wouldn't have been unhappy had they remained childless, and I knew what she meant. Judith was their daughter, but in a proximate sense. They raised her to call them Len and Carol, not mother and father. Their attachment to her was based on duty, kindness, and habit.

Len was twenty years old when his sister Lottie died, and Carol was eighteen. Once Judith told me she couldn't understand how their marriage had survived the arrival of an unexpected child, but I could see how. They knew their limits. They never risked their own relationship by forming too close a bond with Judith.

They were a hardworking, hard-playing couple. Len sold pianos, quite successfully; even during the Depression he had lots of customers. He was affable, and he knew his instruments. Carol managed a large sheet-music store frequented by local musicians. When they weren't working, which they were six days a week, Len and Carol liked to go out — usually to midtown or Harlem clubs, where they listened to big-band music or solo piano and drank into the small hours. Jazz and gin were their two passions. As a child Judith learned to heat her own supper, carefully assembled by Carol, and clean up afterward. Early in the morning she would hear the Rubins enter the apartment and whisper outside her door, and the next day she'd find two half-finished nightcaps and a full ashtray on the coffee table, and a recording of Fats Waller or Count Basie on the record player.

43

When I first met the Rubins, in 1945, Len showed off a for-midable collection of Ellington albums and made me the stiffest martini I had ever encountered. He and Carol and I got along; they thought I was a bit peculiar and I found them slight, but we liked one another. Yet Judith and I rarely saw them. They had us to dinner at their small apartment on Grove Street a few times each year, and Carol called every month or so. If Judith was out, Carol would ask about her in the cheery, unencumbered tones of a friend of the family, and I would have to remind myself that this was the woman who had brought my wife into adulthood.

When Judith was twelve, Len told her that he was her uncle and Carol her aunt. The story of her parents' death came, she said, as a relief; it accounted for the avuncular quality of Len's affection, for Carol's big-sisterliness. Judith had observed her schoolmates' parents, and she knew that for some reason Len and Carol were different. The news of her status answered the question and freed her from a large burden of guilt: she had wondered if the problem lay with her. Clearly it didn't. It lay with circumstance — with the sudden, unintentional swerve of a truck on lower Broadway that had demolished instantly the grey Ford in which Lottie and her husband Sam sat unsuspecting. Sam had purchased the Ford just a few weeks before his daughter's birth, to the reported de-light of Lottie. In photographs (Len had given Judith several), Lottie looked very much like her child would look at the same age.

But at twelve Judith hadn't been able to see herself in the pic-tures of the black-haired woman or the tall, rangy man; they were merely interesting strangers. She knew they had everything to do with her existence, yet they were no more her mother and father than Carol and Len were. She asked Len to tell her about Lottie and Sam, but he said he hadn't spent much time with them. She couldn't make his random details — the brand of whiskey Sam

44

drank, Lottie's aversion to dark turkey meat — cohere into portraits of two people who were supposed to have been the most important in her life.

They cropped up in her poems, her Lottie-and-Sam visions — as representatives of what Eliot called *the still point of the turning world:* the safe center, home in an inner sense, which Judith sought above all else. I encouraged her to write about Lottie and Sam, to imagine them, but my urgings were purely intellectual; I'd never equated parents with safety, and I couldn't empathize with Judith's need to do so. I felt she was fortunate in having no memories to tamp down, no voices to silence — most of all, no sensation of chronic disappointment to endure.

In my own still center was the image not of a mother and father but of the Cross. I believed that God had planted that image there as if it were a tree — a sturdy tree on whose limbs I could clamber and then rest, as if in a pair of arms. I'm surprised, looking back on that image (for I no longer hold it within me), at its sacrilegious dimension: I actually envisioned myself perched on the Cross like some boy in his favorite oak or maple, safely surveying the world from the vantage of the instrument of Christ's death.

During my last visits with Judith at Hayden, she occasionally reminded me of that death. She was always medicated, but she could still say things that would rouse me later from a deep sleep, or catapult one of my dreams into a nightmare. *Don't forget,* she would say, *when you killed him you killed a Jew. One of us redeemed you, and you murdered him. Now you've tried to murder the rest of us.* She had purplish half-moons under her eyes, and her hands were chapped, the nails broken. *Lottie and Sam. How do I know where they died? Broadway? That's what Len says. What does he know? Broadway! Balanowka, Bergen-Belsen, Buchenwald, Bar, Belzec . . .*

45

W ELL," SAID ROBERTA. Her voice placed the word on a border between question and declaration.

She was sitting at a small table across from my desk — the seat she'd occupied during an hour of conversation that morning, and the morning before. After our off-campus breakfast I had guessed, rightly, that I'd be seeing more of her. When she showed up at my office door twenty-four hours later, I hadn't been surprised. Our morning chats had assumed, in the three days since that breakfast, the quality of a familiar ritual, and their ease owed much to Roberta. She was bright, well-read, and humorous. Despite all the warning lights that flickered within me whenever I thought of our first tense foray into the Mason Room, I awaited her visits with growing eagerness.

"Well what?" I said. We had just finished a short but animated debate about Robert Frost, whose poetry she claimed to dislike — though she knew it well enough. I was ready for a renewed argument, but Frost was no longer on her mind.

"It's been three days," she said.

"Since what?" I asked.

"Since we last talked about the letters," she said.

I decided to deflect her gently. I didn't want to antagonize her. Deliberately I put my hands behind my head, leaned back in my chair, and stared at her.

She stared back. She had become familiar to me physically as well as intellectually; I knew her dark brows and good coloring, her predictable black clothing and noisy shoes, the large hands, the slope of her neck, the slight overbite of her upper teeth. I was familiar with the details, yet she eluded me. Something to do with her motives remained completely beyond my grasp.

"Roberta," I said. "What do you want me to do, now that three days have passed? Roll away the stone?"

"Spare me," she said.

"I could say the same to you," I answered.

"Who's the fucking archivist around here?" she asked, leaning forward. "You are, after all. No?"

Her color rose — not in shame, I knew. She was obviously, unabashedly mad at me.

I too leaned forward. "Yes. I am. But there's no need for hostility, is there? After all."

She sighed. "Please, Matt," she said. She had used my first name before, but never in so personal a tone. Much as I wanted to, I couldn't convince myself that she was pleading. She displayed too much self-possession. Pleading never works with me, but authentic and angry self-interest does.

"Let's talk about this," I said.

"Fine," she said, settling back in her chair. "What do you want to talk about?"

"Not about the letters," I said. "At least not immediately. I want to talk about you."

She frowned — an appealing half-grimace, like a child's. For one panicked instant, I thought she might stand up and walk away. Then the frown lifted and her lips opened.

"So," she said, "what do you want to know?"

I pushed on with a kind of automatic urgency. "Tell me why you write poetry. Why you like Eliot."

She closed her eyes, and my office grew still. When her eyes opened, they were a brighter-than-usual shade of green; I had put her on guard.

"I don't have a short answer to the first question," she said. "As to Eliot — I never said I liked him. What does it mean, anyway, to like a poet? I think of Eliot as unavoidable. Sometimes I think I hate his work. And him too, the man — such an uptight snob! It's hard to believe the trouble he got himself into, first with Vivienne and then with Emily. Like a teenager, really."

I laughed. "I've heard Eliot called many things," I said, "but never an adolescent."

Roberta again leaned forward, her forearms on her knees. She gazed away, as she often did before speaking. Her pose was curiously male; it reminded me of the way young men sit on the subway, their legs carelessly spread apart. I was conscious, for the first time, of her hips, the round swell of them in black jeans as she sat with her body inclined in my direction. Her hips were large, in balance with her broad shoulders, her large hands.

"Let me tell you some stuff about Eliot," she said. "The proper gentleman, right? More British than the Brits. Punctual, formal, wry, all that. But some other things too. When he married Vivienne — impetuously, in his early twenties — he wrote to his father that he owed Vivienne *everything*. And then, after she began to get sick all the time, when the psychosomatic weirdness began in earnest — the headaches, colitis, panic attacks — he just couldn't deal with her. He couldn't respond to the craziness, the need, most of all her rage at him for denying her. Because what he'd said to his father was true, and crazy Vivienne knew it: he *did* owe her everything. She'd given him his first chance to break out.

"She loved his work, his mind, his body. The body — that's where he really fell apart. To be needed bodily — always the demands of the physical — her body in sickness, their bodies in sex — it terrified him, it appalled him. And the worse she got, the worse he got.

"From what I've read, it was one hellish marriage. Vivienne asking for more and more, Eliot giving less and less, till finally he couldn't take it anymore. Apparently he and her brother, Maurice, had Vivienne committed to an institution in London. Out of sight, though of course never out of mind. She's everywhere in the verse."

She paused, bringing her knees together and slipping her hands between them. "He knew Emily first," she said quietly. "And better, too."

"What do you mean?" I asked. It was becoming difficult for me not to glance at her hands nestling between her legs. I focused briefly on her eyes, but that too was difficult.

"He met her in Boston," she said. "Emily was a friend of some relatives. They were both sixteen or so. He sent her flowers after a recital she gave. She sang, you know, and acted; in fact, she was involved in theater all her life. Hard to imagine. Vivienne was the histrionic one; Emily was quiet and repressed, just like Eliot, until she got on a stage. Then it came out — the tougher self, brassy and smart, fun-loving. She was apparently a terrific actress. Eliot heard her sing, sent the flowers, they took garden walks, they corresponded. Then he left the States. They fell out of touch for quite a few years, during the worst stretches of his marriage. But he couldn't forget the moments of connection. It's Emily he's talking about in the first section of 'The Waste Land,' you know. Not Vivienne. That stanza about the hyacinth garden . . ."

She smiled briefly; when she spoke again, her voice was softer. "What a peculiar, powerful remembrance . . . It was inevitable that Eliot would seek her out again. That they would move once more toward intimacy. And that he'd back off again."

Beyond my office, the Mason Room was silent. It was noon. We were alone.

"Why?" I asked.

"I have my hunches," Roberta replied. "But they're just hunches. Which is where you come in."

I drew a long breath. She watched me inhale.

"Not yet, Roberta," I said. "Not just yet."

EDITH BEARDEN STOPPED ME in the hallway one afternoon a few weeks later to tell me about an upcoming meeting of the library's board. I was on my way to find Roberta in the cafeteria for our afternoon spot of tea, as she called it.

"Where are you headed?" Edith said.

"A meeting with a researcher," I answered. "What's up?"

She looked a little distracted, as she often does. Edith is my diametrical opposite. Her life is full of people and activities: her husband and sons, several grandchildren, golf and tennis games, season's theater tickets. My life, in her eyes, is a miracle of tranquility. Edith comes to me for steadying, and I go to her for a kind of vicarious upheaving — the sensation of being more of a player, perhaps, and less of an observer.

"Too much happening," she said. "This board meeting is going to be a total free-for-all. I'm running around like a chicken, and Tim's sick at home with a fever, and a part of me wants to catch whatever he's got so I have an excuse to avoid all this crap."

I put my arm around her shoulders. "You poor kid," I said.

"And to make things worse, I'm on my way right now to the damn bookkeeper's office."

"Just make nice to him," I said. "I don't want him knocking on my door. By the way, I can skip the board meeting, right?"

Edith stopped walking and turned to me. "No such luck, pal," she said, still smiling but shaking her head. "They're expecting a report on all bequests. Which reminds me," she added. "I've been meaning to ask you something."

I glanced at my watch. I could picture Roberta waiting, frowning.

"What's that?" I asked.

"I was going over the sign-in sheets for the Mason Room — doing a head count — and I noticed the name Spire kept cropping up. Then last week this woman came up to my office, introduced herself as Roberta Spire, and asked if she could talk with me about the Hale letters. She wanted to know how we store them."

"How?" I repeated. "You mean she wanted to know where they are?"

"No, not exactly. Or at least I don't think so. You've met this woman, I gather?" Edith threw me a puzzled look.

"Yes," I said, shrugging. "A poet, very keen on Eliot. I showed her a few manuscripts." I was acutely conscious of what I wasn't telling Edith. The skin at the base of my neck felt tight and damp.

"Um. Well, she struck me as a bit odd. She wanted to know if we kept the letters in the same packaging in which they'd arrived. I explained all about storing old letters in sets of clear plastic sleeves — she seemed interested. Then she asked a strange question."

"Oh?" I said.

"She wanted to know if we'd saved the envelopes. I said, you mean each individual letter's envelope, and she said yes, and I said of course, we have to — for the addresses and postmarks, you know. And then she said she wanted to see the Hale envelopes."

I was almost sure I could feel droplets of perspiration collecting on my throat.

"What did you tell her?" I asked.

"Obviously I told her no, and explained the policy. She seemed perhaps a little impatient at that point, but she was gracious enough. She thanked me for my help and then she left. What do you make of that?"

I was surprised at the ease with which I manufactured my careless tone of voice; beneath its skin my throat itself felt clammy, constricted.

"It takes all kinds," I said. "She seems to be a pleasant person. She likes libraries."

Edith nodded, then gave me another quizzical glance.

"Everything OK over there?" she said, tilting her head toward the Mason Room.

"OK?" I feigned incomprehension.

"Secure, I mean."

I laughed and touched her shoulder lightly. "Edith," I said, turning her name into a reproach. "Really."

"Oh, I know, Matt, I'm being silly," she said, walking off. "Forget I even said it."

JUDITH LOVED JAZZ. Len and Carol had communicated to her their passion for it, and she embraced it early. She understood the music of her generation as few people I knew did; it had sustained her, and she acknowledged the debt by paying the music a deep, close attention. As a child she whistled the Art Tatum tunes she knew by heart. She could move her hands and feet in perfect imitation of Jo Jones.

Len and Carol occasionally brought her along to hear big bands playing in uptown clubs where she sat surrounded by adults, the only child. Judith would sip sour pink lemonade through a straw and eat the chocolate cigarettes that Carol gave her. Finally, at midnight or one in the morning, she would fall asleep, and Len would wrap his jacket around her and carry her out to the car. Once, she told me, she awoke to find herself alone in the backseat of the DeSoto, which Len had parked just east of Broadway. She sat up and saw the street sign at the corner, its white-on-black letters spelling the name that later would become synonymous, in her mind, with death; but she didn't yet know about Lottie and Sam. She knew only that she was alone in a car on a poorly lit side street, somewhere off Broadway. She thought of screaming but decided against it, sensing that the sound would hurt her ears and summon no one; and she sang to herself instead — like Bessie Smith, she told me — until Len and Carol

54

showed up an hour later, filling the car with the reassuring smells of gin and smoke.

It wasn't that Len and Carol weren't to be counted on. They were always eventually there. They weren't the type of guardians who would abandon a child. They had drawn the boundaries of their affection and concern, and as there was never any question of going beyond those lines, Len and Carol were without any bitterness toward the child in their charge. And the child, it seemed, understood this, and also the unbridgeable gap that lay between them.

Judith and I had this much in common, different though our upbringings were: the people who raised us were profoundly distracted. My parents were essentially unhappy, and Len and Carol were basically happy, yet these states made no difference to me or to Judith. What we were denied, as children, was a particular kind of attention, which neither happiness nor unhappiness are guaranteed to bring about.

It had never occurred to me, before I met Judith, that anyone else would be able to understand the peculiar sensation of invisibility I had experienced in the apartment in Washington Heights. When Judith and I first shared stories of our childhoods, I felt an odd, immense relief: here finally was someone who knew precisely what it had been like. *Overlooked,* she said — we'd both been overlooked by the people who raised us.

Sometimes, though, Judith's judgments seemed severe. Childhood hadn't been so bad, I once said to her. My parents didn't stop me from pursuing my own pleasures.

What pleasures, she responded — books, you mean? — is that all? When I reminded her that books had been everything to me, as jazz and poetry had been for her, she told me that I'd just put my finger on it.

Much of what Judith said was true, but I didn't take it as significant truth. I loved listening to her, regardless. She had a musical voice, big-ranged and reedy, and I found it tremendously attractive. Certain syllables in her mouth were chords. Her laughter was pitched low and spilled out in dense waves. Occasionally, as she spoke to me, her words would become a wash of color and light that bathed and restored me; and I would lose track of their meaning.

In 1946 and 1947, stories of the camps, of DPs turned away from America and refugee boats from Palestine, began slowly to be told. In stores and restaurants and offices there was talk, as there hadn't been during the war itself, of deaths — not hundreds or thousands but millions of deaths, and not of soldiers but of people, an entire culture. At one of our small dinners in the winter of 1946, two friends of Judith's read a letter they'd received from a relative in Holland, a man who had briefly sheltered a Jewish family. One sentence in that letter was striking in its directness: "It's over — European Jewry has been snuffed out like a candle." When our guests left, Judith fell silent. As she stood over the sink, washing plates and handing them to me to dry, her face paled. I asked her what she was thinking, and when she opened her mouth to speak, she began to cry instead, quietly at first and then fiercely, her entire body trembling. She would not let me hold her.

The war's truth terrified us both, but Judith was the one to register the terror — not in words, for we couldn't speak of it directly, but in actions. It is difficult for me even now to pinpoint the changes in her. They were neither large nor consistent, and often I wondered if I were imagining them. She began to write more, and to show me less of her poetry. Sometimes she stayed up late, drinking and smoking heavily. At other times she went to bed soon after dinner, complaining of headaches. And the music she listened to began to change: less ensemble and large-scale swing, more solo keyboard — Monk and his young protégé, Bud Powell.

Several times in the late 1940s we went up to Minton's in Harlem to hear Powell. Even then, still young and raw-edged, he played with depth and force. I lacked Judith's keen musical ear, but I believed her when she said that Powell was literally changing jazz piano, widening its possibilities. I also knew he was quite unstable — and because of that, I disapproved of her attraction to him. Stories of his behavior circulated in all the clubs: of uncontrolled laughter during other musicians' riffs, of things thrown around in bars, days of incoherence. I didn't trust him, and his playing scared me.

When Powell was institutionalized for the first time, some years after we heard him uptown, Judith found out his address. She sent him several poems — a few of her own, a few by Langston Hughes and LeRoi Jones — and some blank composition paper, along with a letter in which she urged him to keep writing music. I realize now how closely she identified with Powell, with his rage and despair, but at the time I was distressed by her loyal concern for him. It was one more thing separating us.

I have an excellent memory, yet the postwar years are for me a kind of blur. People speak in retrospect of recovery, of how the nation pulled itself together and resumed its life with a renewed sense of purpose, but that was not my experience. I went to school, graduated, worked, read books. I didn't pray or attend church, though I persisted in a belief — unarticulated, unquestioned — that Christ's intercession would govern the course of my days. I did not wish to know how, or why.

There were moments when panic broke through, when I was overcome by a pure sensation of my own powerlessness. At those points I felt myself to be absurdly ineffectual, and that quality itself seemed evil. I loved my wife, yet could only approach her — could approach but never reach her. And that failure, too, felt sinful; and frightening.

Yet on the surface we weren't in pain or trouble. We got along well. Our marriage floated as if on a glassy sea, reflecting off its serene surface the muted pearl-grey tones of Manhattan's streets and sky. The city that was our home thrived, or seemed to, and we took our cues from it and carried on.

When Judith began rereading some of her books on the Kabbalah, I assumed she was doing so to gather fresh material for her poems. I was wrong: theodicy had begun to obsess her. She was looking for a way to understand evil, not as a metaphysical abstraction but as a reality — the war's reality, whose contours swelled and sharpened with each new piece of information we received from abroad. Judith sought proof of a beneficent God. I had settled for evidence rather than proof of His goodness, having convinced myself that the latter was unnecessary and in any case unavailable. For Judith, such a compromise was unacceptable.

We didn't know what was happening to us. Emotions we could hardly acknowledge to ourselves, let alone to each other, dominated our shared life. Judith's preoccupations troubled me, and my passivity upset her. The one outward sign of our relationship's distress was my reluctance to have a child. "Not yet" was how I put it, though I could construct no image of myself as a father.

The issue, I knew, wasn't Judith but my own inertia. I read Eliot's "Christianity and Culture" in 1949; written ten years earlier, it still shook me. Referring to "the events of September 1938," the essay ended on an ominous note. Eliot spoke of a new, unexpected feeling of humiliation that demanded personal contrition: "What had happened was something in which one was deeply implicated and responsible." Reading this, I recognized the feeling Eliot described — the queasiness I'd experienced during the war years. I hadn't served; many men my age had served and died. Even more, I had avoided learning what was happening in Europe. My deliberate ignorance had indeed implicated me. And I realized I had no idea what contrition meant — what acts it might require.

In the early 1950s, Judith began writing about the Kabbalistic myth of God's exile. One evening I asked her to explain this notion. How could a divinity responsible for all things be in exile? How could He be separated from Himself?

It happened with the Fall, she said. Adam disrupted what had been whole — God and His Shekinah, the male and female, the apple and its branch.

I scoffed at this. Do the Kabbalists think that Adam had so much power? Of course the eating of the apple was evil. But did this act have the power to exile God Himself? Surely that stretched things.

Remember, she said: He created Adam, so naturally Adam possessed real power. Adam was meant to receive his partner, Eve, as holy. Instead he shattered the union, and part of God went into exile. Each of us has something to offer the Creator, and it isn't belief. It's the returned Shekinah — the bridging of masculine and feminine, life and death. It's redemption, in which each of us is called to participate. Nothing else matters.

Listening to her that night, I was determined to close the gap between us. Undoubtedly all marriages had something like this at their core, I told myself — some issue on which both people are unbudging. But this gap wasn't philosophical. It was a rift in feeling, experience, perception. And it had its parallel within me as well. Judith's interest in Kabbalism awoke in me memories of my mother's urgent, alienating faith. I had never been able to tolerate it. Yet I also hadn't succumbed to my father's cynicism. I recognized the utility, even the elegance, of doctrine.

After hearing Judith's explanation of God's exile, I made a final play for compatibility. Look, I said, we're not so far apart in our views. Christians think of their one job as the service of Christ. All acts are an homage to Him. And reparation for the first sin. What's the difference between that and the return of the Shekinah?

Christianity, Judith answered, is a lie of consolation. There's no consolation for what we've already lost — all of us . . .

Her voice trailed off, and then she turned and looked directly at me. Her eyes were a deep green; they held me as if they were hands — hands that would not release me even if I were to resist.

You should grasp this, she said.

Why, I said.

Because of your name, she replied. Matthias replaced Judas, right? And Judas was really just another version of Adam — the same man in another guise. Both of them betrayed the Holy One. What are we supposed to do — are we meant simply to take Judas's place, to eat his dinner and wear his clothes and carry on?

I hadn't realized that Judith knew the story of Matthias, and I'd never expected that she would throw it at me. I became angry. Judith's eyes left my face, and our conversation stalled. Soon after, I walked out of the room and then the apartment, desperate for my solitude.

Sudden as it was, my withdrawal scared Judith. When I came back, several hours later, she was gone — once more to Boston. The next day I called her office, as her brief note had instructed me to do, and told her colleagues that she was ill and would be out for a week. I spent the next seven days reading voraciously — mostly novels, nothing to do with my life and its questions. I read, and I suppose I waited. The time passed easily, a blur of distraction.

Judith's return this time was not unlike the first; we took pains to patch things quickly. But once again I'd tasted solitude as an alternative to the life I was leading, and the possibility of its permanence scared and attracted me.

In those days I wondered sometimes about Eliot. At that time, of course, I knew nothing about Emily Hale, but stories of Eliot's trials with Vivienne had been in circulation among literary scholars for some time. I'd heard from a visiting English researcher that the Eliots were separated, that Vivienne was unbalanced, that Eliot was reclusive, private, unlikely to change his almost monastic life. When I read "Four Quartets," it was Vivienne who seemed to lurk in all the painful allusions to intimacy — as in "The Waste Land," where the details of a woman's life, "her hair / Spread out in fiery points," could unnerve and arouse, just as Vivienne had always done.

So I assumed it was Vivienne whom Eliot had in mind, writing that line in "The Dry Salvages" that sometimes broke into my consciousness when I thought about my own wife: "We had the experience but missed the meaning." I thought I knew precisely what Eliot meant by that, and I wanted to bring about a different fate for my marriage. I decided that I had to accept Judith more completely than I'd managed thus far — to make amends and be done with arguing over religion and other intractable matters.

But I was withholding. When Judith read aloud to me, when she whistled Roy Eldridge riffs as we walked through the park on Saturdays, when she turned toward my back in bed, draping one arm across my shoulder, I might have grasped more at what was being offered . . . We didn't know how to teach one another to do these things together, and it wasn't enough that we loved each other in tender ways, like the old friends we were not.

We missed the meaning. I know now that Eliot wrote the line not with Vivienne but with Emily in mind. After finally finding himself unable, after so many years, to pursue the promise of the rose garden at Burnt Norton, the promise of intimacy.

61

Emily waited patiently, but the man she loved couldn't offer what was needed. She saw this at last and was nearly undone, yet survived. She and he were products of the same culture, and she would not disgrace him or herself by breaking down publicly. She walled out all feeling and carried on, consummate actress that she was.

Emily, whose hands were large. She cupped his face easily, gently, in her hands, as no one else had ever done. Not his mother, not Vivienne — no one.

I would meet you upon this honestly.

Emily, he said: *Love is itself unmoving.* But he could not move. *There was a door, and I could not open it.*

What must she have thought, reading that letter?

What might have been is an abstraction.

THERE ARE PEOPLE whose interests and knowledge range widely, whose talents are diverse, yet who are impelled by one preoccupation that shapes nearly everything they think, do, or imagine. Roberta was such a person, and her preoccupation was conversion.

The story of the conversion to Protestantism of Kurt and Trudy Spire was told to me by their daughter, whom I encountered after my talk with Edith. We met in our usual spot in the library's cafeteria, which occupies part of the basement of the main building. The cafeteria is a good venue for storytelling. Ambiguously situated, half aboveground and half subterranean, it has small oblong windows at eye level through which you can observe many sets of feet tramping by as you sit at round wooden tables and drink coffee. Or, in the case of Roberta and myself, tea. We'd discovered that we both preferred strong tea to weak coffee, and as the cafeteria's coffee was notoriously dilute, black Lapsong had become our beverage of choice.

After we'd settled in with our steaming mugs (Roberta's laced with sugar), I asked her to tell me about her parents. She was an only child, as both of her parents had been. Kurt and Trudy were artists. They supported themselves with a house-painting and interior design business, collaborating in their spare time on large canvases, religious in theme, which they sold (for decent money,

Roberta said) to various churches around the country. Their work was abstract and rich in allusions to New Testament narratives. Roberta described it to me as compellingly ugly. Apparently she hadn't arrived at this judgment until she'd come to the university and taken several art history courses, after which she concluded that her parents' work left her feeling annoyed and uninspired. Under closer questioning she confessed that as a child she had loved the busy, lurid paintings that filled her parents' walls, but after entering high school she'd begun disliking them. She hadn't admitted this even to herself, however, until her early twenties, when she made up her mind that visual extravagance might be compelling but didn't make good art.

Yet she continued complimenting her parents' efforts. By then, she said, they were accustomed to her praise: they took it for granted. And in turn they praised her poetry — simply, she said, because she had written it. For them it had always been sufficient that she claim the identity of a poet. She didn't have to be a good one.

Her parents had left Berlin in early 1940, not an easy time for two nineteen-year-old Jews to flee Germany's capital. They had escaped with the help of a neighbor of Kurt's. The street in the Charlottenburg section in which his parents lived had also been home to the sister and brother-in-law of Dietrich Bonhoeffer, the German pastor who was killed by the Nazis in 1945 for his role in the "officers' plot," and whose letters from prison made such a strong impression on postwar theologians. It was the pastor's brother-in-law, Rudiger Schleicher, who arranged through friends in the Resistance for Kurt and his girlfriend, Trudy Lansmann, to travel on false papers first to Munich and then, circuitously, to Maastricht, in the south of Holland.

Kurt and Trudy had needed no persuasion to go; they knew they were in danger. Their parents, however, had refused to leave

Berlin. In 1942 they were sent to Flossenburg, the camp where (along with Bonhoeffer himself, as it happened) they were killed at the end of the war. In Munich, Kurt and Trudy were denounced as Jews by a stranger who didn't like their looks, and they avoided imprisonment only by virtue of the high quality of the identification papers given to them by Herr Schleicher. After arriving in Maastricht, they were hidden for a time by an elderly Catholic couple. Between 1943 and 1944, they lived clandestinely in the city's only synagogue. The century-old building had been locked up by the occupying Nazis, who for some reason hadn't smashed the synagogue's windows but had merely boarded them up. Thus, the interior had remained relatively dry, warm, and free from infestation by rats. Members of the Dutch Resistance had broken in through the basement trapdoor at the back. They kept the door covered with boards and brush so that neither the Germans nor the local collaborators knew that the decrepit temple was an important safe house in Maastricht. In the second-floor women's gallery, Kurt, Trudy, and several other Jews were secretly encamped, fed by Resistance members who made weekly deliveries of bread, cheese, apples, and a few tins of jam and jars of water and soup.

In the winter of 1943 the water pipes in the synagogue froze, and its inhabitants didn't bathe properly for several months. In the spring the air in the shuttered gallery was hot and close, and Trudy developed the shortness of breath that was to plague her for years after the war. Yet they survived. For reasons they could not fathom, no one had suspected that the dead-seeming temple might actually house living Jews, and their presence went undetected until the city's liberation in 1944.

The eventual emigration to the United States of Kurt and Trudy Spier — who were married, in a civil ceremony, in Maastricht at the start of 1946 — was no less complex than their exodus from Berlin. They were helped along each difficult step of the way by Dutch Christians — Protestants who gave them shelter and food, then work and money, and finally contacts in America. In 1948 they arrived in Hoboken, New Jersey, on a Holland-America liner. The small port across the river from Manhattan was full of Dutch immigrants and felt familiar, like the country they had just left. They settled in a tiny apartment on Washington Street, near the busy docks and the train station. Kurt found employment as a house painter, and Trudy worked for a Dutch bakery. They had little money but plenty of fresh bread, and they were thousands of miles from Europe. They set about building a life in which fear and despair would be relegated, as Roberta put it, to the basement of their consciousness.

For this effort they sought new identities. A little over two years after their arrival in Hoboken, Dietrich Bonhoeffer's letters from prison were published posthumously. Kurt Spier received a copy of the book from a Dutch friend who knew of his boyhood connection with the pastor's family. The letters had an effect on Kurt and Trudy that their daughter described as incendiary. Bonhoeffer's experience of separation and uncertainty spoke directly to their own, and his affirmation of spiritual vitality — of the power of Christian faith — seemed to carry the promise of a transformed existence. The two immigrants had led thoroughly assimilated lives as German Jews; they knew almost nothing about Judaism as a faith, practice, or culture. As teenagers they had considered themselves bohemian, inheritors of the work of Oskar Schlemmer and other Bauhaus artists. Being Jewish meant one thing only: being targeted for extermination by fascists. The people who had helped them during the war were Christians — men and women of the Resistance whose acts of bravery and sacrifice had saved many lives, and whose piety had grounded those acts.

Kurt and Trudy Spier talked of nothing but Bonhoeffer's theology for weeks after reading his book. They discussed it intensely with several members of the local Dutch Reformed Church who invited them to attend services and Sunday-night meetings. Kurt and Trudy participated in heated debates on the direction of postwar Christianity. They heard members of the congregation discuss Bonhoeffer's views on a Christian life in a religionless world, his conviction that God lay not on the boundary but at the center of human life and action — "beyond in the midst of our life." For the first time in their young, overwhelmed lives, they felt the possibility of community, and they seized it as if grabbing the baskets of food extended by anonymous hands through the cellar trapdoor of the synagogue in Maastricht — hungrily and in gratitude. In 1950, after changing their last name to Spire, Kurt and Trudy were baptized into their new world, into a new life.

Roberta was born five years later. The family moved into a larger apartment on one of Hoboken's narrow side streets. Kurt's small painting business had begun to flourish, and they could afford the light-filled rooms in which Roberta spent the first decade of her life. Kurt hired several men to work with him, and Trudy took design courses at the local polytechnic college. Her instinctive decorative sense and familiarity with the principles of Bauhaus design made her an excellent student, and she soon added her skills as an interior designer to her husband's business. She also proved to be a sharp entrepreneur, and through her efforts, Manhattan opened as a market for the couple's enterprise.

Their daughter entered their world as proof — the largest, brightest proof — of the rightness of their choices. With emigration and conversion everything had changed. The war years were an inexplicable lapse from the grace to which they had been restored as followers of Christ. Loss was a caesura in a larger rhythm of gain and growth, of prosperity.

Roberta stressed to me that her parents were quiet people, disinclined to proselytize. The war had taught them to keep to themselves — a habit of being that altered, in America, only insofar as they allowed themselves to join in the activities of their congregation. They had almost no friends or acquaintances outside that safe circle. Their expressions of faith took the form of practical acts centered on the maintenance of the house of worship itself — an unconscious throwback, Roberta felt, to their experience in that other holy place that had sheltered them against all odds. Every third year Kurt painted the church and its rectory, and Trudy designed beautiful altar cloths and choir gowns.

Yet their Christianity was not confined wholly to the narrow locus of the church building and its congregants. They understood that they had larger responsibilities, ones that rippled out to the world they had left. They read the New Testament every day and subscribed to several periodicals dealing with the urgent theological questions that Bonhoeffer's writing had initially raised for them — ethical and political questions about which they held strong if silent opinions. They considered themselves both politically aware and liberal. Theirs was an intellectual Christianity, but they believed deeply that Christ was the guarantor of all human survival. The absurdity of their own survival had at last been made bearable.

Roberta grew up surrounded by Dutch, Irish, and Italian immigrants. The decade after the war's end brought Germans and Eastern Europeans to Hoboken, including some Jews. One childless couple, the Rosens, lived above a small market they owned on Washington Street, across from the first apartment Kurt and Trudy had rented. As a girl Roberta went into the market every day. Mr. Rosen stood behind the meat counter; he had thick hands covered with curly grey hair, and on his left forearm was a number in dull blue ink. Mrs. Rosen gave Roberta hard candy and spoke to her mother in German. Between the two women Roberta sensed a strong affinity and an equally strong tension. It was not until many years later that she realized that their bond was the result of a recognition that neither woman could express, and the tension an outcome of what one woman suspected and the other denied.

Denial was necessary. Kurt and Trudy Spire treated the tangled threads of history and identity as if they had always been and would always be separate, two skeins that did not braid. What had happened to them had nothing to do, now that it was over, with the individuals they had become. Conversion meant not that they had once been Jewish and were now Protestants, but rather that their having been Jewish was — and here Roberta quoted Eliot as she struggled for the right words — an unattended moment, a moment in and out of time.

"But any shrink will tell you," Roberta added at this point in her narration, "that while denial is useful, it has its price. There's no such thing as identity without history. My parents think they're living in the present, but actually they live in a dream of the present — a dream that their past continually threatens to break open."

She rubbed her eyes briefly; the gesture suggested her tension. "Maintaining that level of denial would take a fair bit of energy, wouldn't it?"

"Yes," I said, noting the creases at the corners of her eyes. "I guess it would."

"You know, my parents are tired so much of the time. Upbeat, deliberately cheery and upbeat, yet tired . . . Their kind of optimism is exhausting."

Roberta's account of her parents' conversion wound down at dusk. We were sitting at a table near one of the windows. The fading light entered the room at a slant, mingling with the smoke from Roberta's cigarette. I helped myself to one from her pack. I'd taken to smoking occasionally with her and found the activity enjoyable, untinged by even a hint of the remorse I might have expected to feel after relapsing into a habit broken years earlier. There is something about being in one's sixties that vitiates such guilt. I didn't want to resume smoking; I merely wished to have a cigarette, now and then, in Roberta's presence.

"So," she said, "you wanted to hear about my parents, how they got here, all that stuff. Is your curiosity satisfied?"

"Well," I said, exhaling, "what interests me is that I asked for the story of their emigration, but what I got is the story of their conversion from Judaism to Christianity."

"It's the same story. And you've put it slightly wrong: they converted from the identity of Jewishness to the identity of Christian-ness, if that makes any sense."

"In a way," I said. "I mean, I understand that they had no be-lief in Judaism, and in that sense naturally they didn't convert from it to another faith. I gather they turned from a life with no faith toward one in which faith could play a part. From darkness to light, one might say."

"One might. I wouldn't."

I decided to push a little. "Who knows what it was like for your parents? You can only speculate."

I waited for her to continue, but she was quiet. After a minute I broke the silence.

"Not long after we met," I said, "you indicated that you found your parents' conversion distasteful."

She smiled, but her face reddened slightly. "One of those un-derstatements I use with strangers," she said.

"So try something else. I've ceased being a stranger."

Her color deepened. She reached for another cigarette.

"Enraging," she said after lighting up. "Enraging."

I didn't know where to go, in which direction to urge her. At various points during her narrative I'd detected anger, the veiled kind that displays itself in certain turns of phrase, certain ironies. Yet I hadn't expected her to admit to feeling it, and its sudden expression was like the presence of a third party. I noted the signals: Roberta's sharp exhalations of smoke, a rapid flicking of ash, the sliding of one black-shoed foot to the carpeted floor, where it tapped out a muted staccato. Her anger lay just under the surface, and it governed. I was foolish to think I could urge or lead her anywhere.

"You confuse me," I said as blandly as possible.

She snorted, then turned and looked directly at me. Even in that oblique light, her eyes were a crisp green.

"Do I?" There was a pause; when she spoke again, her voice was somewhat less sharp. "I confuse myself, too. I mean, I'm thirty-five, did you know that? — you'd probably guessed something close, hm? And still locked in combat with my mother and father. Oh, we get along, at least on the surface. But I haven't talked with them about anything serious for at least two years — since just before I came back here to do graduate work, in fact."

"Why?" I said.

"We had a large fight. I was working at the time, in Manhattan, for a small poetry press. I'd gone to visit my parents, and I was looking through some photo albums when I came across a couple of pictures of my grandparents — both sets, the Lansmanns and the Spiers. I'd known those photos since I was little. There were several of the Spiers, all taken on Marienburger Allee in Charlottenburg — right in front of their house. But the one photo of the Lansmanns, the only one my parents had kept, was taken in another neighborhood of Berlin. I began wondering where. At first I thought Kreuzberg, which is close to Charlottenburg, but then I remembered my mother telling me that her par-

71

ents' house had sat on a steep side street — Kreuzberg is quite hilly — and I figured the photo must've been taken somewhere else, because the background wasn't right. My grandparents were standing to one side of some kind of big building. It had the look of a church — and it had obviously been badly damaged. All its windows were busted and there was a lot of fire damage. The picture was taken from across the street — a wide one, like a boulevard — so the Lansmanns themselves were small and not too distinct. But the building was so big that it didn't all fit into the picture. I was staring at it, wondering. Then I flipped it over and saw that my mother had written 'November 1938' on the back. With parentheses around it.

"And I got it. Something about the date, in parentheses — it was those parentheses that did it. I had this weird feeling inside my rib cage. For a minute I had trouble inhaling, I felt a little dizzy. Suddenly this possibility had entered my mind, this suspicion, and it was such an immense thing with so many implications that my body kind of seized up, like a clutch you shift too fast and the gears lock, you know, and the engine stalls. I felt stalled.

"My mother came into the room just as I was sitting there, holding this photo. My parents had told me lots of stories about my grandparents, about life in Berlin. My mother's stories were of walking along the Spree, of long Sunday-afternoon picnics in the Tiergarten after church. My father's stories were of the Schleicher children, his playmates in Marienburger Allee, and their uncle Dietrich in jail, murdered for his Christian ideals. And I'd believed everything: the church stories, picnic stories, the stories of how both my grandfathers — men in their early fifties — had managed to evade military service by faking illnesses; the stories of Berlin bombed, of electricity blackouts and coal shortages and the constant hunger. And the stories of my parents' move to Holland after the war finally ended, to make a better life. And of how they'd heard about the deaths of their parents, my four grandparents, between 1946 and 1949. All four died of natural causes, my mother had said.

"All of it — I'd swallowed every word, and suddenly here was this familiar photograph with a date in parentheses on the back, written in pencil by my mother. The whole house of cards came tumbling down. I looked up at her. She must've noticed something was wrong because she said *what?* quietly, and then again *what?*, and I kept staring at her. Finally I was able to use my mouth, which had gone all gummy and dry.

"*Kristallnacht,* I said. *This is that synagogue in all the history books. On Orianenburger Strasse.* And after a moment, she said *yes.*

"*You were,* I said — and I was shaking my head in disbelief but I knew I was right — *no, are, you are Jewish. No,* she said, *were, we were but that was in another life.*

"I looked away for a minute and the room sort of lurched and I looked back. My mother was very pale.

"*Why didn't you,* I started to say, but she cut in with something like *why should we, what's the point, it's all past, over, don't you see, we made a new life here* — and then her face crumpled and she started crying, and something in me snapped and I began to scream, like in a movie. My father came running in. He saw me holding the photo, back-side up, and he figured it all out fast. He started trying to talk to me in his warm voice that always used to calm me down, but I kept yelling and flailing my arms around. He couldn't get near me.

"I'd never felt such pure shock. They'd tricked me. I couldn't trust anything they'd told me: all their stories were lies. I pushed the photo in my mother's face, but she had her hands cupped over her eyes; and I said *where, where did they die!* And finally

73

my father said *we were told they died in the camp in Flossenburg,* and I said *and yours, your parents* and he whispered *Flossenburg, we heard they also were sent there.*

"I left the house. The next day I came back, and they told me some of what had really happened to them during the war. A part of me still didn't believe they were telling me the truth, but if it wasn't the truth it was perhaps something close to it — the version I just told you. And I said nothing. They begged me to forgive them, they'd only tried to spare me from hurtful things. This went on for hours, it seemed, while I sat there unable to say anything at all.

"It's been polite between us, but not much more, since that day. I go back to Hoboken a few times a year. Never around any of the holidays, theirs or mine —"

"— what do you mean by that?" I interrupted.

"Just what I said. Theirs — the Christian ones — and mine — the Jewish ones. I'm Jewish. I haven't made that clear?"

I raised my hands, palms up. "It depends on what you mean by Jewish, doesn't it?" I asked. "I understand the birthright part of it, I get the facts. But you haven't said anything about what being Jewish means for you, so I can only guess."

"Guess, then," she said.

"No, Roberta," I said. "Why make me put the pieces together? What's the problem with telling me straight out?"

She looked a bit taken aback, perhaps as much at the heat of my words as at their substance.

"Well," she said, lighting another cigarette. "I figured you're an archivist, you probably enjoy a little guesswork."

"Archivists aren't detectives," I said. My face felt hot. "You've set it up so that if I say something about your being Jewish that you consider wrongheaded, you're likely to become irritated with me. And I can do without that. A little straightforwardness —"

74

"— all right, Matthias," she said, taking in a long draught of cigarette.

I waited a beat or two, watching her, watching myself watch her.

"Good," I said. "I like it when you see my point."

"Have a smoke," she said, extending the pack and holding a lit match between her second and third fingers. "Too much heaviness, hm? As to my Jewishness —"

I broke in again, waving away the cigarette. "Wait," I said. "It's getting on toward dinner, and I'm hungry. I take you out, you talk. I listen. I even pay. Is it a deal?"

The look on her face was one I couldn't then or now describe except as a peculiar mixture of fear and relief, with an underlay of what might've been amusement. I couldn't pretend to myself that I trusted her, or deny that I wanted her company intensely — wanted to continue watching her eyes crease at the corners, her fingers spin her cigarettes to dislodge the ash, her feet tap out their tension like a code.

"Yeah. Sure," she answered. "Deal."

I T WAS MY TURN to choose the place. I drove Roberta and myself to a restaurant in town, a quiet Italian trattoria I visit regularly on my own. The maître d' greeted us politely, revealing none of the surprise he must have felt at seeing a woman at my side. Roberta had turned up the collar of her trench coat; one of her bright silk scarves announced itself at her throat, the only color in her all-black uniform: V-neck wool sweater, jeans, thin suede belt. She wore flat shoes (also black, with pointed toes) instead of the usual heels. Dangling from her earlobes were a pair of gold-filigree hoops. They glinted in the dim light as she removed coat and scarf and ran her fingers quickly through her hair.

"This way, please," said our host as he took our things, and we followed him. I watched gratefully as he seated Roberta and lit the candles on our table. Their steady flickering gave me something other than Roberta's pale throat to attend to.

"So," she said. "Can I have something to drink?"

"Of course," I said, relieved to be inserted into my role. I ordered wine and, after consultation with Roberta, a plate of grilled mushrooms to begin our meal. She was evidently hungry. Her careful reading of the menu made it clear that this was to be a full-fledged dinner. She objected to the pasta I suggested as a first course — the veal we had chosen would have cream in its sauce, wasn't a salad preferable? — and noted approvingly the array of cheeses. A sweet dessert, she stated, was a far less satisfying way to end a meal than fruit and cheese followed — not too quickly — by espresso. I agreed, all the while wondering how a woman who didn't place her napkin on her lap until she was halfway through a plate of mushrooms bathed in olive oil and garlic could display experience with the shape and pace of a good meal.

"I love to eat," she said, using some bread to mop up the oil.

"So I see."

She glanced at me critically. "You look like you could do a little more in that department," she said. "A bit thin for your age, aren't you?"

Somewhat unnerved, I laughed. She had never remarked on my appearance.

"It depends how you measure things," I said.

"I was thinking of pounds. And years. You're around sixty-five, right? And you must weigh about one-fifty. But you're tall — maybe six feet? Most men your age begin to get thick around the waist. From inactivity. Do you exercise?"

"Exercise? Do you mean jogging or some such thing?" I shook my head. "I'm active enough."

"Oh yes," she said, "I know. You putter around, tend your books."

"I object to the word putter," I said, smiling at her. "Where do you get your notions of how much a man should weigh?"

"From my father," she replied. "I get most of my ideas about what men are like from my father. Not all of them conscious, of course."

"Spoken like a good Freudian."

"Why not? It all makes sense, as long as you don't overdo it." She emptied her glass and nudged it in the direction of the bottle; I refilled it.

"Thanks. A nice red you chose, by the way. Let's make the next one a white — a Gavi, perhaps? Good." She twisted her neck in a rapid circular motion, and her eyes closed briefly. "I like to drink, too. Wine, mostly. Beer when it's really hot, in summer. My parents don't drink at all, so they worry I drink too much."

"Do you?"

"Not in recent years, but in my twenties I used to. Now I drink to relax, not to obliterate. It's a tricky thing, though. You drink often?"

"Nightly," I said. "Two glasses of wine, one before and one with dinner."

"That sounds civilized."

"I like to keep it that way."

"A model of decorum," she said, smiling a little. "Any drinkers in the family?"

Her directness startled me. "As a matter of fact, yes," I said.

"Father, mother, wife?"

"The first and the last," I said.

"Interesting," she said. "You've answered another question I've had. I've been wondering if you're married."

"Was," I corrected her. "My wife died in 1965."

"Ah." Her expression said nothing. "Any children?"

"No."

She nodded, looked away briefly, then attacked the near-empty plate in front of her. The last mushroom, speared on her fork, was about to disappear, but she held off and spoke again.

"So you've been alone for a while now. You like it?"

I concentrated on the grey-brown button at the end of her fork, which she held in midair.

"It's fine," I said. "I'm very used to living alone."

The mushroom vanished. She chewed noisily and drank some more wine. "Terrific," she said, pointing with the fork at her empty plate. "I live alone, too. The privacy is right for my work, but I need to have other people around. So I'm out a lot. With friends, often at the movies. I hate watching videos at home. You like films?"

"Not particularly," I said. "I prefer books."

She rolled her eyes. "Too much of a good thing, maybe?"

"Never." I poured us both some more wine. Our salads arrived. I was glad to see that the portions were small. Roberta ate hers in an instant, and I had the waiter clear away our plates.

"You didn't finish — you didn't like it?" she asked.

"It was very good. I'm a smaller eater than you are," I said. "I'm saving room for the veal."

She pulled out her cigarettes. "Will it bother you if I —"

"— not at all," I said. "I'll join you."

"Good. It's tacky to smoke between courses, but I do it anyway." The lit match was extended toward me. I bent my head over it and cupped the flame with my hand, careful not to touch her wrist. We settled back into our seats, and I felt a definite release of tension. Roberta's earrings glinted as she exhaled, her mouth pouting. A line of reddish lipstick banded the filter of her cigarette.

"So what did your wife do?"

"Do?" I inhaled deeply, paused, and blew several smoke rings. Roberta began laughing.

"I can't believe you're doing that."

"Why not?" I said, ending the act. "You must have yet another preconceived idea about archivists. Or men. Does your father smoke?"

"He quit. He used to smoke tons, but he never blew rings. I don't know many people who can."

"Can you?"

Unexpectedly, she blushed. "Sometimes. Usually not. Like when I blow bubbles with gum — I can't be sure it'll work."

"Oh, go on," I said. "Try it."

She shook her head. I wanted to push her but decided against it; seeing her flustered was enough.

"Anyway. Your wife," she said. "What did she do? Apart from drink?"

"She wrote," I said. "She was a poet."

Roberta's dark brows lifted. "You're kidding me," she said.

"No," I said. "Why would I?"

"True. Sorry — go on. What kind of poems did she write? Did she publish anything?"

I was at a crossroads. Some choices had to be made.

"She wrote long narrative poems. A few were published, in decent journals. She also worked as a legal secretary — not with any enthusiasm, as you can imagine, but because the money was good. We couldn't have survived on my salary alone. But she thought of herself as a poet."

"Did you think of her as one?" The question had a honed edge; I felt it as a small, sharp thrust into my memory.

"Yes," I said. "A good one, too, if you like that kind of verse. These judgments are very subjective, you know."

"Oh yes, I know," she said. "And did her drinking affect her work? Do you mind if I ask?" she added.

I put out my cigarette before answering.

"No," I said. "But I don't have an answer, any more than to the question of how it affected her life. Or our life together. The problem got worse after the war. I began to drink less, she more — we were responding differently to various tensions. She did publish one poem in the midst of a particularly bad drinking period, so I suppose that says something. Her writing didn't become gibberish."

Our dinners were brought to us by the maître d' himself, gracious as always. He called for a waiter to serve our bottle of Gavi and smiled at Roberta's praise of the mushrooms. Then we

80

were alone again. I took the opportunity to redirect the conversation.

"Did you know," I asked, "that T. S. Eliot was quite a drinker at one time in his life?"

"Um," Roberta said, her mouth full of veal. She paused to swallow. "This is great food, Matt. Very good choice." She used her napkin for the first time, patting her mouth roughly before speaking again.

"Yes, I've read about Eliot's drinking. Heavy during the marriage and then the war, off and on throughout. I'd drink a lot too, if I had a wife who kept having psychotic breaks and stank of ether."

"Ether?" I said.

"Yeah. Apparently she used it like perfume. Some weird self-medicating thing. Vivienne had a few crackpot doctors and lots of her own ideas about medicine. Some people said she went crazy because of all the drugs she took for various ailments. Of course the line between psychosomatic and physical illness was always pretty blurred for her."

I passed a basket of hard rolls to Roberta, who was eating with gusto.

"Have one," I said. "And slow down. We have all evening."

"So we do," she said, fiddling with a roll. "A bad habit of mine. I picked it up from home — my parents eat too fast. Probably because of their time in Holland, when the food wasn't exactly plentiful." She put down her fork and knife and placed her hands awkwardly on either side of her plate.

"Do go on," I said. "You know quite a bit about the Eliots. You've investigated them."

"Lots of reading," she said, twirling the stem of her wineglass with a restless hand. "A couple of biographies, a bunch of letters in the collection at Harvard — you're familiar with it, I'm sure. They let me look at some stuff Eliot wrote to his family in the States. This was not a man with a lot of deep loyalty to old friends! Ezra Pound was a huge help to Eliot at the beginning of his time in England, but once Pound started going off the deep end, Eliot dumped him. And Vivienne — well, it gets extremely complicated with her. His motives, I mean.

"It's Emily Hale I want to know more about. And not just because I'm interested in the story of her relationship with Eliot. For me the important thing is Eliot's conversion — how it happened and what Emily knew about it."

She picked up her glass, again revolving its stem. I continued to eat, slowly, while Roberta talked about Eliot. The substance of what she was saying didn't surprise me, but I was struck by her grasp of Eliot's complexities. She did know a great deal, and she painted a colorful picture. Her animation began having a tonic effect on me, and I regained my appetite. When Roberta paused to sip at her wine, I reached for the bottle.

"So how," I said, refilling our glasses, "does all this relate to you?"

She gazed across the room without answering. I watched as her brows pulled together for an instant, her lips pursing slightly. Her face was peculiarly expressive. I gazed at her, and an inexplicable gratitude welled within me. I heard Eliot's incantation in "Ash Wednesday": *Rose of memory/rose of forgetfulness . . .*

The moment passed; our waiter arrived, napkin over forearm, to announce the dessert offerings.

Roberta shook her head at him.

"A nice cheese, perhaps?" she asked him. Her expression remained concentrated.

The waiter suggested a parmesan with pear slices. I ordered espresso; Roberta asked the waiter to bring hers in a little while. The bitter aroma of the coffee calmed me; I sipped at it while Roberta ate cheese and fruit.

"So then. I'd like to answer your question," she said, pushing away her plate. "But I'm unsure." She spoke more softly than usual. "It's like this. I keep going back to Eliot's work because it has something to teach me. About craft, obviously, but more than that. The hollowness that Eliot could describe like almost nobody else. But even that's not all.

"In the poems he wrote during the forties, after Vivienne was locked up, there's this counterweight: an urgent move toward atonement. Toward release from all that daily pain and tedium. I'm talking about the period when he was closest to Emily. She was the one who listened, who accepted his trauma and made no demands — the utter opposite of his wife. And this was also the time when his conversion became a reality, when he committed himself to the Church.

"Something just doesn't add up. Vivienne dies in 1947, and there he is, a hugely successful poet — a man released from an awful marriage, with a woman friend who would marry him instantly and gladly. And what does he do? He rejects her completely, isolates himself for a decade, and lives like a hermit. And at the end of the decade he suddenly marries his secretary — a woman almost forty years his junior.

"I mean, he had his conversion to give him strength, and he had his secure place in the world. He seemed as ready as a man could be to settle into a mature, intimate relationship. Yet he repudiates the one person who had consistently loved him through everything, who knew his darkness and could actually bring out his playful side. A lot of those little cat poems were for Emily, you know. How can you explain this?

"My guess is she must have had something on him. Like Vivienne did. They both knew things he couldn't bear them knowing. And I have the feeling that his faith was no match for an obsessive self-protection — his need to reveal only the self he could control. Vivienne had threatened to expose the naked man, and he just wasn't going to let that happen again.

"He converted in 1927; he left Vivienne in 1933, and she was institutionalized in 1937. She died ten years later. He and Emily corresponded throughout those two decades. I'm sure his letters to her give a sense of what was really going on with that new faith of his — that anti-Unitarian, anti-rational faith that was supposed to deliver him from his tormenting memories. I want the details: how his belief protected him from overwhelming emotions. I need to understand this, Matt. I need it for my own work, and I need it for my life."

"I don't follow you," I said.

She leaned back in her chair and tilted her head so that she was staring up at the ceiling.

"My parents' conversion . . . it has me paralyzed, in a way." She lowered her head. "In my early teens, long before I learned I was Jewish, I started dreading church. The liturgy, the kneeling and standing, the prayers — whatever meaning these things had had for me began draining out of them, and I couldn't locate the rupture in that comfortable sensation I'd always had when I sat between my parents and sang hymns with them. That feeling of being safe.

"Eventually, my discomfort got so strong that I told my parents I didn't want to go to church any more. They asked me why, and when I said it made me feel uneasy, they just said I was free to do as I liked. I'll never forget that conversation — so brief, so strange! I was fifteen, and terrified of this unexpected divergence. Yet my parents were totally calm, as if we were discussing someone else's not very interesting dilemma.

"It hit me then that they were telling me I'd better fend for myself. And it was only much later, when I found out about their conversion, that I saw why they'd been capable of such detachment. For them, converting to Christianity meant that they'd made a leap — only it wasn't a one-time thing; this leap would have to be continous, a constant recommitment. They understood that they'd have to sever ties with anything that threatened to

84

hold them back. Including, if necessary, their child. Because the leap was the most important thing. It's like what Eliot wrote in 'Marina' . . ."

She paused, then recited from the poem's closing lines:

> *let me*
> *Resign my life for this life, my speech for that unspoken,*
> *The awakened, lips parted, the hope . . .*

"But there's a price to pay, isn't there, when you resign speech? My parents couldn't acknowledge my spiritual distress while continuing to affirm their newfound faith. As they saw it, they had to make a choice. So they chose a lovely, long, entirely believable string of lies."

She ran her hands quickly through her hair, shaking out its tangles.

"In Eliot's case, you know, it was Emily Hale who got in the way. And I think it's so stupidly sad. She could've been at the center of his new life. She loved him. She was strong and funny, tolerant, clearheaded. There he was, terrified of the dark, and she would've illumined everything."

Her gaze swung toward me; I could feel its charge, an electric longing. "Can you seen now why I'm so interested in Eliot's conversion? And why I want to know what he actually told Emily about it?"

She lit a cigarette and exhaled; smoke clouded her face. I reached for the pack. She held out her match, offering its flame for my cigarette, and I bent quickly over her hand — acutely conscious of its nearness to my face.

"If you want to know how Eliot's conversion worked for him," I said, "I think you should stick with the poems. The real story's likely to show up there. Eliot's letters are notoriously unrevealing of his deepest feelings. You probably saw that from the Harvard collection. He made a point of staying near the surface when he wrote letters. I see no reason to expect anything different from the Hale correspondence."

Roberta didn't respond. The check had been placed on our table; I slid it to my side and took care of it quickly. Roberta looked directly at me and spoke a soft thanks.

"My pleasure," I said. "Let's walk a bit. I'm not used to such eating."

"Don't get the idea that I do this all the time," she said as we rose. "It's been a while since I've been taken out for such a meal."

Our host helped her into her coat. Suddenly I needed to be outside, released from role and decorum. Roberta's focus on the letters, expected though it was, had drained me. The night air was warmer than it had been earlier, and I was glad that we'd parked several blocks from the restaurant. I put my hands in my coat pockets and fingered my keys. We strolled at an easy pace, our bodies several feet apart but moving in tandem, as if we had linked arms. I caught occasional notes of her perfume. She wore it lightly; it was almost undetectable.

"Who else did your wife read?" she asked.

I was used to her rapid shifts of topic, but I wasn't expecting Judith. I glanced at Roberta. She was looking at the ground.

"Poets, you mean?"

"Yes."

"Well," I said, "she used to read most of the poetry journals published in New York at the time. In the fifties she became quite excited about what they now call the Beat writers. Allen Ginsburg, of course. And later, LeRoi Jones."

We had arrived at the car. I opened Roberta's door for her. The car's interior felt damp and noticeably cooler than the outside air; I shuddered slightly, but Roberta appeared not to notice. She sat with both hands in her pockets, her legs crossed.

"Your seat belt," I said, and she put it on, straightening her legs. Her actions set off another small but definite wave of perfume.

"Tell me where you live," I said.

"Waldorf Street," she answered. "Number ten, just past the corner of Plains. In an ugly apartment building. You know how to get there?"

"Yes," I said.

"And you?"

"The other side of the university. Anderson Road."

"Nice," she said. "I should live in such a neighborhood."

"All in good time," I said.

We rode in silence. I found her building easily. She lived in a neighborhood I knew well, having rented an apartment there when I'd moved to town over twenty years earlier. I remembered the quiet of that space — a large, ramshackle flat with high ceilings and little heat. I'd been too absorbed with my new job to care much about how cold it was, but now I remembered and shivered again.

I pulled up in front of Roberta's building.

"When I first moved here," I said, "I lived a just a few blocks away. On Pine Avenue."

"With your wife?" Roberta lit two cigarettes. "A final smoke," she said, passing one to me.

"No, not with my wife," I said. "She'd just died."

"Oh." She pulled open the car's ashtray and flicked some ash into it. "How?"

"How?" My temples pounded in a muted but unpleasant rhythm.

"Yes," she said.

I didn't know then why I told her, and I don't know now. The voice emerging from my mouth did not sound like my voice. I felt oddly separate from it, from my entire body, and from the self who'd experienced the substance of the words.

"She killed herself," I said.

Roberta exhaled slowly and very softly.

"How?"

"Roberta," I said. "Do you really —"

"— tell me," she said, in the most gently emphatic voice I'd ever heard.

I obeyed her. "She cut her forearms with a razor and sat in a tub and filled it with warm water and died maybe an hour later."

"Did you find her?"

"No. This happened somewhere else. I was told about it."

The street was dark, the car's interior even darker. We sat for a while in silence. Her face in profile was a shadow among others, yet I sensed its approach — sensed before actually feeling the quick, direct pressure of her lips at the juncture of my jaw and ear. A short swift kiss, essentially mysterious. There are no words for what such contact communicates. If I could've translated, I believe I would've heard Roberta saying something about an unbreachable solitude. The car door opened. I heard instead a murmured good night and her quickly receding steps.

THE WASHINGTON HEIGHTS APARTMENT in which I lived until I was eighteen wasn't a prison, but my life in it was that of a prisoner. My book-filled room, the small but well-stocked kitchen, the square living room with its corduroy-covered chairs and long sofa — these weren't oppressive spaces. They were utterly familiar and comfortable. As a child I spent far more time indoors than outside, and I knew the apartment as an extension of myself, the natural setting of my inner life. Prisoners live in full awareness of the existence of an external reality, but the cell is of greater significance.

My mother was the gatekeeper. She arbitrated between me and the exterior. Knowing that my father was too advanced in an alcohol-induced depression to play this role, my mother tried to do what she felt had to be done so I could survive on the outside: teach me the love and fear of the Lord. She succeeded in arousing in me something only superficially akin to these emotions — a kind of clinical interest in the details of Christ's life and an aversion to those of his death.

Both of my parents had been unpopular teenagers — my mother because of her already too-strident religious beliefs, my father because of his cynicism, expressed with an unmodulated relentlessness that echoed, in another key, my mother's Christian ferocities of opinion. They shared a profound distrust of the social world of their adolescence, the middle-class Manhattan of the 1920s, whose narcissistic culture was completely unprepared for the inevitable tumble from grace that the Depression brought about. This distrust had alienated my parents from their peers, and adulthood did nothing to change their uneasy relation to the place they chose not to leave. Washington Heights had always been their home. There was nowhere else to go. They clung to a hope — increasingly diminished as time wore on — that their marriage would provide some relief from loneliness. It could not do so, but they were bound to it.

I was brought on the scene to mitigate their stress, but instead I added to it by refusing their diagnoses of the world's ailments. I knew the dangers of too open a rebellion. If I were to push too hard, my parents would become even more frustrated and anxious, and I didn't want to harden them completely to my actual isolation. I thus spent my childhood in the grip of the prisoner's constant worry about antagonizing the wardens.

Perhaps all children are solipsists; perhaps I was merely more of one than most. I don't know; I know only that when I was eighteen, reading for the first time those astonishing lines in "The Waste Land" — *I can connect / Nothing with nothing* — I felt that T. S. Eliot had stated exactly the terms of my life. Yet I cannot say I was unhappy. I didn't understand the meanings of unhappiness or happiness, those paired conditions I came across in novels and stories and poems. I guessed at what they might involve: anxiety and relief from anxiety. In this I was my mother's child, preternaturally conscious of the cinching and loosening of my nerves. Happiness might be the heavy sleep sometimes induced (if I was lucky) by warm milk; unhappiness the light sleep, dream-punctured and unrestorative, with which I was far more familiar.

*   *   *

My mother's poor health was a constant, like my father's drinking but with less predictable consequences. My father and I both understood, though we didn't speak of it, that the person my mother should have fussed over wasn't me but herself. As she grew heavier and paler and more short of breath during my adolescence, my conflict with her enlarged to incorporate — always in wordless and unconscious ways — a lack of patience with her physical ailments that was simply the other side of my disdain for her brand of Christianity.

My mother was the person who introduced me to the New Testament: to my namesake and the other Nazarenes, to Paul and his epistles, to election and witness and grace. From her I learned of sin, transgression, and repentance, of abnegation and atonement, redemption and eternal salvation. And, of course, eternal damnation. My mother lived with a barely suppressed anxiety about her status with respect to the life to come. The good acts she might perform would never, she believed, fully counterbalance her various sins. The roots of my mother's faith somehow managed not to encounter sustaining soil, the come-what-may of forgiveness. Her spiritual doubt was not of the sort that characterizes — even legitimizes — most faith. It was dark, neurotic, urgent. At times it shaded into hysteria.

I discovered early on that my mother's God wasn't mine. I saw His intercession, in the person of Christ, as perpetual, unvarying, and utterly reasonable. Human beings might be capricious, but God was not: He was bound to deliver on His promises. On this issue I developed a way of thinking that merged elements of both my parents' worldviews, and by my twelfth year I had constructed for myself a deity to whom neither parent could give any credence. The God I knew was tolerant, relaxed in the knowledge that He and eternity were coterminous, and preoccupied with more weighty matters than my sins — which were unremarkable, and in any case carried with them their own punishment: isolation, my childhood enthrallment.

My father, who as an accountant had witnessed many massive reversals of fortune in the late Twenties, had no patience with self-deception, financial or spiritual. For him, the central question was whether and how other people, in their greedy stupidity, would make his life more difficult than it already was. Scotch on ice was his armor. Wearing it, he felt free to rail at the world. His hope for me was that I would become the renegade he couldn't be, except when drunk, and his disappointment (which gradually became indifference) sprang from his feeling that I too had opted for stopgap measures.

What my father didn't see was how extreme my divergences from my mother really were. She knew this, however, and undertook all possible manipulations to bring me back onto the solid ground of Protestant doctrine. My refusal of church would offend the Lord. My sense of His holiness was too inward. The discipline of spoken prayer was necessary, she insisted, to avoid the pitfalls of pride. That was it: my relations with God were too confident — and too tacit — to be trusted. Christian faith without community was dangerous.

Neither of my parents could possibly grasp the imaginative force of my god-concept — the exuberance of it. The God I had imagined was capable of anything and obliged to do nothing, although He would do whatever needed to be done, and only He knew what that was. This God would leave us to our own devices. His forgiveness was never in question: He had offered Christ, to make that clear. We had our Savior; what remained at issue was what we would do with Him — whether we would allow Him to save us. It seemed clear to me that God had stepped to one side of this question and was simply waiting for us to make up our minds.

*   *   *

Adolescence conferred power, but in a limited and crude sense. I stopped accompanying my mother to church when I was fifteen. In my sixteenth year I told my father that I wouldn't leave New York to go to college. I had no interest in Harvard or Yale. Instead, I was determined to know the city in which I'd lived almost like a visitor — and especially to spend time downtown, where my parents seldom took me and where I hadn't been encouraged to wander alone. I decided to apply only to schools in Manhattan, and after being accepted at New York University, I made it clear that I wouldn't remain at home but would live in an apartment building with other students.

My education was thus formally removed from my parents' control. Once I left home, I inhabited what is sometimes referred to as a parallel universe — a Manhattan with which neither of them, tied as they were to the Heights, was even remotely familiar.

During my four years downtown (I lived off Washington Square before moving, after my graduation in 1940, to the West Side), I read constantly and walked the city each day. I knew exactly the hour at which the sun, on a clear afternoon, would throw Broadway into shadow at the base of the Flatiron building. I knew when I could hear, for free, the NBC Symphony rehearse at Radio City, and who in the main Public Library could get me an advance ticket to an Auden poetry reading. I could hum the Sunday-morning belltones of all the churches on the West Side from Fifty-ninth Street to Harlem.

While at NYU I experienced most of these things on my own, but I wasn't entirely alone. I had several male friends who shared my interests and toward whom I felt affection. I learned how to eat out, and how to be entertaining. After our graduation one of my friends helped me find a job at Brentano's bookstore, where I worked for six years. By the time I left Brentano's in 1944 to begin graduate school, I had become one of the store's managers, and it was evident that I had a natural talent for finding and selling good books.

In those years I slept with a few women, all of whom I told myself I liked without admitting that they confused me, and that the pleasures of their bodies in no way mitigated the fear they inspired. Although I formed no lasting attachments, I always made sure to part on amicable terms. When I met Judith, soon after my twenty-seventh birthday, I'd been alone for several years, and it didn't seem worrisome that this was so. I was used to long stretches of solitude. Certain things seemed immutable: my often aching lower back and the late-evening walks I took in Riverside Park to ease my discomfort; the difficulty of my encounters with my father after my mother died; the eruptions and reverberations of memory; the relief of books; and above all, my ignorance of God's motives, which I was not in any case in a position either to abet or oppose.

My mother's death, after her prolonged illness, had lifted a burden of guilt. She had felt betrayed by me. I'd called her regularly but visited seldom, and she knew I'd resolved not to enter the turmoil of her dying. She told me about repeated nightmares, hoping somehow that I would transmit the calm of my own belief. But that was precisely what I couldn't do. My calm was a function of passivity. I could transmit nothing, even had I wanted to.

In January of 1943 my father was diagnosed as having cirrhosis of the liver, the disease that killed him by the end of the summer. I'd watched him decline after my mother's death and had urged him to cut back on his drinking and smoking, but he would hear nothing of it. As removed as he'd become from my mother during the course of their marriage, he still missed her. She had been the touchstone of his embittered life, the only person to whom he could display the full range and depth of his frustrations. Scotch dulled his need for her presence.

He was a man of unusual intelligence, but because his anger was so diffuse, he couldn't make full use of his incisiveness. It was continually subverted by his need to confer harsh judgments. I suspect he knew that he'd made a profound mistake in choosing to become an accountant. His choice had really been a compulsion — the result of a powerful, unconscious urge to force balance on a world dangerously out of kilter. And the work itself only heightened his sense of ineffectuality. He knew that what he did made no difference — it too was a stopgap measure. He too was powerless.

My father's disappointment in me was somewhat reduced by my ascent at Brentano's. The fact that I became, at last, a manager gave him some measure of satisfaction. Before his hospitalization we would meet, now and then, in one of several midtown bars near his office, and talk politics. He was predictably pessimistic about the war, though he was glad when the United States finally entered combat in Europe. It was about time, he said, that Americans put themselves on the line for their supposed ideals.

We didn't mention my mother. There was nothing to say. After her death he had given me all her books and her engagement ring. We'd taken her clothing and other belongings to the Salvation Army. I'd kept a few photos of her, and her Bible. The ring I sold (without telling my father) almost immediately. I never visited my father in the apartment on 180th Street; we always met downtown.

With my mother I'd known where I stood. I knew that her love for me was actually fear for my emotional safety, masking her own profound insecurity. I had pitied her, not wanting to. I knew, even as a child, that pity wasn't a useful response to her, but I couldn't help myself. I'd wanted even less to hate her for what she had been — my well-intentioned jailor.

With my father, however, everything was reversed. I hated him, not wanting to. I wanted even less to pity him. And I couldn't be certain that his reluctance to love me was not some-how my fault. This uncertainty was as old as my earliest memo-ries of my father's stern blue-grey eyes, his deep-chested voice telling me to come to him, the impatient movements of his hands as he pulled on my overcoat and mittens, and his long-stepped stride (with which I scrambled to keep up) as we walked the streets of Washington Heights on cold Saturday afternoons, os-tensibly to do errands but really so that my father could have a few quiet drinks in the company of other taciturn men — I was always the only child there — in a bar on 176th Street.

Sometimes I wondered whether he would notice if I were to slip away and run out the back entrance. How far would I get be-fore he realized I was missing? Unlike my mother, I had never doubted God, but I did doubt my father.

My father died just a few weeks after the Allies' disastrous raid on Schweinfurt, about which he'd been enraged: how could we not have known that the Germans were waiting for us? During my final visit with him in the hospital, he told me he was glad I'd been unable, because of my back, to serve. I'd probably already have been killed, he told me, and for nothing.

Listening to him, I understood that he wasn't celebrating my present safety but predicting and promising future dangers, and I felt a purer sorrow and loss at that moment than at any other. When the hospital called to tell me he was gone, I went out and bought a fifth of his favorite scotch. I'd intended to distract my-self, but my first drink had the unavoidably bitter taste of my fa-ther's life, and I couldn't finish it.

I did, however, drink a good deal in the year after his death — a year I spent reading poetry. I relished the problems that poems presented, and I enjoyed the effort of figuring out how and why

96

each one managed or failed to move me. I discovered that I wanted to be moved. All this I undertook along with my graduate work, at which I excelled. It was easy for me to do well in something that had always consumed my interest and energies. Having decided that I wanted to work with literary archives, I traded in my goal of becoming an archivist at the Library of Congress for that of working in an elite academic setting, where the collections I would supervise would be diverse and of high quality.

My labors appeared to be restorative. In spite of my drinking I ate and slept well, waking on most mornings to sensations of vigor and directedness: I knew what the days held for me. I didn't often want or seek the company of others, preferring (when I wasn't tucked away in one of several libraries I used for my work) the anonymity of bars. I had come to appreciate the reality of solitude and the illusion of community that bars provide. Like my father, I developed a few favorites, including the Five Spot, uptown, which offered some of the better jazz in Manhattan.

It was there, in fact, that I met Judith. She was sitting alone at the bar, reading Auden's collected poems, which had only just come out; I had a copy on order at Brentano's but was surprised to see one in the hands of a stranger. She wore a dark blue cashmere cardigan over a tan broadcloth shirt, rather male in cut and finish but softened by a necklace of gracefully linked silver leaves. Her hair was pulled back by a silver clasp. She wore small pearl earrings. I remember perfectly these neutral but elegant colors: that deep blue sweater, the dun of her shirt, the creamy circles on her earlobes, the silver's glint at the base and nape of her neck. These things stood out then as now, but the long leanness of her body was less apparent. She sat as if curled around the book she was reading, placing it at the center of her body, and she didn't notice me noticing her, then sitting next to her, ordering my drink and straining to see which poem she was reading. When I finally spoke to her, she started in surprise. I remember how ambiguously colored her eyes were as she stared at me for a moment, trying to identify me.

"Do I know you?" she said, and I shook my head and introduced myself.

"Which poem are you reading?" I asked.

She handed me the open book. My eyes landed on the lines to which her red-tipped forefinger pointed:

> *We are lived by powers we pretend to understand:*
> *They arrange our loves; it is they who direct at the end*
> *The enemy bullet, the sickness, or even our hand.*

I read and then glanced at her.

"Overstated," she said without self-consciousness, "but still scary."

Her eyes were neither grey nor green. I was instantly, irrevocably drawn in.

THE MORNING AFTER MY DINNER with Roberta, I found two messages in my campus mailbox. One was from Edith, asking me to meet her for lunch to discuss the monthly report to the Board. The other was from my dinner companion. Roberta's note said that her mother had suffered a mild heart attack and was in the hospital. Roberta would be in Hoboken for a few days.

I went to my office and called Edith to confirm our lunch. Then I decided to take a walk around the quad, to ponder Roberta's news. I was surprised that she'd felt the need to share it with me — and surprised, too, by my own revelations, the night before. The only people who'd known about Judith's suicide, apart from the staff at Hayden, were Len and Carol. I'd told everyone else who knew Judith that she'd died suddenly of pneumonia. Her friends were aware that she'd been weak and unwell, and they didn't doubt my account. I justified my lie by telling myself that Judith herself would have countenanced it.

Her death had saddened but not shocked Len and Carol. She had been at Hayden for six years, and they'd seen little of her in the decade before that. They knew about the psychotic breaks that had periodically interrupted her depression. They knew that by the time she entered Hayden, in 1959, Judith hadn't been able to go to work or even to eat regularly; that at Hayden she would sometimes refuse to dress or bathe, and that she always insisted on having a light on in her room. After their infrequent visits with Judith (conducted, as always, in a spirit of unresentful but fundamentally disengaged duty), Len and Carol had reported to me the same things I'd observed. Judith was reading various Kabbalistic writings. She was playing albums of Bud Powell and John Coltrane on the record player Len and Carol had given her. She was keeping a journal. She was sleeping a great deal.

Len and Carol understood that the woman they'd raised was retreating from the world the three of them had experienced together. Although they were distressed by Judith's evident pain, they didn't believe — they'd never believed — that there was anything they could do about it. It was a given, like Lottie's and Sam's accidental deaths and their own subsequent responsibility for Judith's physical welfare. Her emotional welfare had never been, in their eyes, their business.

My move from New York to assume my post at the university broke my social links with them, and with Manhattan. I found myself finally in solitude, the point at which I seem to have been aimed all along, like an arrow that after much delay had finally found its target.

The university was and remains my haven. Naturally there are individuals with whom I have reason and desire to interact — Edith, of course, and others here and there. I'm no hermit, I like the sound of voices, the refreshment of conversation and laughter. I'm very fond of stimulating exchanges with particularly fine researchers. But behind or beyond these comminglings, I have safeguarded my solitude. It is essentially intact.

Books never cease to astonish me. When I was a child, I knew — in the incontestable way that children know things — that God was an author who'd imagined me, which is why I (and everyone else) existed: to populate His narrative. My task was to imagine God in return: this was all He and I owed each other.

Between people it is less clear what is owed. Yet perhaps what's called love is really an empathetic and hungry imagination. One must be willing to enter other stories — even terrifying or dangerous ones, or those of uncertain outcome.

Judith imagined too readily, and I too cautiously. Now I am no longer so afraid, but that doesn't matter. Our shared life is not, after all, some story whose end I can keep rewriting. It was brought to a close.

T HE BOARD," said Edith, "is at it again." She had ordered her usual lunch — an ungainly tuna sandwich surrounded by potato chips, which she pushed into small
mounds on the plate. "Honestly, Matt, you'd think they have
nothing better to do than pretend they're archivists."

As I watched her play with her chips, I could sense Edith
preparing to spill her anxiety about the Board's latest inter-
vention. She reached for the salt shaker, but I gently restrained
her.

"Your blood pressure," I said. "You've told me to remind
you."

She frowned and blushed, obviously exasperated. "You're
right, I have," she said.

I smiled at her. "Calm yourself," I said. "It's not worth ruin-
ing your lunch." I sipped at my coffee, wishing it were stronger.
Edith's tension wasn't contagious, but it required a certain kind
of management, and I was tired. The night before, I'd drunk several more glasses of wine than usual, and they (along with the
cigarettes, no doubt) had taken a small toll. I was conscious of a
thrumming in my temples.

"They're such pompous fools, those Board members," Edith
said, taking a large bite of her sandwich. Tuna salad spilled out
from either side.

"Shit," she yelped. "I'm sorry, Matt. I guess I'm feeling a bit frayed. You know it's not like me to —"

"— stop," I interrupted. "It's completely understandable. You're under a lot of pressure. You don't have to explain."

She stopped toying with her food and looked straight at me. "It helps knowing that. It really does," she said, beginning to compose herself. "Thanks for your patience."

"No problem," I said. "You're plenty patient with me."

"Am I?"

"Yes — when I'm cranky, which I probably am a lot."

She laughed. "Constantly," she said. "I'm always complaining to Tim about you."

"And what does he say?"

"He says I should be glad I've got someone to complain to."

"Tim's right, you know. I guess that makes us all lucky."

Edith leaned back in her chair, and I could feel her getting ready to say something probing. She's so seldom directly personal with me that I can always detect the impulse; her physical movements give her away.

"Not exactly," she said. "You're the one who doesn't have someone to complain to at home. Matt — do you ever think about finding someone?"

"A person, do you mean?" I began laughing, and Edith's face reddened.

"Of course," she said. "I'm not talking about a dog or a cat."

"That's good," I said. "At least with a person you don't have to worry about buying enough canned food or refilling the water bowl."

"Quit fooling around. I'm talking seriously here. I mean, when was the last time you took someone out on a date?"

"Last night, as a matter of fact." As soon as I spoke, I realized that I could neither lie to Edith nor tell her the truth.

"You're kidding."

103

"No."

"Where'd you meet her? What's she like?"

"In the neighborhood. She's too young for me. No — that's not it. I'm too old for her."

"Oh for God's sake! What is she, ten or something?"

"Three times that. But not the older-man type."

"Don't count on it. I have to say, Matt, I'm really pleased to hear about this. It just seems wrong to me that you spend so much time alone. I mean, solitude's fine, but it can get to be a bad habit." She paused. "How long has it been since Judith died?"

I was caught completely off guard by her question; it'd been years since either one of us had mentioned Judith. I had to look away. After a moment or two, my eyes focused on a large, brightly colored canvas on the far wall of the cafeteria. In its garishness, the painting reminded me of Roberta's description of her parents' work, and this association only fueled my consternation.

"Too long," I said.

Edith was scanning my face closely, attempting to read it. "What exactly does that mean?" she asked softly.

"It means too long to remember, and too long to forget." Suddenly I felt acutely sick — not to my stomach but in a deep, bone-and-muscle way, as if my entire system were registering an invisible assault. With it came a wave of dizziness. I closed my eyes briefly; when I opened them, Edith was giving me a concerned look.

"Well then," she said. "As long as you're not turning into a hermit." Her tone indicated she wouldn't press further.

"No, no," I said, still feeling light-headed. I needed Edith to keep talking while I collected myself. "Tell me about the Board. What's their scheme now?"

Edith moved briskly into gear. "I need some advice on how to handle the latest attack on our independence. It involves you rather directly."

"Yes?"

"It's ridiculous, but I'm afraid it's also a fait accompli. Darnton and a few others on the Board called Lewis and convinced him — I mean, can you *imagine* a more spineless president of a university? — to go along with their newest scheme, which they're billing as 'student involvement.' The idea is to appoint one grad student from each of three departments — English, History, and Computer Science — to serve as so-called library guardians. They're supposed to work closely with us to maintain, preserve, and expand — those are Darnton's words — the Mason Room collection. Darnton insists this has nothing to do with your performance, Matt. He's as pleased as always with you. It's a matter of giving capable students a closer look at how institutional resources are developed, as he put it. Have you ever heard such crap?"

She paused and shook her head. "I mean, how on earth can three grad students with no prior experience in library science be anything but a nuisance? And what's worse, we don't even get to pick them! That's left up to the three department heads. Which means that we'll have several complete strangers milling around, sticking their greasy fingers into everything." Edith pushed away her half-eaten sandwich in disgust.

I was able, by this time, to chuckle. "You have to look at the funny side of this," I said.

"There isn't one," she moaned.

"At least two of these guardians are from the humanities," I said. "We're relatively safe. Only one will try to talk us into putting the whole collection on disk or some such nonsense. Can't you hear it? I mean, who needs Eliot's galleys when we can fit the entire 'Waste Land' onto a microchip?"

Edith started smiling, but she wasn't finished worrying. A fresh cloud of anxiety blotted her face.

"Actually, it's the Eliot material I'm thinking about," she said. "And the other more or less modern items. I mean, even the

105

Board won't let a couple of grad students paw over the older stuff. All of the Poe letters, the American Transcendentalist manuscripts, the slavery archives — those are clearly off-limits. But the modern stuff — well, the Board doesn't mind using the twentieth-century portions of the collection as a learning experience for these three students. Darnton said something about how their first assignment should be to write some flashy descriptions of our recent acquisitions for the alumni magazine. Of course he's working the fund-raising angle, and he smells some free labor. He specifically mentioned the Mencken papers, the Harlem Renaissance photos, and the Eliot letters. Darnton wants his guardians to become familiar with those acquisitions."

"What is there to become familiar with?" I said. "These things have all been indexed. That's it. There's nothing else for anyone to do but wait until the stuff is out of mothballs."

Edith shook her head again. "I know. And Darnton knows that too. But he wasn't really listening, he was thinking about the fund-raising."

She stared off, lost in her frustration, and I finished my coffee. My stomach felt tight. The usual comfort I find in Edith's presence had deserted me, and I needed our lunch to be over. But I had another question to ask.

"Edith," I said, "have the three students been picked already? Do you know who they are?"

"Yes, they have — and yes, I know them. Their names, that is. The computer scientist's is something unpronounceably Japanese. Actually, I've met one of the three — and so have you. The English department has bequeathed Roberta Spire to us. She happens to be one of their shining lights, you know. Apparently an excellent poet. I guess she'll get to see the envelopes of the Eliot letters after all. She'll be glad for that, won't she?"

I had my answer.

"Oh, yes," I said. "I'm sure she will."

Two

1959

Hayden House
April 20

Light came first, then words: in the beginning the luminous mirror. First light, then language; first the *en-sof*, the unknowable, then the letters of the Torah all jumbled, from which somehow we were supposed to construct a world — somehow! — though how did He expect us to do this once Adam the dust-man had broken the sacred vessels and scattered the light like motes of his own pale dust everywhere, leaving what the Kabbalists call shards. Leaving us broken incomplete wordless, each of our souls attached to a letter in the Torah but still unconnected — separated in the Here and Now?

Eliot:

> *I can connect*
> *Nothing with nothing.*

The Holy One cannot fail to see how lost we are, how our souls' letters form not a language but only gibberish. How opaque and dull the light has become. (Always I keep the bulb lit in this little room, but it does no good; I do it only as a gesture toward Him.)

Hayden, my nicely landscaped hell. I am utterly infantilized here. It seems they think I am the baby the cops delivered to Len and Carol after those two deaths on Broadway, some dead couple's helpless child.

Today the doctors talked to me about eating; yesterday, bathing; tomorrow, dressing, combing my hair each morning. Also they speak of what they call my episodes, and I can read the fear in their eyes — as if they and not me were experiencing all this.

I want to forgive Matt for bringing me to this place, but I don't yet know how.

April 29

All my books have arrived. Matt packed them carefully, on their sides or with spines up, to spare the bindings. One of the attendants — black, the color of bitter chocolate, around the mouth he looks amazingly like Bud Powell! — brought in the boxes, and a good-sized bookshelf. He helped me shelve all the books. Later I counted them, one hundred and seven.

My typewriter sits on a table in the corner, across the room from the bed. I have plenty of paper, my fountain pen, two bottles of ink. I will use the pen for letters if I ever feel like writing to anyone. I can't imagine that.

For myself I will use this machine. I need its metal solidity, the clacking it makes.

I can't picture the living room of the apartment without my books. There are gaps now in the shelves where my books

110

were, but soon Matt will buy as many as it takes to fill the empty spaces. He thinks that will work, but it won't. His new books will give him no pleasure because they'll remind him of where I am and how I got here.

I've organized the titles by subject, just as Matt would do: top shelf, poetry; middle shelf, Kabbalah; bottom shelf, miscellaneous, including art books and my records. Eventually Len and Carol will bring the record player they promised me, and then I can listen to Powell again. For now I hold my favorite tunes in my head. I can hear all the lines, all the changes, all the shadings, all the fury sadness loss and that stunning virtuosity, the truth of the playing.

I have to force myself to eat. When I manage to sleep, I dream of the apartment.

It looks the same, but Matt and I aren't its tenants. Lottie and Sam live there, and they have a child who is me but not me, a dark-haired girl who's safe.

May 2

Yesterday I threw out the book of Auden's poems I was reading the first time I saw Matt. The attendant who empties the trash (a different one, surly, not the man who reminds me of Powell) tried to make me take it back when he found it in my basket, but I refused, and then the bastard told Dr. Clay, and I was pressed into one of those predictable dialogues in which Clay tells me my actions are "emblematic" — how psychiatrists love such words! — of other refusals. This time I told him in a deliberate, malicious way to fuck his mother, I could discard whatever I liked.

That seemed to unnerve him. I could tell I'd made him angry, but I also knew *he* knew he couldn't be openly angry at me, couldn't show it. It's easy to turn the tables on these people.

But I'm alone, so the tables are turned on me.

May 3

Poetry. The actions of reading and writing it seem so remote. I can bring myself to read Eliot but most of my other favorites scare me, they're so much less controlled. (Matt likes Eliot precisely for that control, but I need him for what slips out in spite of it, and for his remarkable cadences: *Teach us to care and not to care . . .*)

I'm having trouble remembering specific poems, anybody's, my own included. But yesterday a few lines came to me from a LeRoi Jones poem, and I hunted for it in several journals and finally found it in a copy of *Beat Coast East:*

> *Or the broad-edged silly music the wind*
> *Makes when I run for a bus . . .*
>
> *Things have come to that.*

I am reading the *Zohar*, the *Book of Splendor*. I am poring over it for clues, as if it were a detective story — though God knows what I can really expect to find in a bunch of obscure epigraphs and homilies written in the thirteenth century by someone named Moses de Leon.

Surprisingly, I find a great deal. This, today:

> *But later, men abandoned the road of faith and left behind the singular tree which looms high over all trees, and adhered to the place which is continually shifting from one hue to another, from good to evil and evil to good, and they descended from on high and adhered below to the uncertain, and deserted the supreme and changeless One.*

The doctors are giving me medications that make my hands and feet swell. I feel distorted. They won't give

112

me any news. I'm no longer allowed to read the Times or the other papers every day because (the doctors say) I get too upset.

How can the *tikkun* occur if we don't know what is happening to us — all of us?

They are hiding the world from me.

Everything is so much more frightening than it was when I was living with Matt. I was beginning to accept — why does Matt feel that *now* is the time for me to be here — can't he see it was so much worse for me ten years ago, right after the war?

Perhaps it's Matt's turn to be frightened, and that's why he brought me here. Matt can no longer count on his Christ. I've talked to him about the *tikkun*, the repair, but he won't hear it. He hears only that the original light was shattered and then dispersed, and the original light seems to him as irretrievable as the first months of our marriage, when our bodies and our feelings were not different things but the same. And he could find redemption, grace, each time we kissed and each time he came into me, looking into my eyes and seeing everything there, not just himself mirrored, tiny and distant; or me in shadow, hazy, recessive: as he sees me now. Through a glass darkly.

I can't reconstruct how it happened, how one day I knew that what we felt was not being told anymore through our touching.

We have become opaque to each other, have lost the lovely irreplaceable translucence of that first feeling . . .

May 9

It has been exactly three weeks since I came here. Today the doctors allowed Matt to visit me for the first time.

He was wearing the striped cotton shirt I'd bought him sometime in the second year of our marriage, when we had no money but occasionally made extravagant purchases for one another. I remember the day I found the shirt — at dePinna's, on sale but still expensive — and brought it home in a flush of guilt and excitement. The stripes were a bluish purple, fairly wide, against a pure white.

When the attendants opened the door to my room, I saw the stripes on Matt's shirt before anything else. I couldn't take in all of him, even though I knew he was entirely there; I felt his presence charge the room. The stripes had paled over the years, but they held their essential color. My eyes dipped past Matt's face and landed on the first attendant, the same surly one who got me into trouble with Dr. Clay.

Leave, I said.

The doctor says no unsupervised visits, he answered in an uninflected voice, just like a machine. So I went after him. I don't recall the exact sequence of events, but in a brief time I had a clump of his hair in my hand, and Matt and the other attendant had me pinned by the arms, and the attendant I'd attacked was telling me (in that passionless voice) to stop spitting at him or he would call Clay. So I stopped.

Then was I able to look at my husband. His eyes were lit now with panic, their blue on fire, and I wanted to punish him by laughing but I knew there was no point. At Hayden everything is pointless but especially punishment.

You're wearing my shirt, I said to him. The one I gave you.

My voice was low, calmer now. I felt his grip loosen, then he let go. The other attendant held on a few more seconds until he was satisfied that I wouldn't move anywhere quickly. Then he took his hands off me, and I stood perfectly still.

Yes, Matt said.

I paused and turned to the attendant at my side. The bitter-chocolate one, Bud Powell. I knew I was safe with him.

114

How long is this visit supposed to be? I said very quietly.

Two hours, he said, also very quietly.

Listen, I said. You stay here for fifteen minutes so you can report that everything began under control. Then you leave us by ourselves for an hour and a half. Then you come back for fifteen minutes so you can report that everything ended under control. Is that a deal?

Yes, he said. If you keep the middle part under control.

I nodded.

He gave the other attendant a signal; the man left. The three of us moved to the corner of the room. Matt took my hand.

I am going to stand by this window, the attendant said, and he moved over to the room's southern corner. And I am going to watch the outside world, and you two are going to talk softly if you don't want me to hear what you're saying. I'll leave in fifteen minutes and I'll come back at a quarter to two. I'll knock once, then enter. Be ready for me.

He looked directly at me, though I knew he was speaking to us both. His eyes were a limpid brown-grey under thick brows. In that instant he was much more real to me than Matt, but when he turned his back on us it was as if he'd already left the room. Matt's hand in mine was damp.

Excuse my outburst, I said to Matt, I didn't mean to scare you.

It's all right, he said, I'm all right.

We sat on the bed as we would've done at home: Matt at one end, me at the other, our legs angled across, only this time not intersecting, both of us careful not to touch although there wasn't much room, the bed being narrow.

I don't know what Matt was looking at because I wasn't looking at him. We said nothing, and after what seemed like little more than a long pause (but it must've been fifteen minutes), the attendant left.

We talked in the middle part, as the attendant had called it. When he returned for the last fifteen minutes, we were again silent. As far as he knew, we hadn't spoken during the entire visit.

I can't remember what we talked about. There'd been so much talking and arguing, so much crying, so much anger and sorrow in the days before Matt brought me here that neither of us now had anything serious to say.

There was something about Matt's work, something about Len and Carol — a leak in their radiator? — yes, but the water didn't damage their record collection, I'll get my record player eventually.

I have no idea how Matt looked as we spoke, or whether he even glanced at me. I was unable to bear looking or being looked at.

He thinks I'll get better here, that I will be restored, as he puts it, and more in control, and less easily upset by everything.

You're not functioning well, he said as we were driving here. I am not interested in functioning, I said, and he said you know what I mean. And I said you mean you can't stand my being this way, as I am; and he said Judith don't keep doing that, and we fell silent again, stuck in the same place.

He wasn't afraid when we first met. But he's become afraid of me.

May 11

Zohar: "At times the Shekhinah tastes the other, bitter side, and then her face is dark."

May 14

Now that the weather's mild, they've let us wander the grounds, which are vast, studded with purple and pink aza-

116

leas, many dogwoods, magnolias. It has been a lush, rainy spring. The border gardens are full of pansies and marigolds and impatiens in all different shades; the pachysandra is thick under the shade trees. The gardener is evidently the only happy employee here. Everything thrives.

I spend much of each morning outdoors. In the afternoon I go inside and daydream about the city, Central Park's flowers in spring, the Botanical Gardens behind the Brooklyn Museum, all the places I miss. It is hideously quiet here.

I don't talk much to the other patients. They are dull, their pain doesn't interest me, I have no desire for connection. It's healthier to be silent.

Matt is my sole real connection. The others have been products of chance; Pam in Boston, Mary and Clara and a few of the couples we know in New York — these are all ties of chance, affectionate ties but weak, easily severed. I know I won't hear from these people much, or for very long, now that I'm here; being here will make clear what divides us.

But Matt is afraid of me now. It wasn't like that at the beginning, when we trusted each other in that animal way. I was the one who got scared first — but not of him. Never of him. He has made me angrier and sadder than anyone else ever could, but he's never frightened me.

No. I was scared of the things I started reading about. Of the camps dotted across Germany and Poland. I was the one who made Matt begin to see the precise science of it, the inconceivably systematic deaths.

The *Zohar:* God is part mercy, part stern judgment; and when His judgment enlarges, it overwhelms.

The Holy One, be blessed, spoke: Man, life you have abandoned, and to death you cleave; truly, death awaits you . . .

117

> *But if Adam transgressed, in what did the rest of the world sin? . . . When man stood upright, all creatures, beholding him, were seized with fear of him, and slavelike they followed after him.*

May 15

I miss whiskey, neat shots of it in the dusk as I listen to Elmo Hope or Monk or Powell.

If Len and Carol don't bring the fucking record player, I *will* go crazy.

Matt shouldn't have worried so much about my drinking. He made it the wrong issue or the issue it wasn't. The real issue was the space the whiskey made for me, a space Matt didn't trust and anyway feared, especially in his own life.

The things he fears, he tries to take away from me. A certain kind of hunger I have.

Matt was right, I couldn't have stayed in Manhattan, I was coming apart, everything terrified me. But I'm still in trouble here: this isn't the safe place Matt wants to think it is. They take away the whisky but the trouble remains and is not (as the doctors would say) susceptible to treatment. I'm waiting for Matt to learn that, so he'll take me back, as I am.

A certain kind of hunger. To know what happened and at least ask why. Because the *tikkun* can't start until everyone asks what happened — not just the Jews but everybody.

The strange thing is that Christ evidently saw this.

Matt's waiting for something, but he won't budge. No one taught him how to take what he wants, so he just waits. I call it a sin not to satisfy your own hunger. Matt's been duped.

> *Teach us to care and not to care*
> *Teach us to sit still*

118

Matt has learned only to sit still, which isn't sufficient.

I want my fucking record player. I want to hear Powell play "It Never Entered My Mind" like the prayer it wasn't meant to be, a prayer of sex and loss. I want to hear how all of a sudden Powell reverses things. And what he lets out! — the hidden life —

May 16

Matt's second visit. This time I put on fresh clothes, earrings. My hair was clean. I can't afford to be fully female here, it hurts too much. I guess Matt can't afford to be fully male either. He showed up in an old cardigan and loose grey pants that disguise what I like best about him. That supple firm leanness of his.

Matt doesn't look like Sam in any of the pictures Len gave me. Sam was even taller, very lanky, boyish. Matt is self-possessed, he holds himself differently, with a certain elegance and guardedness I can't find in the pictures of my father.

Father. When I write *father* or *mother* I split in two. One of me is incredulous and the other is enraged, and when I try to push the two selves together a sensation of panic inserts itself between them, and this I think is a defense against a sadness so profound I can't even begin feeling it.

Matt wanted to know what I was writing. I told him that all I can do is keep this journal. I told him what I've been reading. He asked me some questions. I knew he wanted to know how I'm really doing. So I told him that the conditions of my life here preclude my talking about it, and he said what conditions, and I said internment — it's a camp here, you know. He got agitated and reminded me of all our discussions about what Hayden could do for me. How I would be able to like my life again after spending some time apart from it, examining it with the help of professionals.

I could recite all his arguments in my sleep, but I haven't accepted them. I told him I still feel betrayed, and he got agitated again. It wasn't that I regretted saying it, afterward, but just that I knew it had done no good. We have this wall between us, unbreachable.

The thing is, he's right, but I am too.

When he left, we were able to kiss one another but it was a passionless kiss, almost like siblings. He told me his work was going well. I believe that; he's always been good at immersing himself in work. I could never get the distance that work requires. How did I do it all those years at the office — typing all day, answering phones, taking letters . . . The daily act of being with others but not really being with them, just as they weren't really with me.

Len and Carol were the ones who taught me how to go through the motions. They're masters at it. But the difference between them and me is that they've always had each other and I never had them, not in a deep trustworthy way.

Lottie and Sam —

May 20

Dr. Clay is trying to make me talk about my childhood. I meet with him once a week and with one of his young apprentices each day. There are three of them, a woman and two men. My little team of sorcerers.

Clay asks me a string of questions. I answer the ones that don't bore me, which is to say about half. For the time being, Clay has accepted this — what he calls my "stalling maneuver" — but he doesn't like it. It leaves gaps in the story he wishes to compose, the one about my life.

Does talking about Len and Carol bore you, he asked me today.

I've thought plenty about them, I answered, I know what they did and why. It no longer interests me.

What do you feel about the fact that they haven't yet visited you here, he said. (Which surprised me. He is cannier than he appears to be.)

I feel just fine about that, I said. Only I do want my record player.

That's how it tends to go. Sometimes I feel guilty for resisting Clay, I try to tell myself I'm here, so why not go along with it? And I can hear Matt's anguished pleading — the only time in our marriage he ever pleaded with me was when he tried to get me to come here — but I just can't believe in it yet, and I can't imagine when I will.

Which is why I feel incarcerated. But none of these headshrinkers understand this.

The attendant who looks like Powell understands, perhaps? Though I'm probably making that up, to feel better. Pretending I see something in his eyes.

I can't do that with Matt anymore. But it was there, a long time ago, something I saw in his eyes.

Once he recognized what had happened in Europe, the thing I saw in his eyes began to dim. I can't see it now.

Matthias was never connected to his Christ through love, only through awe. The *Zohar* says that through the second we come to the first, which is loftier.

Awe is safer, though: you don't have to risk the terror of loving a God who turns His face.

May 29

Matt's third visit was a blur; I can remember only the end, when the attendant, the one who's like Powell, came back into the room and I was begging Matt to take me home, and Matt was crying but not letting me touch him. He was slumped against the wall next to the window, just where the attendant stands at the beginning and end of our visits.

His face in his hands. He never sobs but I can tell when he's crying.

When I came back from Boston, after the first time I left him, he cried and then I saw in his eyes the fear I'd never noticed before, not from the crying but from what he'd suddenly felt: a need to keep separate from me, to protect himself. It must have terrified him.

I never wanted to keep separate from him. But after a time it began to dawn on me that the question isn't what one wants but what one can bear.

The attendant stood quietly in the doorway for the last fifteen minutes of the visit while Matt finished crying and I stopped begging. We were finally silent, sitting side by side on the bed (like two people waiting for a train to arrive), when the announcement came that our visit was over.

That much I do remember: the two of us sitting in what could be called communion because love persists between us, but which must also be called separation because fear now reigns.

June 3

Len and Carol. Some New Yorkers wouldn't last twenty minutes outside the city; they take their whole life from it. Len and Carol are that kind. I can't remember going anywhere with them except Jones Beach. When Pam invited me to Boston for a weekend, sometime in the fall of our sophomore year, Len was skeptical. Why do you want to go there, he said, if you want history and old buildings you can always run up to the Cloisters.

And when I went to Boston and came back, Carol said welcome home, and I knew then that she didn't mean *home* as the three of us, as the apartment on Grove Street; she meant New York, a larger home, where we three were thrown in with people but didn't need to engage with them.

If you don't want them to be, New York's intimacies aren't personal.

Len and Carol are utterly assimilated Jews, but this is how their repressed Jewishness has always manifested itself: in their desire to stay in New York without ever having to think about leaving it, about uprooting. There are enough Jews in the city to afford a kind of protection — safety in numbers — but not enough to require affiliation.

When I was fourteen, Carol took me to a synagogue for the first time. You should at least see the inside of one, she said. You're at the age where religion might interest you. And besides, you should know where some Jews go every Friday night and on the Holy Days, when Len and I don't have to go to work because — well, because we don't!

Carol's nice infectious laugh. Sometimes it was like a first snow, refreshing and unexpected. At other times her laughter repelled me with its high-pitched insistence.

She hid behind it. She and Len are good at hiding. Manhattan suits them. They work hard and drink and club-hop, and no one asks them any questions they'd rather not answer, because no one gets that close.

Happily lost in the shuffle.

They do know how to have a good time. But they also know jazz, which means they know something other than a good time.

123

But they aren't talking.

And over the years they've moved away from music that's too unsettling or subversive. Swing has become their idea of jazz. They aren't keen on bebop, they don't know what to make of Miles or Coltrane. After the war, all they wanted was energy, technique — the brilliance of Bird's runs without any of the excruciating pain that buoyed the playing, kept it airborne.

Len and Carol don't hear pain. For them there's never been anything painful to acknowledge. Especially since the war.

That first visit to the synagogue, in 1932. A couple of years after the Crash. Manhattan: a deflated balloon. Probably lots more people than usual were attending church or temple back then, scrambling for solace — though on the day Carol and I walked into Central Synagogue, the place was deserted.

I remember thinking less about its physical features than about its wonderful quiet, so different in quality from the quiet of the few churches I'd entered.

Carol got bored right away and walked out. The only cool dark places I like are jazz clubs, she said.

I stayed, poked around a little, found a shelf in the entrance foyer with some printed material on various subjects. Reprints of newspaper articles, mostly. Matt would've appreciated my persistence: I dragged Carol back in — she was smoking a cigarette on the corner of Lex and Fifty-fifth — and asked her if I could take some of those papers on the shelf.

You mean this stuff? she said, thumbing it. It's just a heap of propaganda. But sure, go ahead, she said, you're Jewish, anybody who's Jewish can help themselves. That's what it's here for. Just don't expect to find it interesting.

I took a sampling of the poorly mimeographed sheets and brought them home and read them. They concerned obscure topics about which I knew nothing: Torah, Midrash, matters of law and observance.

But there were two short articles that interested me. Both were from German newspapers, awkwardly translated. One announced a lecture series taking place in Berlin on "the Kabbalah, or the study of the Tree of Life and its hidden secrets." I had no idea what that meant, but the image of the tree and its secrets captured me. The other article was about Ernst Thälmann, the Communist who was making a bid for the German presidency. His most dangerous opponent, the article said, was Adolf Hitler — a known Jew-hater; progressive American Jews should provide moral and financial support to the Communist party.

Oh, Christ, Carol said, when I showed her the article.

I had heard her and Len discussing the situation in Germany, and I knew they disliked Hitler and his party. I figured she would find the article enlightening, but it only annoyed her.

Look, she said. People here are barely keeping body and soul together. Why are these people after *us* for money?

She put the article aside and turned to me.

The thing to remember about most Jews, she said, is that they don't know how to leave well enough alone. I mean, they're over there in Germany, and here we are in New York, and still they've got to stretch their arms across the ocean and try to pull us back into their troubles. Who needs it?

I remember watching her light a cigarette, then exhale noisily.

Your grandfather worked like a bastard to get over here, she said. His son doesn't need to be harassed by a bunch of shtetl types all in a tizzy because some Communist needs money. Ernst Thälmann's not even Jewish, for God's sake! We've got our own damn troubles.

I hadn't ever heard her refer to my grandfather, the father of Lottie and Len. There was a shock in this, in the sudden realization that I had a history that involved a language and place that were foreign and thus — to me — exotic, attractive.

Carol was still irritated.

Don't let anyone tell you there's anything wrong with being Jewish, she said. But don't let anyone tell you there's anything right about it, either. The world these days is not a safe place.

More surprises. Carol had never been given to large pronouncements. She left that to Len, who did most of his pronouncing on the topic of music, not politics or religion. But here was Carol suddenly not taking something lightly. And there I was, torn between the pleasure of discovering more large secrets and the fear that the next revelation (there had to be more!) might not be harmless.

But there weren't any more.

When I think back, I see how I got through the 1930s: just as Len and Carol did: work and jazz. I listened to music all the way through those days.

I had my first drink with Len and Carol the night Ernst Thälmann was thrown in jail by the Nazis. We heard the news on the radio, and at first Len said nothing. He fixed three strong, cold martinis. I had just turned sixteen.

Thälmann died in a camp at the end of the war. Later I heard he was a Stalinist and probably an anti-Semite. I remember Len, his first martini gone, pacing the floor of the living room, cursing the Nazis, cursing Thälmann, cursing all of them. He was scared, as he damn well should have been.

Carol laughed at his cursing and told him to forget about it — what good did it do to get so riled up?

The war, when it came, was a sorry thing. That's how Len referred to it: a sorry but necessary thing. This Hitler guy's insane, we have to stop him from taking over all of Europe, don't we?

And the Jews? I can remember Len's words: Yeah, seems they're having it especially rough. But who can tell what's really going on over there? Rumors — who can tell?

No new revelations.

That day at the temple Carol had said all that Carol would say on the subject of Jewishness, which wasn't much and amounted to this: Leave me alone.

Eliot: . . . *human kind / Cannot bear very much reality.*

June 5

Clay tells me I should be putting this time at Hayden to good use. He is suggesting something about what I'm not facing, what I'm hiding. As if in the middle of nowhere, hours from home, in the company of strangers, I am supposed to reveal important secrets about myself.

As if. Everything here is as if.

I keep telling him that whatever secrets I contain are nothing compared to the average German's secrets. Just what *was* that smell carried south from Sachsenhausen into the village? Somebody had a father, mother, sister, brother who looked the other way. What are my secrets as against theirs?

June 29

Matt's visit this week, another failure for me, though perhaps not for him. I can't tell how things register in him. The pain is there in the way he only glances at me when we speak. None of those long stretches I remember, when our eyes would lock in an easy languorous embrace. Matt's eyes so blue, a deep navy. His brows haven't turned color yet. His hair and mustache are greying, but those brows still have their first sandy shade, that earliest smoothness.

I would stroke them with my index fingers, over and over, one finger on each brow as we lay on our sides talking, our eyes embracing. The hair beneath my fingertips incredibly soft and smooth.

Those first months of marriage — a kind of dream now, in which I want so desperately to believe. They did happen, I wasn't dreaming them; so why do I feel obliged to call those months a dream?

I began waking up slowly into history, from which we do not emerge as from other nightmares.

During the visit I asked Matt to ask Clay to let me read the newspapers again. He refused. You're on their side, I told him, it feels to me like a conspiracy.

There's no conspiracy, Judith, he said.

I saw how it exhausted him to say it but I didn't care. I kept pushing and finally he got angry. He told me he'd thrown away all my files.

I couldn't believe it.

For your sake and mine, he said. I couldn't bear having those files in the apartment anymore.

They weren't yours to throw away, I said.

It doesn't matter, he said.

It does to me, I said. I was trying to hold his eyes, but he pulled his gaze away and I was suddenly overwhelmed with loss: all my dwindling connection.

We didn't speak any more, and then the attendant who is like Powell came in and told us to say goodbye, and we said it. Then Matt left quickly, quietly, like any dream evanescing.

July 3

Today Dr. Clay played God and handed down his judgment upon my head.

We have arrived, he said, at a diagnosis of your condition, which we would like to share with you.

Keep it to yourselves, I said.

We think you should know, he said. So we can talk about what it means for your future.

My future is not a function of your diagnosis, I said. With all due respect.

That may be, he said (quickly) and then (more slowly) but you can look at the diagnosis as a resource. Something helpful, useful. A way of thinking about what lies ahead.

Go on then, I said.

You are suffering from manic depression. It is a fairly common disease characterized by high and low moods, erratic emotion, intense shifts from elation to despair. It afflicts many people. It cannot be cured — or rather, we don't yet have a cure for it — but it can be controlled through certain therapies.

Such as, I said. (Stiffening.)

Shock therapy for one, he said. A treatment that can be highly effective, although it is not without risks to the system.

What system, I asked.

Physical and psychic, he said. Body and mind. Here at Hayden, before we administer shock therapy, we need the consent of the patient's nearest relatives.

You mean the people who brought the patient in, I said.

No, he answered, not necessarily. You came here of your own volition. Nobody committed you. But we need your husband's consent to treat your illness.

And have you asked my husband, I said. (My neck's tendons like bone.)

Yes. He is opposed. On what we accept as reasonable grounds. He doesn't think such an approach is necessary in your case. He is in favor of an ongoing program of medication to help you become calmer, more balanced. He is worried about the effects of what he sees as a radical strategy.

I exhaled and felt myself breathe out the name like a prayer of thanks: *Matt!*

I did come here freely, I said. My husband and I have agreed to a trial period of separation. We will decide together when it will end. Not you — just the two of us. And I will decide what if any of your strategies I will follow. And what if any diagnosis I will accept. Or whether the words strategy and diagnosis will have any meaning for me.

(These are the exact words I spoke. Odd how I can recall, word for word, my conversations with Clay, but not those with Matt.)

It's not that simple, Clay said. Your condition is not something to be taken lightly. It has the potential to become rather debilitating. If you want to be released from the manic-depressive cycle, you will need to be open to certain realities. Beginning with the fact that your diagnosis does have meaning for you, whether or not you accept it. The same holds for your treatment. If you cannot open yourself to it, you will find it almost impossible to gain release from your mood swings. Your husband understands this.

Don't tell me what my husband understands, I said. (Look at you trying to insert yourself into my life, your dirty doctor's hand up my skirt into my darkness, *mine!* — but I held off saying this.)

You grow angry quickly, Judith, he said. Has it been like that since the miscarriage?

And then I saw where he was headed.

Listen, I said. We are not talking about the miscarriage now, we're talking about your fucking diagnosis, your strategies, your cures.

No, he broke in. I already told you: manic depression has no cure. It only has controls. You accommodate this illness. You do not recover from it. It's a way of being.

I felt my strength and my will start to slide from me then, slipping like the glutinous, wine-red effluence of my inmost self in which the fetus whose existence I had not even suspected was dislodged, sent down, expelled from me. The same slipping sensation. Something mine and not mine, departing.

I'd thought I wanted a child. Then the war years, and I stopped wanting it; then Matt came into my life and I wanted it again, briefly, a kind of flickering — until the war's aftermath, which was for me the war's real occurrence. Then the desire to give birth was suddenly unsustainable, and Matt in any case was unready, his own fear so palpable.

October, was it? In 1946? That month passed and I was late, and when it came, my period was not a period at all but something viscous and dense and significant as it had never been before, and I saw I was losing a pregnancy I hadn't even recognized. I hadn't known the baby was there — often I'm late, irregular — I had no clues in body or feeling, and suddenly what had begun was gone, vanished.

My will and strength leave me as easily as Lottie and Sam left, as unexpectedly as the embryo: no pain at the instant but then the wordless shock of discovery, after the fact.

131

July 10

Clay is on me all the time about my childhood. Details, he wants details. I prefer spinning them out on these pages; with Clay, I'm never sure where my words go. Here I can write as if for him, or for other listeners I don't have.

Letters are still too difficult. Pam has written twice; I send back short postcards, nothing real. I can't stand the solicitude in her letters.

It's not that I don't register her affection. Or Len's and Carol's. It's there between us, a slack filament on which we pull now and then, to make sure somebody's at the other end. Fondness, yes I feel for them a certain fondness.

Love is what I reserve for Matthias.

> *Who then devised the torment? Love.*
> *Love is the unfamiliar Name . . .*

Until I came here, Matt also wanted details. He is happiest when he doesn't have to handle abstractions directly. Which is why he likes libraries. And the early work of Klee and Picasso. Robert Frost's poems. But not Bud Powell's music, because no matter how full of particulars it is, it's always got something abstract going on.

Matt was afraid of Powell from the start. Did he see me in Powell, in those fits of rage?

Poetry: where I encounter what is not in memory but arises through a kind of instinct, deep-running, inventive. Recognition of something I don't know I knew; something I know only as I write and a poem begins to deliver itself, to assert a reality, startling but oddly familiar.

Until I came here. There are still mornings when I wake up and cannot believe I'm in this room, my books neat on their shelves, my typewriter, clothing, hairbrush, nailpolish —

everything mine but in the wrong place; it's not our apartment, there's nothing here to remind me of Matt.

Who is he? I must conjure him, which is different from remembering. When he arrives each week, he doesn't match either my conjuring or my memory.

During the last visit he said my hair was growing in nicely, and I asked him if he knew why I cut it off, and he said he could imagine why, which at first I took to be an extension of sympathetic understanding until I realized it was a way of fending off further details. He can't bear the specifics of my existence here, how I go from session to session with Clay as if on a desultory stroll; how I lose hours wandering the beautiful grounds, my mind lulled, reciting a litany of plant and flower names — epimedium, columbine, portulaca.

They're treating me with Miltown. I wonder if they know that poem by Robert Lowell, how it starts (so scarily!)

Tamed by Miltown, we lie on Mother's bed

and goes something like this (once I knew all of it by heart)

All night long I've held your hand
as if you had
a fourth time faced the kingdom of the mad —
its hackneyed speech, its homicidal eye —
and dragged me home alive

Matt and I have faced the kingdom always, though not squarely; but Matt isn't here to hold my hand.

Details. Matt's thick fine hair, sandy-grey, brushed off his forehead with that smooth careless movement he makes with one hand.

133

Our hands together, large, broad, coiled as we lie in bed; his hands reaching for mine when he dreams and wakes sweating, his entire body inarticulate, only his hands able to speak such uncertainty.

His hands are questions.

I guess at the questions.

August 1

Matt didn't have bad dreams until after the war, when I started keeping my files.

Why are you doing this, he asked me.

I told him I wanted to know what had actually happened, and he said he didn't see why I was keeping so many articles and photos. It seems morbid, he said.

Morbid. I'll never forget that.

My survivor files.

By '47 all the New York papers were running feature stories on people who'd made it through the war. The Boston papers, too. When I left Matt that first time and went to Pam's, I looked through lots of back copies of the Globe and the Herald, and there were some articles I could hardly believe, about rural children who'd been hidden in barns or potato cellars, people who lived for four years in cemeteries like Weisensee right in the middle of Berlin. People holed up in the crypts of bourgeois Jews.

Pam hadn't read any of those articles. She said, I skip that type of story when I read the news, and you should, too. The war's over, time to move on.

Or something like that. And so we spent our weekend together drinking gin martinis as in the fun old days at Barnard.

*　　*　　*

Matt and I had our own separate wars. Matt's was the one he had managed to elude physically, the one he felt guilty about not fighting. Mine was the one I refused to acknowledge until it was over.

Our shared shame was that we'd turned away from overwhelming evidence. We couldn't read what was in front of our eyes, couldn't speak about what we had heard, couldn't act.

Len and Carol spent the war years in clubs, drinking. Matt and I (we didn't even know each other yet!) spent those years reading. At work, nobody talked much about the war except when Nora's son was wounded in France and we took up that collection for him. As if there were an unwritten rule not to bring the war too far into the office.

But there were a few lapses.

Jack Schwartz — that summer day in '43 when he came in and told me he'd heard Chaim Weizmann at the Garden, heard him shouting that two million Jews had already been exterminated and what were we going to do to save the rest?

Two million lost, Jack said, looking at me (and for the first time I understood: as one Jew looks at another Jew). And I said, what exactly did Weitzmann mean by exterminated?

Knowing that I should not have to ask this question.

August 10

For fourteen years my words have been wrapped up in Matt's, my speech inflected by his. I have been afraid to speak in a language I might want to call my own. Because if he can't or doesn't understand, what then?

It has been easier to borrow than to lend words.

With Clay I don't borrow anything. I don't lie to him; in fact sometimes I tell him truths. But I never know where it all goes.

In this notebook I write and write and never look back, never re-read.

Then there are the poems. My stubborn little offerings. Maybe one day I'll send them out again into the world; for now I clutch them to myself.

August 15

Matt asked me today if I felt I was changing.

How, I said.

Do you feel calmer, he asked. You seem calmer. You seem not to be fighting with everything so much.

He was thinking about last winter, before I came here. That was the worst time for him because I wasn't even trying to not lash out; I flared at everything.

That afternoon at the library. The secretary told me he'd gone home and I knew he hadn't, I knew he was in some bar, one of those dives near Columbia, drinking to avoid everything, and I yelled at the secretary — abusively, Matt said later — to make her tell me where he was. Then he walked in on us.

He'd been at a meeting in the dean's office.

I blew up, called him names, threw books around, made a mess.

He pulled me into his office and shut the door and told me to stop it, didn't I see I was out of control?

I saw.

What Matt didn't see: how lonely I was, how much I needed just to talk, how I'd been working for weeks on a difficult poem and I thought maybe I would read it to him, it'd been so long since I'd shown him anything.

If I seem calmer, I said to him at the end of our visit today, it's because of the Miltown.

He looked upset then, and I could feel him forcing himself to paint a bright picture for me. Listen, he said, I know you've never liked tranquilizers but it does seem that you're calmer, you look more rested.

Matt, I said, I didn't come here for the rest. I'm not after tranquility.

I understand that, he said. All I'm saying is I'm glad you're looking more relaxed. It makes me confident that we made the right choice for you to come here.

I don't feel like I chose anything, I said.

Matt took my hand in both of his; the palms were dry.

You couldn't keep going as you were going, Judith, he said. (So quietly I could hardly hear him.)

You weren't eating or sleeping. Here you've been taking care of yourself.

I'm confused, I said. I think it's the Miltown. Lots of times I don't have any idea why I'm here. Sometimes I don't know what day it is. I feel uprooted.

But it's necessary, he said. (Still holding my hand in his dry palms. Soft and dry like his voice.) You need to pull up some of those roots. The dark entangling ones — like you wrote once — remember?

He was gazing off now. That one phrase, he said. So startling.

(And I realized — a quick small shock — that my poems had affected him powerfully, that it was absurd for me to think they hadn't. Even the ones he disliked.)

Matt, I said, if I'm going to stay here, I need the newspapers.

No, you don't (his voice agitated now), you don't have to dig there any more. It's over and there's nothing to be done, you're not responsible.

He stopped, his face suddenly haggard. He'd been fighting this one as long and as hard as I had, but with a different motive: to suppress the questions, to banish doubt so he could say simply *I'm unworthy*. As if it sufficed to be humble.

Humility is endless, Eliot wrote. But that's the trouble with it.

The door opened. Time to go, said Bud Powell.

August 29

Recent daydreams, memories: the interior of the Five Spot, Chet Baker's horn on "It Could Happen to You," and then the street afterward, dark and windy as we walked downtown at 2 A.M. in silence because Baker's playing had overwhelmed us. The aching pull and reach of his trumpet . . .

New York's permanence. The facade of the Met, austere, grey, immutable. Bryant Park, those straight-spined trees behind the Public Library, a stand of green and brown sentinels guarding all those books. Matt clambering on one of the stone lions in front of the library, in that season when we wandered the city like lost happy children.

Matt's body was draped easily over the lion as if he'd fallen asleep on it. I sat at its base and tilted my head upward, and Matt looked down at me and began whistling "I Didn't Know What Time It Was," slow and languorous — I'd never heard anything like it. And then he slid slowly off the lion's back and sat down and held me from behind.

Sitting there with him, both of us looking down Forty-first Street in the middle of the dead-quiet night, I knew that whatever linked us was wordless, and would be hard to break.

Eliot:

> *Before the urban dawn wind unresisting*
> *Beyond any meaning we can assign to happiness*

September 5

Len and Carol's first visit.

Well, it took us long enough, Len said, but here we are.

Yep. Here we are, and here's the damn record player at last, said Carol, smiling, then breaking into one of her quick trills, and Len laughing with her. I laughed, too, though not exactly with either one of them. Or at least it didn't feel that way. But it *was* laughter, and profoundly strange because I never laugh here.

They brought some wonderful albums. Joe Morris's orchestra, and Monk and Bird. Dizzy. Oscar Peterson. Coleman Hawkins. And Powell, a double set. I almost asked them to leave when I saw the Powell records. I just wanted to listen, alone. But Len started talking like he does when he's got nothing much to say, that easy rapid chatter kicking in automatically, and I knew they were bent on getting their full visit out of me. So I settled back.

We heard Art Blakey the other weekend at the Vanguard, Len said. Terrific set. He's got a real bunch of hot-shots now. Couple of new horn players working with him — Carol, what's that one kid's name?

And also, said Carol (ignoring Len and looking me up and down to see how much weight I'd gained or lost), we heard that sax player, what's-his-name, yeah, Coltrane. You'd mentioned him once. He was at the Gate, so we checked him out. I don't know, he's not my taste.

Though he can blow, said Len. He can definitely blow, but we didn't like how he broke up the melodies. It sounded odd, kind of pretty sometimes but just not — well, you know, Judy, you always like that kind of oddball stuff and we're just a couple of conservatives. Give me Dizzy any day.

Carol stretched out on the bed. She can get comfortable anywhere.

The city was a mess this Labor Day, she said, and you wouldn't have believed the traffic. Washington Square just stood still. I swear, the Village isn't what it was. Sometimes I tell Len we should get the hell out — move uptown, or to the Heights or Kew Gardens or something. You know, a little room, some peace and quiet. But then Lenny reminds me I'd get bored in Queens.

Christ, Carol! (Len's laugh now, low and gravelly from too much smoking.) You'd last maybe a day there. You know, we live in the absolute best part of the city. Even better than your neighborhood, Judy.

(And he looked at me directly for the first time since he came into the room, and I couldn't keep focused on his eyes; I ended up looking at the door and wondering when Powell would open it and tell them to leave.)

The West Side is a real nice place, Len said. Matt seems to like it there even after all these years. He says it's still right for him. For you two (he added? — I couldn't tell whether he'd really heard the slip and was trying to fix it).

And Matt's keeping up the place, Judy, you don't have to worry about anything. I stopped by a few weeks ago. Matt and I had a quick drink and I could see he's doing fine. Nice new set of oak bookshelves he just bought, he told you about them? — they look swell in that corner by the blue chair. He's a real neatnik, that guy, he doesn't let anything get messy in the apartment like we do sometimes.

He paused, lit up, passed me the pack; I lit up too. Carol abstained.

I mean, there are nights when we're just too tired even to feed ourselves, Len said. And so we order in some food and spin a few tunes and then we forget to go to bed. Wake up in the middle of the night on the fucking sofa, for God's sake.

And sometimes we don't even know where we are, said Carol. (Still on her back.) You know that feeling, when you wake up and for a minute everything's a blank, it's like you could be *anywhere?*

Oh yeah, I said, I know.

And for a few seconds we were all silent, and I had a glimmer of what they've been sitting on — the suppressed unease, futility . . . Then Carol snapped back into place, reached for the pack of cigarettes, lit up, exhaled, picked up the reins again.

So anyway, she said. Some things never change. You know we still have that pair of loony squirrels in the trees out behind the building, remember? — the pair that chase each other and dive from one tree to another like they're birds. Christ! One of these days, one of those little suckers is going to lose his footing. And I'm going to feel sorrier for the other one, he's the real loser. I do get a kick out of watching them. A scary kind of play — what's a good word for it, Lenny? — we've been trying to improve our vocabularies lately, Judy, we're tired of the same old words so we use the thesaurus sometimes.

Len frowned, lit up, jabbed his cigarette in the air.

Cavort, he said. Those squirrels cavort.

No, I said. Not scary enough.

She's right, said Carol. Something's missing. The squirrels are testing each other, it's a kind of pushing to the edge —

— oh I got it now, exactly the right word, said Len. Brinksmanship.

Yes, I said. That's it.

Yes yes, said Carol, excited because she likes little games like that.

Then they told me about how their jobs were going, and I filled them in on Matt's work. As if nothing had changed, as if I were still in on the details, and we just happened to be meeting here in the middle of nowhere two hours from Manhattan instead of on Grove Street or at some coffee shop in Sheridan Square.

Len talked a little politics, and I took the opportunity to ask him if he had a newspaper on him. Both he and Carol looked startled and said No, simultaneously, so I know they're in on it too: my news blackout.

Carol stood up and looked out the south window.

Nice view you've got, she said. The grounds are spectacular.

Yes, I said. I walk a lot.

Good for you, said Len (a little too fast). Now you have your LPs so you can stay inside if you want, listen to great music all day long. Never get bored.

That's not a problem here, I said.

Good, said Carol.

They both looked so relieved then that I nearly started laughing but managed not to: it would've been too much trouble to stop.

The door opened, the familiar deep-brown face inserted itself, the usual quiet voice (the only one here that calms me!) spoke: Time to go.

We three parted as Powell stood by.

I was reminded of that scene in "The Waste Land." *Ta ta. Goonight. Goonight.*

A rushed farewell, essentially meaningless.

It was worth it for my record player.

They asked nothing of me.

October 2

My record player is saving me. They try to make me stop listening at night, when I need it most. Clay sends one of the attendants to check on me at eleven. If it's Powell I'm OK, he just opens the door and puts one finger to his lips and I lower the volume; but the others are stooges. *Lights out, music off.* If I protest, they stand around and cross their arms on their chests to show they aren't leaving until I turn off the record player. So I do, and when I hear the hall door close, I turn it back on and keep it low.

During the day I close my eyes when I'm listening. At night I want a cigarette and a little whiskey, but these are not necessities.

It is possible for me to distinguish between what I want and what I need. Clay thinks I can't, but he is hopelessly predisposed in his judgments. He has to fit symptoms with diagnoses, adult effect with childhood cause. He is looking for a way to put the whole picture together. He enjoys making connections.

So do I, I tell him, but only when they're interesting. Past a certain point it is not interesting to think about childhood as the central drama and adulthood as its reprise.

Sometimes my existence up to 1939 seems like an unconscious waiting, an extended anticipation. Almost as if I sensed something unimaginable was descending, and nothing real could begin until it had ended.

I've been reading Rabbi Luria's myth of creation. It's one of the best Kabbalistic stories. It has a certain lyric economy. I can't resist it.

God inhaled and withdrew from the world, contracted Himself to make space for the world: an act of self-purification, to free Himself from evil. But the evil was mixed in with other divine powers, and when it flew outward in Creation it shattered the vessels, the lights of primordial humankind, and everything was dispersed — the original pure lights and all their impure forms too. And so everything Made

143

was mixed, the constructive and the destructive laced together. And as the descendants of Adam Kadmon, the primordial one, we are given breath to gather the shards, the evil as well as the good pieces, and return them to their right places.

This is the Repair: our only meaningful work. Not just His work but ours, too.

I told the story to Matt, not long before I came here. He said he liked its images — God breathing in and withdrawing, the broken vessels — but not the myth itself, because it made no allowances for redemption. And I argued that yes, it does, it's just that there's no single Messiah to redeem us. There's only the messianic aim — the end of exile.

I can't buy that, said Matt. It's too vague, it leaves too much room for pseudo-saviors.

Everything gets worked out here, I said. Not on some cross but here. On the ground. Between human beings. In our exile anything can happen.

I remember how his face darkened slightly then.

Why do the Jews focus so much on their exile? he asked. It seems arrogant to me.

Arrogant? Suddenly I opened to anger — such tremendous anger, larger than anything I'd ever felt for this man; larger, more heated, frightening. I felt it as a creeping sensation on my skin, not unlike gooseflesh.

You're in no position to talk about arrogance, I said. I mean, Christianity's a religion that claims all nonbelievers are damned forever. A religion that used to kill off the same nonbelievers it had already damned, just to prove the point.

Judith, Matt said (interrupting me, shaking his head, his tone urgent). Why do we get into these things? Don't throw all of Christianity at me, you know that's not fair. Don't oversimplify.

144

Right, I said. But isn't that exactly what Christians do?

Some Christians, he said. Not all.

Action, I said, tell me about action. Tell me what you're supposed to do once you've taken the place of Christ's betrayer — you're in that man's seat now, it's your turn, and it's not enough to talk about salvation, is it?

Careful, he said.

Don't back me off, I said. Don't try to shame me.

I'm not, Judith (his tone so weary now), you know that.

Millions dead, I shrilled at him. A whole culture obliterated in less than five years, and Christians still talk about salvation? Where was everyone in Europe? All those Christians standing around wringing their hands, inwardly sighing with relief, saying to themselves *good riddance*.

He turned away from me. You insult many innocent people, he said. You have no right to do that.

The white heat pulsed at my temples.

You can't have it both ways, Matthias, I said. Either you're a Christian who admits that most Christians in Europe looked the other way, or you're not a Christian at all.

You're on thin ice, Judith, he said. If you're going to talk about Christian complicity, you'd better also talk about Jewish collaboration. There was plenty of it. Right inside the camps.

I said nothing. Matt said nothing.

We'd been in such a place before, deadlocked, separated, silenced.

My temples thrummed. I remember picking up a glass.

Forget Christians and Jews, I said. You know what I'm talking about. We both know what *we* didn't say, how *we* didn't act. It's not just the war I'm talking about — what about afterwards, when the refugees started coming in, when we avoided them on the street!

He walked toward me, his eyes on the glass.

Judith, don't, he said.

How can you tolerate it, I said (only it was not speech, it was a wail bursting from me, a keening as if at a death) — what we've done together, this pretending, both of us! Damn it, Matt, why don't you see?

His hand went out in front of his face as the glass left my fingers. I hadn't felt the release but the glass was gone. It was directly before his face, deflected by his hand; it glanced off his forehead and then arced up, down.

A shrill sound of breaking. Shards on the floor.

On Matthias's forehead a small cut, a thin bloody rivulet.

I approached him but he backed away.

No, he said (softly, as if without anger), no. Leave me alone.

Matt, I said, please, let me.

No, he said. Go. Please.

I left him five times altogether; this, Hayden, is the sixth.

The first time I left without warning. I knew I had to. I felt him wanting me to. When I came back from Boston, he said he'd been unprepared, shaken, but I knew he'd wanted me to go. He needed his aloneness. It had restored something in him which I'd eroded.

Each time after that, he asked me to go, and each time there was nothing for me to do but go. We would arrive at some impasse, a wall we could not negotiate. I would come apart; he would ask me to go.

His voice low, quiet, unrefusable.

I threw something each time. Usually a book, once a coffee can.

I didn't aim, I just threw. The glass was the only time I hit him. I didn't mean to. I think that time I just needed to hear

146

the sound of our life splintering, and see the real shards: not myth but the actual bits of glass, waiting for me to retrieve them.

November 16

The high holidays came and went. I've put nothing on paper since then.

On Rosh Hashanah they gave me and each of the handful of other Jews here a prayer book, but I let the Days of Atonement pass, uneventfully, like any other stretch of time.

Atonement. I don't think I believe in it. It's an impossibility, a ruse. Why do we even try it? So we can make the vows each year and then break them?

The thing the Jews have going for them is they don't start wars to convert people. They don't kill to spread their faith; they ask to be left alone to practice it. But too often they suppose that their God will protect them. Which thus far He has repeatedly failed to do.

The ones deported — what did they think was happening? How did they explain things to themselves? Was it only terror — was it not also complacency to which they surrendered? As if He were just around the corner, watching?

God set certain things in motion when He inhaled and withdrew from the world, and now we bear the consequences.

I picture Len and Carol in Vienna or Cracow or Munich in the 1930s, selling pianos and sheet music. Two Jews, benign and genial and undistinguished, not much different from their Austrian or German or Polish gentile neighbors.

Len and Carol wouldn't have left. Any more than they'd leave New York now, if it were happening here. This was their life. *Is* their life.

147

I can picture him saying to her: *We do not leave such a life.* And she would nod, say to him: *There's nowhere to go.* And they'd stay, knowing they had no choice.

Lottie and Sam? I might guess now that they would've left, but that's easy to say because they're gone; no risk in being wrong.

Their dying was an accident of time and place, nothing more. Like being Jewish in Vienna or Cracow or Munich in the 1930s.

Accidents. The car heading down Broadway was part of it, part of *such a life.* I too, I was part of it; but I wasn't in the car when the truck swerved into it.

A quick careening. An error.

It was just one of those things
Just one of those crazy flings

December 31

An hour before the decade ends.

Tired of fighting with Clay. He refuses to see my side; this is pure pig-headedness on his part, it has nothing to do with his training or skills (which I accept as considerable, I tell him; but he must hear a certain irony in my voice, he looks uncomfortable when I say this).

Why did you do it, he asked yesterday, almost before I'd sat down.

Yesterday: our first session since Christmas Eve. I removed the tree from the lobby on Christmas Day, when most of the staff and patients weren't around. The gardener found the remains of the fire the next day. I figured they'd tell Clay then, but apparently he didn't hear until yesterday that the tree had been burned. That it was a sweet-smelling heap of ashes in which (if one looked hard) one could pick out little bits of colored ornaments: a Santa's hat and arm, part of a reindeer, some tinsel, the horn of an angel.

Clay figured it out right away. There are dozens of patients here even during these holidays, and a good many are in far worse shape than I, but I give Clay credit: he knew immediately who'd burned Hayden's Christmas tree.

Why, he asked.

I could ask the same thing of you, I answered him.

What do you mean, he said.

Why did you put the tree in the lobby, I asked.

The Christmas tree is a symbol, he said. Of hope and goodwill. A familiar symbol of the season. Not a threat, Judith — just an ordinary object.

Bullshit, I said. It's only familiar and ordinary to some people. I don't have to tell you that Hayden is not a Christian institution.

He was silent.

The tree did not belong in the lobby, I said.

It's a secular symbol, Judith. You read too much into it.

If you were Jewish you'd see it a little differently, I said.

He frowned in annoyance.

Come now. None of the other Jews here burned down the Christmas tree, he said.

None of the other Jews here had matches, I said.

That flustered him. I felt a sudden surge of pride. A manic arousal, Clay would call it. Perhaps. But I felt the Miltown lift, felt *clear* for the first time in weeks.

Yes, he said. And I want to know where you got those matches. You know they're forbidden here.

You needn't remind me, I said. I know the rules.

And?

I've had the matches for months. Since Len and Carol visited, in fact. Len is a sloppy man, he's always scattering his things. He didn't leave his cigarettes in my room, unfortunately. Just his matches. I've had ample opportunity to burn this whole place to the ground. I think you should take seriously the fact that I haven't.

You acted on a destructive impulse, he said.

Listen, Clay. (I stood up and paced his office as I do when he angers me, to throw him off.) It's simple — the tree didn't belong in the lobby. Non-Christians shouldn't be subjected to Christian symbols in public places.

You should've asked if the tree could be taken down, he said.

Asked? (I stopped pacing, laughed. The current still carried me.) You didn't ask the Jews here whether they objected to your installing it. Why should I ask whether the Christians would object to my removing it?

You did more than just remove the tree, he said.

(I stood very still. The current was all at once cut off.)

The Nazis did more than just remove the Jews, I said.

He tugged on his pencil with both hands as if it were an object he could pull apart, separate into its constituent parts.

Judith, he said quietly, a bit warily. We've talked about this — how you must break that association, how it is not the underlying truth of your condition.

I'm not talking about my condition, I said. Why are you?

It's what we're here for, he answered. We need to figure out why you had to burn the Christmas tree. We need to get to the bottom of this thing.

(The Miltown settled back over me, a miasma. It's a powerful drug. It hits me in waves throughout the day.)

This thing is bottomless, I said.

No, Clay said, it's not. But you're resisting.

Today I didn't talk so much. We sat in silence for long stretches, and Clay's face darkened, but I stopped glancing at him during the silences. I gave myself over to remembering how the tree's flames rose and fell in a peculiar syncopation that reminded me of Monk's playing, those lovely staccato jabs at the notes . . .

I burned the tree at dusk, in a fairly remote corner of the property dotted with some low scrub brush and not much else. I found a safe clearing from which the fire wouldn't spread. The tree was small; I carried it easily on my shoulder. No one saw me. The air was very cold and there was no wind, no noise except for the crackling as each dry green branch was consumed.

I realized, sitting in Clay's office, that the fire had calmed me as nothing but Powell's voice ever does, here.

For whatever reason, planned or circumstantial, it was Powell who escorted me back to my room afterward.

Eight minutes to 1960. If I knew more about gematria, I would play that Kabbalists' game with the numbers, one nine six zero, and make them come out to something good. Make them bode well for me.

As I approach the new year, I am aware mostly of a deep and wide anxiety. It is discordant with what I want to think of as my reality (*I'm getting better, I'll be back with Matthias soon*), and thus extremely compelling.

In fact, the anxiety is the most believable thing.

Matt told me yesterday, during his visit, that tonight he would go to the Village Gate by himself, listen to Lou Donaldson's quartet, and raise a glass exactly at twelve.

151

To you, he explained.

And us? I asked.

First to you, he said, to your becoming happier.

But we both knew that wasn't the word for it.

And now I see him at the bar, quiet amidst the other revellers, alone among them, and frightened: at having to think of me.

1960

January 1

I have under my bed a copy of every Sunday Times from the start of September through the end of the year.

Len and Carol showed up this afternoon — out of the blue, looking a little the worse for wear but clearly pleased with themselves. Len was carrying a blue duffle bag.

Jesus, said Carol, surveying my room (which was a mess because I'd decided that morning to get rid of a lot of clothing I no longer wear. It amounted to several piles, not very neatly stacked). You planning a trip to the Salvation Army? Why don't we take this stuff for you, there's a drop-off joint around the corner from us that takes donations for the needy, especially at this time of year — no, of course it's not a problem! Glad to do it (easing off her boots and curling up on my bed after pushing a couple of my books to one side).

And look what Lenny brought you, she finished.

He was in the middle of lighting up. One hand cupped the match held with the other hand.

Happy New Year, kiddo, he said.

The cigarette jangled at the side of his mouth as he spoke. He pushed the bag toward me with one foot.

Had to sort of smuggle this in, he added (exhaling, a grey haze around his head). Guy at the front desk said *what's in there,* so Carol says *sheet music, I sell it,* and then we get walked over here by that same Negro who was here last time, and he kind of glances at the bag like he's wondering, but he doesn't say a peep. So you got lucky, I guess. No confiscations.

It occurred to me that they were both a little drunk. I looked at Carol.

What did you two do last night? I said.

Oh-h, Carol breathed. Too much.

Wasn't a club we didn't catch, Len said. Some great playing — I mean truly great. Must've been the end-of-decade thing, everybody was on a roll. Especially Lou Donaldson — terrific, what a saxophonist! He was at the Gate. Place was packed.

Did you see Matt? I said.

Matt? No. Past his bedtime. We came in just before closing. Carol's boss knows the owner, so they let us stay. Jesus! We heard incredible music, Judy. After everyone cleared out.

He wore the happy, distracted look he gets when he's stayed up all night for music.

So then, said Carol (taking over — she doesn't like to lose the rhythm), we'd had a lot to drink and not much to eat so we went to the Brasserie and had steak and eggs, and by that time it's seven-thirty so we go home and crash for maybe two hours, but we're so used to getting up for work, we can't ever really sleep in. So Lenny says *let's take a drive in the country,* and I say *why not visit Judy,* and we climb into the car and in a couple of hours we're in Centreville and there's this wonderful little inn, did you pass it when you first came here?

My eyes must've scared her. She let the question drop.

So we decide to hop out and have lunch. Which of course on New Year's Day is also a matter of a drink.

She smirked at Len.

Hair of the dog that bit us, Len said. That bartender makes a fine martini. Warmed us right up. It's cold out there. You been outside today? — no? — well after we go, you should take a nice walk. Get the blood circulating. Put some red in those cheeks.

Jesus, Lenny, said Carol. Listen to you talking like some kind of football coach. Leave the poor girl alone, for God's sake.

He lit another cigarette, ignoring Carol.

Now go on, open the bag, he said to me.

I opened it.

Newspapers, a deep stack smelling of ink and dust. The Sunday Times.

I knelt next to the bag and flipped through: September to now. I took one off the top. Only the important sections, all the junk removed: just as I would've done it myself. Len knows certain things about me. When I looked up, he was smiling, a smug, conspiratorial upturning at the corners of his mouth, not at all like his usual loose grin.

Why? I said.

What do you mean, why, he said. It's obvious why! You need some news. I said to Carol on the way home last time, you know, we should get Judy some news. It's ridiculous that a person should be denied the Times.

A New Yorker, Carol broke in, you specifically said that a New Yorker should not be denied —

— yeah, I did, said Len (the smug smile returning), and in September I started saving the papers. The Sunday ones. I figured they were all you really needed.

To keep things in perspective, said Carol.

Nothing like the Times for that, said Len. Except maybe a dry martini.

He walked over to the window, gazed out, turned back to Carol (still on the bed, curled up in her usual ball).

So, he said, let's hit the road, Carol. We got a drive ahead of us, remember?

Yeah, said Carol (unwinding stretching standing; suddenly looking small and tired, her blond-grey hair limp, her eyelids blue-tinged, puffy).

And I need a good cup of coffee, Len said. Let's go back to that inn, I can tell they make it strong there.

In a fast minute Carol took the papers from the bag, stuffed my discarded clothing inside, and slid the papers under my bed. She knows how to straighten things up no matter what shape she's in.

I could say nothing, could think of no words.

They stood before me like two boastful truants.

We'll bring more, said Len. Only not right away. I hate to drive in winter, you'll have to wait til spring but we promise another batch, a big one just like this —

— if you're still here, that is, added Carol (in the voice of one saying what must be said).

Oh yes, Len said. Of course. So we'll just wait and see.

He lit up again. Carol pulled on her boots and tossed Len his coat.

Guess you'll need to keep it a secret, Len said. The Times, I mean. You know, I think a dose of the real world is good for everybody, I don't see why they —

— never mind, Carol said (taking his arm, propelling him doorward), it's not ours to figure. So bye now Judy, you take care.

Powell was right there, waiting, when Carol opened the

door. Like he knew I needed him to take them away. I saw in his eyes that he understood about the newspapers, he wouldn't tell Clay.

I looked directly into those dark brown eyes.

Thanks, I said. Really.

Len and Carol thought I was saying it to them.

And I closed the door, and an image of Matt's face flew from nowhere into my head like a lost bird wheeling and plunging across the spaces there. And for the first time in weeks I wept, the tears carrying off the silt of these months, leaving me empty and dry as any stripped bed.

February 3

I've read the papers. Everything, even the fashion pages, the recipes, the ads.

I don't like the skirts they show this season, the way they stop at the knee — an absurd length that flatters nobody.

I haven't missed the clothes I gave away. Each day I wear the same things: dark wool sweaters, skirts cut on the narrow side, or pants. Cream-colored shirts cut full. No prints, no patterns.

When Matt visits I wear my blue cashmere cardigan and my pale yellow blouse. Colors he likes.

I don't miss my pearls either, I'm glad I gave them away. Pearls are useless here. This is not asceticism, it's the Miltown, which makes me tired of too many stimulations.

Matt hasn't asked about the pearls, but if he does I'll tell him the truth.

Within me, truth assumes so many shapes that I find relief in objects, which have certainty. Pearls, books, record players. Newspapers.

I have in my possession Manhattan: the smudge and smell of the New York Times. It took me a long day to read all fifteen papers. I started at dawn and didn't stop until dinnertime, and it was only when I went to wash my hands before eating that I saw how I'd actually absorbed what I was reading, through my inked fingers.

I've had to be careful not to mention to Matt or Clay any of the news I've read. Sometimes I ask Clay questions about what's happening in the world, and then I compare his answers with the newspaper accounts. This has yielded (as he would say) interesting disparities.

But my latest information is now at least a month old.

I can tell what Matt is focused on — now more than ever: reviews of books and music, some art shows, the occasional poetry reading. He has little to say about world news. I'm sure he knows what's going on, but he doesn't want me to think about it.

I'm not sure what he wants me to be thinking about.

I almost asked him if he'd heard LeRoi Jones read at Corinth Books, but I caught myself. Matt seldom goes to such things. He prefers reading about them. But he didn't mention that particular event, even though it had a little write-up in the arts section, so I suspect he's being selective — taking care to avoid anything too reminiscent of me. Staying with what he can bear.

He comes and he goes, each week, and after he leaves I'm numb, not so much depressed as simply empty. We embrace at the end, we kiss one another, and I can't feel anything. But after Matt leaves, there's always another moment when suddenly I'm back in his arms, their pressure and warmth around me are absolutely real, and it's like imagining — in complete, faithful detail — a missing limb's sensation. As if it were really there.

As if it really were, or could be.

*   *   *

Last week I asked Matt what he misses when he finds himself missing me. He paused for a long time.

It's hard to name, he said. Your presence. The way things feel when you're home.

You didn't always like the way things feel, I said.

He didn't look at me. He stood at the window, staring out.

No, I didn't, he said. You're right. But that doesn't matter. I still miss what's not there.

(Not wanting to say *what's gone.*)

How do you sleep? I asked.

(His body curved along mine, one arm under my pillow, the other crooked over my midriff, forearm between my breasts, palm cupping my collarbone; his breathing low and deep until one of his bad dreams, then shallow, faster, more urgent, his forearm pulling me closer to him, his entire body pressed hard, seeking refuge; his breathing an echo of his mother's at the end, her ardent wheeze, that indrawn suck of air — unavailing, painful, pointless.)

I don't sleep much, he said.

His profile at the window, a clear silhouette.

Do you want me to come home, I said.

What I want (his head turning, his eyes finally meeting mine) doesn't matter.

If it doesn't, what does?

I don't know (his eyes closing), I don't know, Judith, why do you always ask —

— because I have to know what you want. If you want me.

You know that, he said. You know that's not it.

Then what is it, I said, tell me, look at me, look at me for Christ's sake!

(Once again spiraling, *balance and proportion* gone.)

I can't, he said, I can't live like this, I can't be with you now. In this way.

What are you saying, I asked.

I'm saying we have to be apart. You have to go through this alone. I have to wait.

The door opened. I can't be sure what really happened next. Something gave way, I heard Matt say *wait* and it wasn't Powell at the door but the surly one, the man I loathe, and I went for him. He must've had to hit me to stop me. I found myself on the floor, he must've thrown me there on my back and I went for his neck but he pinned my hands and I closed my eyes and felt Matt's breath at my ear, heard his terrified voice — *for God's sake Judith don't, please not this!* —

— but I couldn't trust that he'd stay, that he'd help me with the Repair. And no one would redeem us. And I couldn't go home.

February 24

Clay has increased my Miltown dosage. He denies it, and the tablets look the same, but I can tell.

In the mornings I try to write, but each poem slides into another. I read for several hours. Sometimes I absorb everything, but often it's a struggle.

My afternoon walks seem to last longer than when I first began them. The snow on the ground is shallow and dirty, but on the trees it remains clean, undisturbed. I spend a long time standing beneath the tallest firs. Their black boughs are frosted white — it's been so cold that the snow is no longer dust but solid, dense and crusty.

Outside, the frigid air makes me sluggish. I'm often warm indoors. I take off my sweaters and pin back my hair to get it away from my face. Sometimes I take a tepid bath to release the heat.

*   *   *

Clay often asks me if I'm angry, and I don't know what to say. The question lies in Kafka's realm. Most of what Clay says is in that realm, in fact.

However, I have managed to escape shock therapy, and I'm left more or less to myself.

Clay asked recently: But don't you feel dislocated everywhere? And I said yes, that's why I feel Jewish even though Len and Carol never told me much about it, only that I was a Jew like them, like Lottie and Sam.

Clay looked bored until I mentioned Lottie and Sam; then he perked up.

Isn't it possible, he said, that your sense of dislocation derives more from that original loss than from being Jewish?

Isn't it possible (inside me my voice was not a voice, it was a shriek of fury at this man this ego this arrogance sitting before me) that my Jewishness explains as much about me as the loss does?

Loss is internal, Clay said. A subjective emotional experience. I think that what's internal is more relevant.

Does history mean nothing to you, I said.

It depends what kind, he said. In your case I think personal history is the most important factor. You feel dislocation as a result of your parents' death. On some level you still cannot accept that it happened so unexpectedly, and that you were somehow exempted. You are refusing this history, which is yours. Other history — the world's, I mean — is not so relevant. You must work on accepting your own.

That is very tidy, I said, and I'm impressed, only you seem not to notice the similarity between my own history and every other Jew's. You seem not to notice that since the war, every Jew has been trying to accept the unacceptable, the unthinkable, every Jew is dislocated.

Judith (his tone impatient now), please try not to widen everything, to include everything. You drag in too much. We are not talking about other people. We're talking about you. No, I said, no we're not. Really and truly, we're not. And I heard those lines from "The Waste Land":

> 'Do
> *You know nothing? Do you see nothing? Do you remember*
> *Nothing?'*
>
> *I remember*
> *Those are pearls that were his eyes.*

April 15

Yesterday, Passover; today, Easter. I didn't mention either holiday to Clay, and he didn't bring them up.

On the Lower East Side, in Brooklyn, the Bronx, Jews at the seder table. *This night different from other nights. Next year Jerusalem.*

I had no desire to share this Passover with the other Jewish people here. Nobody here interests me much, including the Jews.

In midtown Manhattan, Fifth Avenue a blur of pastel dresses and hats, floats of white flowers. The Easter parade. Celebration of a ghost's rising.

I once asked Matt if we could have a seder at our apartment, but he said it would make him uncomfortable. I pressed him to explain why, but he couldn't. If you feel you must, he said. No, I said, it was just an idea. Then I'd rather we didn't, he said, it would feel false somehow.

I remember being shocked by the word *false*, the clarity of it, the way it illumined Matt's fear. Matt's been terribly afraid all his life, and Christ is a cage for the fear that he knows will escape someday. His faith is like that line in Frost, *a momentary stay against confusion . . .*

May 20

Matthias hasn't visited since the end of April. Powell brings weekly messages, brief notes from Hayden's main office: Mr. Lane has called to say he's got a bad flu. Mr. Lane has called again to say he's still recovering from his flu.

Each note ends: He says to say *I think of you.*

Ben Webster and Art Tatum on "Night and Day" — I can hear it as if I were sitting there, across from the piano in the Bohemia, as they braid the melody, each of its lines crisscrossing, everything tangled, despair and desire inextricable.

Whether near to me or far
it's no matter darling where you are

A third message, tonight. Mr. Lane will come with Mr. and Mrs. Rubin this weekend.

Saturday or Sunday, I asked Powell.

He shrugged gently.

May 29

Len and Carol looked the same as always, but Matt looked tired.

Are you feeling better, I asked him. Oh yes, he said, only it takes time.

Yes, I said.

Our eyes met. In the mid-afternoon light, his were a deep aquamarine. Even when he's exhausted, his eyes remain clear, but the skin around them shows more shadows than usual. He smiled at me — a wan smile, to match his face — and I smiled back. Then our gaze faltered, broke.

How've you been, said Carol. You keeping busy with all these books? Christ, Lenny, will you look at this stuff on Judaism and Kabbalah? I think she's seen the Jewish light or something, I mean this looks like some yeshiva kid's bookshelf, doesn't it?

Matt had moved quietly to the shelves. His fingers drifted over the books' spines.

Where did you find these, he asked.

Sam Wiser's bookstore, I said, the one with the occult books — Broadway at Forty-eighth Street.

Yes, he said, I know it. You ordered these by mail?

I nodded (watching Len from the corner of one eye as he poked around the room). Sam Wiser knows me now, he's given me a tab.

Oh boy, Len said, wait'll that bill comes in, Matt.

I'm not really in a position to complain about anybody else's book purchases, Matt said.

Yeah, Carol piped in, that's right, all this man ever buys is books! Take a look at his sweater, would you? I think he's forgotten how to dress himself. When Judy comes home she'll have to retrain you, Matt. Just like Liza Doolittle, only in reverse.

(*Home:* a low-register chord, like one of Art Tatum's.)

So tell me what's happening, I said.

Whadya mean, Carol said (a note of alarm in her voice, small but undisguisable).

In the world. Out there, I said.

Oh, said Len. Well, you know they found Adolf Eichmann in Argentina. Two weeks ago. Took him off to Israel.

Who did, I asked.

Israeli secret agents, said Carol. It was like a movie. A

group of Nazi hunters tracked him down in some city where he had a fake name, and they stuck him on the next plane out. He's sitting in a jail in Jerusalem, waiting to be charged.

Incredible, Len said. When Ben-Gurion made the announcement to the Knesset, the whole place was stunned. The papers said you could've heard a pin drop. After all these years they just couldn't believe it. Eichmann, for God's sake.

I looked at Matthias. His face unreadable.

The Argentine government wants Eichmann sent back, he said. They claim the Israelis violated Argentina's sovereignty by kidnapping him.

Those Catholic bastards, Len said.

Well Lenny (Carol frowning, smelling trouble), it's a tough call, I mean you can't always go picking people up just like that, no extradition warrant or anything.

Oh come on, said Len. This is a war criminal, this is the last of the big Nazi murderers! The Israelis should just hang the guy. No questions asked.

Lenny, listen to what you're saying, this is completely undemocratic.

Len's face dark. His lighter in one hand, a cigarette in the other.

Fuck the Argentines, he said. Eichmann is Israel's. Now we'll see some justice.

The lighter's flame, a quick flare; Len's harsh indrawn breath and long exhalation. His eyes darting around, not resting on any of us.

Carol's gaze on me for a moment, nervously.

I suspect we will, said Matt.

Will what, asked Carol.

See some justice. The Israelis will get to keep him, and they'll give him a fair trial. They'd have to, so no one complains.

Complains about what, said Len.

About a biased judiciary in Israel.

Jesus Christ, Len said (flicking his cigarette ash on the floor).

I'm not saying it's a sound complaint (Matt's eyes on Carol, his voice steady), I'm just saying this is how they'll have to handle it.

Well it's interesting, said Len, that the Israelis have to prove how fair they are. Nobody asked that of Mr. Hitler.

Len, said Carol, we fought Hitler, we defeated him. That was better than asking him questions, wasn't it?

Len said nothing.

I decided it was my turn.

If there were questions to be asked, I said, they should've been asked before war broke out. They should've been asked in the mid-thirties. When everyone kept silent. Even the Jews.

They all looked at me.

I looked at Matt, who looked away.

Len passed his hands over his face and rubbed his eyes.

Well, he said, if they don't try Eichmann soon, some Israeli will get to him in jail and whack him, and that'll be that.

Meanwhile, back on the farm (one of Carol's favorite nonsensical segues, she knows just where to insert them), always something new — you know I got a new job, Judy? I work at Schirmers now. Best music store in the city, only I have to sell real collections now. No more sheet music. I kind of miss my old beat, but the pay sure makes up for it.

Can you imagine Carol selling classical? said Len (his big loose smile back, the Eichmann cloud dissipated for the time being). I mean, what does she know from Chopin, all that waltzy stuff?

I'm going to take music history lessons from Matt, said Carol. He doesn't know it yet but I'll make him my chief advisor. It's true, I don't know squat about the stuff I'm selling. God forbid I should have any customers as ignorant as I am, but so far they all seem to know just what they want.

Judith knows a fair bit about classical music, too, said Matt.

Oh, but not like you, said Len. Judy's the expert on bop. You're the one who knows the old stuff. Old music, old books.

I'll take notes, said Carol. And Judy can send me a quiz. You know, we haven't had a card from you in a while — you still writing?

Now and then, I said.

Letters? asked Matt.

(And I could hear in this question other questions, and I knew he wanted to know but couldn't ask me: *has it been silenced yet, your pain, has it stopped interfering?* And I wanted to scream at him: *no, it hasn't, and it's yours too, it's ours, damn you!*)

No, I said. Poems, now and then. I keep a journal, too. Not every day.

That sounds good, said Carol. As good as sending letters. I mean, for God's sake don't feel you have to, on our account.

I don't, I said.

Good, said Len. Who needs such pressure?

He picked up his jacket.

You'll be seeing us, kiddo — whatcha say, Carol, maybe in August we'll come up again, get the hell out of Manhattan. The city's so damn hot by then.

Yeah, said Carol, sounds good.

She pointed at Matt, looked at me.

Him you'll see before then, I'm sure, she said.

Matt's blue gaze on me now: love, fear, questions.

Yes, he said.

I couldn't keep looking at him. I looked out the window.
See you, I said to them all.

Powell led them off. But in a few minutes it happened, predictably: Len came back to the room, in the company of Powell (and slightly out of breath), holding the duffle bag.

He stepped inside the door.

Here, he said (in a low voice, and pulling from the bag a bundle of newspapers tied in string), I told Matt I forgot to give you some new records. No need for him to know, right?

I nodded.

This guy straight? (jerking his thumb in Powell's direction).

I nodded again.

Fine, he said. A person should be able to read the news undisturbed. Bye now, you take care.

This would be amusing to tell Clay, but I want the newspapers, so I'll keep it to myself.

June 1

The paper says they arraigned him at a court in Jaffa.

The charges: crimes against the Jewish people, war crimes against humanity, membership in a criminal organization.

Matthias is right. They'll get to keep him. The Argentine government will back down, the Israelis will give him a fair trial. The world will get to see how scrupulous the Jews are in matters of law.

I've tried to envision this man in his fifties ("slight, balding," according to the Times) in a cell that is continuously guarded, always lit. But I cannot imagine what kind of thoughts he could be having.

What kind of memories.

He oversaw the whole thing. The Final Solution was his. He managed it, made sure it worked.

Even though they've found him, even though they've charged him with his crimes, I still can't believe he exists at this instant. That he has actual thoughts and memories. That he talks and eats and drinks.

The paper says he plans to defend himself by arguing that it wasn't just him, it was everyone together, it was the Reich.

I speak sometimes to Clay about guilt, but he is less interested in guilt than in anger, which is for him more palpable. (Naturally. I display no guilt in his direction, and like any good narcissist he takes as his first concern the feelings I have toward him.)

He thinks my angst (as he calls it) over what I might've done and didn't do is indicative of a deeper, more important despair. Over who I am. Whose daughter. Whose wife.

I find these questions numbing, I tell him.

Why? he asks. Is it because you feel you must protect yourself against them?

No, I say. It's because a person never discovers who he is. Only what he might have been and what he failed to do.

You speak too abstractly, he says.

You aren't really listening, I say, and please don't protest.

For whatever reason, he does as I ask. I have never experienced an impasse as total as this one with Clay. Yet I go to the sessions with him; they are a familiar exercise, like my daily walks around the grounds, my nightly baths: physical, necessary, purposeless.

June 30

I've read my newspapers.

A short review of a recording session in Paris, a tribute to Cannonball Adderley. Don Byas on tenor, Powell on piano. Just the two of them.

It must've been astonishing. So much exchanged, so much said. Because such music would speak: for Cannonball, his instrument, his presence, the loss of him and the regaining: the man restored by the playing of the music. You don't mourn, you play. You answer the death with the music.

Byas and Powell did mostly ballads, the reviewer said. Beautiful ballads: *Moonlight in Vermont, I Remember Clifford, I'll Be Seeing You.*

I Remember Clifford. Another tribute, said the review, *in memory of Clifford Brown, trumpet player. Dead in a car crash, four years ago this month. So young, so gifted, so much missed.*

I remember that death. I remember reading the paper that morning in June, in New York, in the apartment. Matt sitting opposite me at our table; the coffee warm, the air warm, the news a wash of benign events — the world's untroubled doings; and then a short column about the accident. Not an obituary, just a little record of the facts. Clifford Brown, trumpet player, dead. In the same car as musician Richie Powell, the only brother of pianist Bud Powell. In the same car as Nancy Powell, wife of Richie.

Nancy was driving. They were traveling late, after a gig in Philly. The car skidded off the Pennsylvania Turnpike and rolled down an embankment; there were no survivors.

I remember not telling Matt. He would've been upset at my being upset. Powell always scared Matt — right from the beginning, that first breakdown at the end of the war, and then all those stories about Powell drawing huge keyboards on the sanitarium walls.

Powell in France now. Paris, Powell's safe haven. I'm sure he won't come back home. If he knows what's good for him, he'll stay put.

I can imagine that session with Byas. The room is empty except for the black piano, the amber-gold sax. The two men

170

enter. Powell sits; Byas bows his head to the mouthpiece of his sax, his fingers move into place. And when they begin playing *I Remember Clifford* for Cannonball, Powell is remembering Richie and Nancy, and Byas knows it. And when the second chorus modulates to that elegaic minor, Powell takes it with him — all his loss — and lays it out in a solo whose runs are spare and so articulate that Byas knows exactly what to say in response. And they bring it to a close together, *in memoriam:* love being the only tribute possible.

But afterwards, in his small flat, again alone, Powell wonders: *How long, Jesus how long can I keep it together?*

August 19

It's been hot. I can't sleep much, or think long thoughts, or write. Only read. I read all the time.

Len and Carol brought me a third batch of papers yesterday.

There's lots on the Eichmann snatch, Len said. The Argentines backed off. Now it's up to the Israelis. Eichmann's going to get his day in court after all.

The stack of Sunday Times, neatly bound in string, in the blue duffle bag at Len's feet.

After you read those newspapers, said Carol, you'll know more about the Nazis than you ever wanted to. I promise. The trial hasn't even started and already the papers are full of the whole thing. The war all over again.

She looked tired; her hair was damp, matted against the sides of her head. Her blouse needed ironing.

The room was airless even with the windows wide open.

Dog days, Carol said (fanning herself with one of my paperback books). Why's it so beastly here? This place is no better than Manhattan, for Christ's sake.

I handed them each a glass of water. Carol held hers against her forehead, then drank it. I refilled it. Len lit a cigarette.

There's no way they won't sentence Eichmann to death, he said. Not after all the evidence. I mean, you couldn't imagine such evidence they're gathering, those Israeli lawyers. You couldn't dream up such a story.

He was in one of his stews, soaked in a single idea. He finds one mental track and glides along, impossible to derail. Carol rides it out, knowing he'll get off that track and onto another if she just waits. Carol can wait any amount of time. She expects nothing. But she also knows that Len will never leave her alone for too long: which is all she needs to be sure of.

She hasn't needed to be sure of me. Neither has Len. It isn't important to him, counting on me as a daughter. But on some wordless level — on the level of his Jewishness — he's uncomfortable with my being cut off. For Len those courtroom proceedings in Jerusalem have the force of revealed secrets, and he can't stand my not hearing them. He wants me to have the news. Like any other Jew.

Carol lay stretched out on my bed, her short thick body immobilized by the heat, her hair unresponsive to persistent fanning.

What do you hear from Matt, she asked.

Not too much, I said. I think he's fine.

Len handed me a cigarette and lit his own, then mine.

Matt gave me a couple of music history lessons, Carol said. It was a little embarrassing. At least now I know that Beethoven was the deaf one and Schubert was the one who died young — I always used to get them mixed up. But I sell them anyway. Business is booming.

That's what counts, said Len.

The cigarette tasted strange to me after so many months of not smoking. Strange, good. It absorbed all my interest.

You know, in the trial Eichmann's going to come across as some kind of cultured guy, Len said. Big on the Old Masters, the German philosophers. I think his lawyers are trying to show that such a smart man couldn't possibly be a mass murderer.

All of the Nazis did that at Nuremberg, Carol said (slightly roused, the topic luring her despite herself). They all wanted to prove how classy they were. Books, art — as if any of it could make a difference.

It can, I said. It can keep a person that much farther from the truth of what he's doing.

Well, maybe so, said Carol (her voice again lethargic — she didn't like this track, didn't want its difficulties).

Yeah, it's true, Judy's right, said Len. I mean, these guys somehow had to rationalize what they were doing. You gas a bunch of Jews and then you read some Nietzsche, and everything's OK.

Jesus, Lenny, it's too hot to talk about this kind of thing, said Carol. Let's drop it. We didn't come all the way out here to tell Judy such depressing stuff.

Yeah, he said. OK.

(I could see it playing out on his face: the battle to suppress, to minimize. What's known but ignored takes its revenge. You bring me the Times, Lenny, you don't want me to be cut off. But we cut ourselves off; and now we pay the price.)

I need some more music, I said. I've played all the records you brought me. Dozens of times.

Well, you just happen to be in luck, kiddo, said Len.

He smiled. (How I envy him, the way he hoofs it loose and easy across the stage, blowing those slick uptempo riffs, *grab your coat and get your hat!*)

We happen to have some new records right here, he said. You're in for a treat.

He dug into the blue bag, handed over the black disks.

173

Johnny Hedges and his band. Charlie Rouse. Bird, Dizzy. Tommy Flanagan's trio. Eric Dolphy with Ron Carter, Roy Haynes, Booker Little. Flute, clarinet, alto: all those sounds in one head! Dolphy the reedman, magical Dolphy.

A new Miles Davis LP: *Kind of Blue.*

With Coltrane and Bill Evans, said Carol. More of that new cool they've been doing. Miles uses a mute on his horn. Sounds good.

They did some kind of game together on that album, added Len. Improvisation, messing with the tempo. Like blues but not really — hard to describe. Not my favorite. See what you think.

She'll like it, said Carol.

Has Matt heard it, I asked.

Yeah, said Carol, as a matter of fact he was at the apartment a few days after I bought it, and I played it for him.

What did he say, I asked.

He said you'd like it, said Carol.

He should know, Len said.

What else did he say, I asked.

Oh I don't know, said Carol. It was too hot, we didn't talk much.

Yeah, but we did talk about Eichmann, said Len. Matt's sure they'll hang him. It's the Jews' turn, he said to me.

Yes, I said.

Matt better be right, Len said.

They left a little later. I gave Carol a final glass of water. She looked wrinkled and dehydrated, in spite of her damp blouse. I remembered her looking like that sometimes when I was young, after she'd been through an especially heavy bout of drinking.

Len's final question as Powell opened the door: What do you do with all the papers once you've read them?

I save what I need, I said. The rest I give away.

(To Powell, who takes them and gets rid of them in perfect silence.)

Well, good for you, said Len. Why hang on to what you don't need?

Amen, said Carol. Bye hon, see you, take care.

Bye, I said, thanks, bye.

October 3

Yesterday, Rosh Hashanah.

Matt showed up.

Shanah tovah, I said.

What's that, he said.

A good year, I said. I'm wishing you a good year.

Ah, he said. Thanks. I'd forgotten — the holidays.

The Days of Awe, I said.

He paused.

Are you marking them in some way, he asked.

No, I said, but they're marking me. I become more anxious during these days. If I knew how to atone, I would. Or what to atone for.

I was sitting on the floor, which is increasingly where I choose to sit; for some reason it feels safer, what with my occasional Miltown dizziness. Matt was standing by the window.

Sit, I said to him, it's hard having you look down on me.

He sat near me. He's always been limber, despite his bad lower back. His frame collapses easily into a cross-legged posture, and when he gets up, the rise of his body is an unfolding rather than a series of movements, without any struggle for balance.

I don't think atonement is the issue, he said.

You believe in redemption, I said. Right?

Yes, he said.

And judgment?

I suppose, he said.

Can't have one without the other, can you?

Probably not.

Well, I said, I want to be inscribed in the Book of Life as one of the righteous. But first I must be judged. No — first I must judge myself. And atone.

That's always the case, said Matt. Not just in these days. But not too harshly, Judith.

I have to write myself in, I said. Into the Book, I mean. It doesn't just happen. First you have to convince yourself of your own righteousness.

The final call isn't yours, said Matt, it's out of your hands, don't be too harsh —

— I know, I said.

He took my hands in his.

Think about something else, he said. About your poems.

My little atonements, I said.

No, no (his hands tightening on mine), don't think of them like that. They're separate.

Nothing's separate, I said.

OK, he said.

He let go of my hands and stared off, his eyes emptying.

Don't make it harder than it already is, he said (so softly, I could barely hear him).

This place, I said. You don't know what it does to me. I need to come home. Matt (my voice rising, I couldn't stop it), if you tell them to let me go, they will. I need my desk, I need the city noise, I need all my records. My own bed. I need to sleep with you.

His eyes alighting on mine.

Please don't, he said, you make it hurt more when you say these things.

They're hiding the world from me. You have to tell them to release me.

Words burst from him, finally. *Judith do you think I wouldn't — oh can't you feel it, don't you see how you're not ready, you know I can't tell them till you're ready, till you're well again — oh please God try to understand me, Judith, hear me —*

His body unwinding, extending toward me. His hands reaching me first, grasping mine, pulling me to him. Then his arms at my sides and around my waist, pulling, the space between us collapsing. My chest against his, the bony armature, his arms still pulling, his hands first in my hair then drawing my face down to his shoulder, into the heat of his neck, its hard basis of collarbone, the tendons running upward to the jaw. His hand on the nape of my neck, thumb and third finger spread and hooked under my jawbone at either side; his legs scissoring mine hard, the bones at the sides of his knees pressing at my thighs, pinning me on top of him, not letting me move, keeping me still, holding me telling me showing me still he loves me, still.

Til I'm well again.

Our breathing uneven, as if we had been making love, as if we had been connected.

Matt, I don't know if I can be well again. I don't know what it means. Do you know what it means?

No, I don't, he whispered.

You have to help me, I said.

I can come see you, he said. It's all I can do.

When you leave me, this is gone, I said. Then I'm alone.

(Strands of his soft brown-grey hair between my fingers.)

I know.

It's not enough.

We have no choice, Judith.

October 31

They've stepped up my Miltown dosage. My entire body is leaden.

Tomorrow I will tell Clay, I'll say to him *you fucking son of a bitch you take me off this shit or I'll* —

I can't finish what I start, the drug short-circuits everything.

Where's Powell? When I need him, when I need his nut-brown bittersweet gaze on me, *oh yes I know you!*

Instead, Matthias. On this of all days, today, Halloween! He showed up in the late afternoon, dusk approaching. A quiet knocking, his *let me in* breaking into the room's grey air.

Hello, Judith.

I brought you some books, he said. From Wiser's.

The Apocrypha. The Secret Doctrine in Israel: A Study of the Zohar and Its Connections. The Kabbalah; or, The True Science of Light.

I couldn't talk. I looked at Matt, trying to bring him into focus. The edges of him were clear but the center wouldn't hold.

He swung one hand back and forth in a low arc while he spoke, a small self-deprecating gesture.

I thought I'd just drop in for a minute, he said. I won't stay long. I don't know, it seemed like the right thing to do, so I came.

His stammering voice, that hand dipping through the air. The books heavy in my arms, my entire body heavy.

Yes, I said. Come on in.

Voices. I needed to hear a voice other than his or mine, so I put Ella Fitzgerald on the record player. The tunes Matt likes. Then I watched him sit in the chair. I tried to sit on the bed but it seemed to be swallowing me, so I somehow found the floor and leaned against the wall.

You look a little pale, he said. Are you all right?

Fine, I answered. Only you did make me think of a ghost. When I first saw you.

He forced a short uncertain laugh.

Really?

No. Not literally.

It's Halloween, you know, he said.

Yes.

Maybe that's why you thought —

— no, I said. But it doesn't matter. They've increased the Miltown, that's probably it.

He was silent.

I don't understand your being here now, I said.

He looked away, a wince. Pain. Between us always pain.

I didn't mean that the way it sounded, I said. I don't know what I meant.

He nodded, but I saw he was keeping his eyes cast down. He wouldn't look at me. Even though I was on the floor. Down there on the floor.

Look at me, I said (the fury ignited, a bright whip-like snap), will you look at me, goddamn it?

(*So I can make you real* — I should've said it — *so it won't be a ghost, our love!*)

I can't right now, he whispered. I just came to be with you for a little while. It's what I can do.

His eyes down, still down.

Leave, I said. Leave me.

Judith, he said, don't.

No, I said, no, just leave.

Somehow he'd gone. I lay on my side on the floor, listening to Ella — her voice so rich and deep and dense on the last few terrifying bars of that absurd ballad —

> *I'd like to gain complete control of you*
> *to handle even the heart and soul of you*

November 16

So what do you think of our new president, I began.

How did you hear about the election results, Clay said.

Don't be an idiot, I said, everyone here talked about the election. You don't need a newspaper or a radio to know the news. Even here. Even with these crazy people.

What do *you* think, he said. Of our new president.

I think Kennedy is young and handsome (I rattled on) but probably smart and certainly preferable to his opponent, who makes me think of certain caricatures I've seen of evil Jews. You know. Big nose, shifty eyes, dark brows, heavy beard growth.

You find Kennedy's opponent compelling, Clay said. Does he remind you of any man you know?

Oh yes, I said (trying to look sincere; I've learned which of my expressions appear convincing to Clay). He reminds me of most of the men I know.

Why is that?

Because most of the men I know are untrustworthy, I said.

Are you reminded of Sam? he asked.

Oh yes, more than anyone else, I said. I'm sure my father was very much like that — crafty, wily, argumentative, a bit morose, self-absorbed. He must've been that way.

180

Why is that?

Because he was a Jew.

You're not taking this seriously, Judith.

But I am, I said. What are you expecting me to say?

I expect you to say what you really feel.

Ah, I said. Well, I feel that Sam is very dead. So I can think of him as a man like Nixon, or a man like Kennedy, or a man like Matthias, or Len, or you. It doesn't much matter, does it?

Yes, he said, it does, because the way you think of Sam helps us see why you have trouble letting him go. Why you still require his attendance at the drama of your inner life.

Oh fuck my inner life, I said. The most dramatic thing about my inner life is how dried up it's become in this place. I can't write here, can't think here, can't stay in touch —

— with what, Clay broke in, with what aren't you in touch? What is it you're really missing? *Who* is it?

All of them, I said (but not to him; only to myself). The millions in Europe, the two on lower Broadway — the ones who might've seen things differently —

December 31

A note from Matt, delivered by Powell.

Missing you, thinking of you.

And then this, copied out from the book of Auden poems I no longer own, the one I threw away:

> *In the depths of myself blind monsters know*
> *Your presence and are angry, dreading Love*
> *That asks its images for more than love*

Yes, I remember that poem; and the two of us reading aloud, in bed that first winter, our legs tangled for warmth. I remember this, too:

On a high chair alone
I sat, my little master, asking why
The cold and solid object in my hands
Should be a human hand, one of your hands.

1961

April 25

Spring. The earth has finally thawed. Its muddy surface is such a relief.

More newspapers. Today, Len and Carol's first visit this year. A quick here-and-gone. They like being the bearers of news, it gives them a reason for visiting me.

Len paced and smoked and told me about Gideon Hausner, the Israeli prosecutor who made the opening statement at the Eichmann trial last week.

A dumpy little Pole, he said, but smart. You'll read about him.

Eichmann's got six volumes of testimony, said Carol. Can you imagine? The lawyers are going to be reading the stuff for months.

No, said Len. Hausner's all set for this. He knows exactly what's in those pages. His team's all set to go.

They say Eichmann wants to make like he was just one of

the foot soldiers, said Carol. You know, the whole following-orders bit.

No dice, said Len.

He sounded tough, but I could see he was nervous. Distracted. When they left, Carol handed me a couple of records and some cookies.

I made them yesterday for Lenny, she said, but he's eaten too many already, why don't you take the rest?

Len stood in the doorway. He turned suddenly and gave the sill a fast, hard jab with the heel of one hand.

They better hang that son of a bitch, he said. And they better not waste any time. Or there's going to be a bunch of very angry Jews in America.

I wanted to laugh at him: Len Rubin, the now-angry Jew who managed to sit out the entire war.

When Bud Powell lost Richie and Nancy, he knew he'd lost segments of himself. And now when he plays, he knows he's retrieving the shards, bits of the *ein-sof*, slivers of light. This is his Repair. Playing is painful for him because slivers enter his skin as he strikes the keys. In his fingertips, up the shaft of each finger, across the palm of each hand are stabs of pain. But he keeps playing, *in memoriam*, for everyone gone.

America is punishment for Powell. He thinks it isn't safe here, and he's right. So he goes to Paris, but even there he meets up with all the deaths when he plays.

LeRoi Jones:

> *Smiling & glad/in*
> *the huge & loveless*
> *white-anglo sun/of*
> *benevolent step*
> *mother America*

Len and Carol swear they're safe. Oh, they swear it. But Lenny grows nervous.

June 9

Matt's here once a month, for maybe an hour each time. We go outside — I still can't sit in the room without ending up on the floor, but outside I feel stronger. We walk, often in silence. Between visits I get little notes from him. They are emptily sweet: *How are you? Hope this finds you calm.* And: *Thinking of you.*

I read them and give them to Powell. I don't care what you do with these, I tell him, but don't even think of saving them. They aren't for safekeeping.

He nods, he understands.

Matt brings books, mostly poetry, things I don't feel like reading. Last week he brought a small narrow box. I opened it; inside was a strand of pearls identical to those I no longer have, but with a different clasp.

I looked at him. He smiled at me uncertainly.

Carol mentioned you'd got rid of your necklace, he said. I thought maybe you'd be missing it. You used to always wear it.

How does Carol know what I've kept or not kept, I said. And why is she telling you?

My voice was a slap bringing color to his cheeks.

Last year you asked her to give away a bunch of your clothes, he said. When she sorted them out, she found the pearls and gave them to me, and I had them cleaned and re-strung for you.

Wait, I said. First you threw out all my files without asking me. And then you and Carol saved a necklace that *I* didn't want to see again, *ever*. Take these fucking pearls away and go yourself, go now!

He must've tried to speak because I began saying *don't talk to me*. It turned out I was yelling without realizing it. The door opened and Powell was standing there, watching me.

He motioned to Matt, and Matt walked out quickly, as if in danger. And I knew it would be a while before I'd see him again.

August 16

Earlier this humid evening, Len and Carol brought the latest news. The court had adjourned after hearing all the Eichmann testimony.

It's going to take a couple of months for them to come to a verdict, said Len.

Carol handed me the pile of newspapers and put the blue bag by the door.

We can't stay long, she said, we want to get back in time to catch Bill Evans's first set.

Where's he playing, I asked.

Someplace uptown, said Carol. Lenny, check today's paper for the club, would you?

Len lit a cigarette and flipped through the paper on top of the stack as Carol chattered about her job, the humidity, a new restaurant on West Fourth Street, her recent disappointing haircut, the prices of sheet music — everything's going up, the city's getting so damn expensive.

You forgot to tell her about the Wall, said Len, looking up from the newspaper.

What wall, I said.

In Berlin, he said, handing me the front page of today's Times.

A photograph showed a city street lined with flat-facaded apartments. Down its middle ran what looked like a fence of barbed wire. Groups of soldiers were building a stone foundation for the fence as other armed soldiers stood by, preventing any crossings.

What's this, I said.

The border between East and West Berlin, said Len. The East Germans got tired of people leaving. The other day they circled the western part of the city with wire, and now they're putting up a real wall, and they're shooting anyone who tries to cross over. They've killed some people already.

They threw the whole thing together overnight, said Carol. Just like that. People woke up and found themselves completely cut off — from neighbors, family, friends. It's terrible. Kennedy's got a real mess on his hands. I don't know what he'll do.

What's to do? said Len. We just have to wait and watch how things develop. See what move the Russians make.

I looked at the pictures. My nerves started jumping inside me, as if somebody had thrown a switch — it wasn't painful, but everything felt overstimulated, uncontrolled.

Wait? I asked them. Are you serious?

They said nothing. Their gazes on me were wary, intense.

You're doing it all over again, I said.

Doing what, Judy, said Len.

You're pretending, I said. Ignoring the evidence. Making believe that no evil will ever come. But you know, don't you? You know if you don't act now, it'll happen all over again.

Judy (Len breaking in, scared now), come on, this is a different situation. They're not going after one group of people, they're not singling out anyone in particular. It's just lousy politics. The Russians want their piece of the pie.

I could no longer tell what my voice sounded like. It was barely mine, and it was very loud.

You fucking coward, I said. You liar. I know you! You see

187

but you won't see. You've never told me anything true. Nothing. Not one fucking true thing.

Carol put her hand on Len's arm. Let's go, she said.

Her voice was neutral, but I had never felt so provoked by her. In my head everything — all her evasions, her glosses, her refusals — suddenly massed together, a noisy chorus battering on the inside of my skull, making my ears ring.

I lunged at them both, pulling her hand off his arm, separating them as they deserved to be separated, forcing them apart as they deserved to be apart, alone, locked in their cells with their deceptions.

It was Powell who came up from behind me, gently pulled my wrists to the small of my back, snapped the metal rings on them, and spun me around gently to look full into my face.

Just so you don't hurt nobody, he said, his eyes greeting mine.

September 22

The humidity still hasn't broken. I spend most of each day outside, walking slowly or sitting or lying on the grass; and there are long merciful hours in which I don't think of Matthias. But always at some point my lassitude is punctured by some image of him, and I think *how could this happen?*

Matt brought me here. And I let him.

December 28

A long gap, and now the news.

Eichmann was condemned to death two weeks ago.

He's appealing the verdict, said Len. Stupid bastard. It's pointless — he's a dead man.

Matt said nothing. He glanced at me, his eyes shadowed in reluctance.

So talk, I said to him. Tell me what you think. No — tell me first why Carol isn't here.

Len jumped in nervously. We told you that already, he said. She's got a bad stomach. Something she ate.

I doubt that, I said. Something's eating *her*.

Well *we're* here, he said. Long time no see, huh?

Yeah, I said. Since the Wall went up, right?

Yeah, he said.

Matt, I said (turning to him, his face in profile, his body angled away from mine). Tell me what you think.

Of the verdict, you mean, he said.

Yes.

There was a pause. Then he swung toward me, and it was like having a too-sharp light in my eyes; I had to stop myself from holding my hand in front of my face.

I think it's good, he said.

A sudden elevation in the current. My fingertips prickling, sweat on my scalp.

I repeated the word as a question: Good?

Yes. Necessary.

Good and necessary are two different things, I said.

I know, he said. The Eichmann verdict is both.

The Miltown was hard at work now.

I would've thought, I said, that as a Christian you would oppose the death sentence. Or at least not call it good.

Matt was silent.

Len inhaled hard on his cigarette. His words emerged from his mouth as smoke.

Jesus, he said. What're you talking about, Judy? Nobody opposes this sentence except maybe a few ex-Nazis.

And more than a few Christians. The death penalty is against their religion, remember, Lenny?

Matt remained silent.

189

Len dropped his cigarette to the floor, stepped on it, picked up the stub, and tossed it in my wastebasket.

Don't insult Matt's intelligence, he said. You know what he thinks about all this.

It's not a question of intelligence. If it were, the war wouldn't have happened.

We got what we wanted, said Len. A death verdict for Eichmann. And we'll get the death too. The guy will hang for what he did.

He didn't look at Matt or me as he spoke. Lost in a fantasy of retribution. But scared. Len knows the questions: *What if it's not enough, the hanging? What if it means nothing?*

The verdict is good, said Matt again. A balancing of the accounts.

Oh yes, I said. But after the fact. I mean, when the deed's done, it's easier to balance everything, isn't it?

Easier, maybe, he said. But still good. Still necessary.

It's not your loss, I said. So what can you possibly know?

Len handed me a cigarette. He lit first his, then mine.

Don't split hairs, Judy, he said.

What are you saying, I asked.

Don't make it worse than it's already been, he said.

His voice incendiary, a lit match at the fuse of my rage. I threw the cigarette at him. He raised one hand to shield himself.

Fuck off, I said. You bastard traitor.

Matt stirred as if trying to wake up.

Let's go, he said to Len.

I began shrieking at them. The words were mine, yet they broke like water on rocks, a spray of meaningless emotion. All the things I saw — Len's stunned face, Matt's vacant eyes, the blue bag full of newspapers — all the details keep breaking up now as they did then, refusing to hold shape, to stay real.

Powell was at my side, his muted alto in my ear.

Now you got trouble, he said.

It swung just right: the downbeat *now,* the quick bridge to *trouble,* each note true.

1962

January 5

Clay told me today, at the end of our session, that visits from family members are to be curtailed.

Curtailed? I said.

It's in the interest of your health to minimize any interruptions of your treatment, he said. We have asked your husband and Mr. and Mrs. Rubin to visit you less frequently so that you can concentrate more fully on your experience here.

I laughed at him.

They hardly come anyway, I said. Matt comes maybe once a month. Len and Carol come a few times a year. What are you saying to me?

Now they'll each come twice a year. Separately — your husband by himself, the Rubins by themselves. You may write to them, but they have been asked not to write back. Naturally I trust you'll want to share with me the contents of any letters you write. We can learn from talking about them.

But communicating with your family shouldn't be a priority. We must focus on your experience here.

Panic rising like a fluid inside my chest, up toward my throat, to the dam of my mouth.

What experience, I said. I experience nothing here. Nothing happens to me here.

That is subjective, said Clay. You must work to restore meaning.

Wait, I tried to say, and the word itself was glue, a viscous lump I couldn't spit out or swallow.

Wait.

Clay stared at me with his blank eyes.

Yes? he asked.

Whose idea was this?

It is not an idea, he said. It is part of your treatment.

Did they suggest it, did they agree to it, do they want it? *Tell me, you son of a bitch!*

His voice: a pall settling over me, soft as smoke.

What your family wants isn't our concern, he said. But yes, they agreed.

Powell stood in the doorway, waiting to escort me to my room.

Where is it, I said to Clay.

Where's what, he asked.

He nodded at Powell, who wrapped his hands (tightly but gently, causing no pain) around my elbows and squeezed them slightly inward to let me know I couldn't move.

My yellow star, I said.

Clay's face: nothing.

Where is it? I asked him. I think you should paint it on my door. Or let me sew it on my coat. So we'll all know who's who, our roles will be clear —

— what roles, interrupted Clay.

I'm the Jew, I said. So that makes you the Nazi, doesn't it? And your husband? The Rubins?

Collaborators, I said. Informers.

Try not to play with such notions, he said. They lead nowhere.

Do you have any idea how much I loathe you? I asked him.

We'll talk again tomorrow, he said.

I felt Powell's grip tighten on my elbows as he headed me toward my cell. I let him impel me. Only in his hands am I safe. At the door he released me.

Take me home, I said, please take me back.

You're there, he said. You're there.

April 27

I've seen Matt once this year. One day last week he came. I can't recall when, or what he said, or if I said anything. Maybe we said nothing.

Touch, did we touch?

The cold and solid object in my hands, one of your hands.

June 1

It's over, said Len, handing me today's paper. Eichmann's been executed.

His face was bright with pride, as if he'd done it himself.

The Israeli police dumped his ashes overboard last night, said Carol.

Outside territorial waters, of course, Len added. They didn't want any chunks of him floating around.

Jesus, Lenny, said Carol. I mean, is that kind of detail necessary?

Nope, he said. I just like thinking of the guy in little pieces. You glad, kiddo?

194

He turned, making himself look at me.

Glad? I repeated.

Look what we got here, said Len. Actual justice, the real thing. Eye for an eye.

Hardball, said Carol. It's a new game now. There'll be more trials. The Israelis will find more of these scum. These guys can't hide forever.

She sat on my bed, reached for my pillow, and lay down, sighing with relief.

Jesus, I'm tired, she said. We stayed out too late last night.

Len laughed. Tee many martoonis, he said.

Most of the Nazis aren't hiding, I said. They're being concealed.

Len and Carol were silent for a moment. Carol looked at Len: *you answer her.*

These people are clever, said Len. They go off to some rancho in Latin America and hide out. You can't expect to turn them up right away. Takes time.

Carol was nodding at him. Oh, they'll be found, she said.

Goddamn right, Len said.

He pulled out his matches and lit up. I could feel him waiting for me: to approve of his jubilation, to condone his false courage. To say *Oh yes, I see how resolute you are.* And *Yes, of course, you've always been that way.*

Len fears me because I know what Carol doesn't: in his deepest heart, Lenny isn't laughing, he isn't drinking gin and having a wonderful time. He's completely disconsolate. After Lottie and Sam were killed, he took me in; but he could never love me. I was his loss, not compensation for it but proof. And when all the other losses started mounting up, he couldn't take any more.

Len stubbed out his cigarette. Carol sat up, as if on cue, and pushed at her messy hair.

195

What do you think, she said to Len.

It's getting late.

Long drive back home.

We should go.

See you soon. Sooner or later. Later. Or maybe not again, ever. Because you never know, do you?

September 13

Clay is trying to make me talk about why I hate him.

We need to get at what I represent to you, he said today.

You represent nothing, I said.

That's not possible, he said.

Oh, but it is. You represent nothing to me.

You must talk about this, he said.

Why talk about what's meaningless?

This has to do with other people, Clay said. You know that. You must confront me in order to confront the others.

I'm not interested. Really. Whenever I sit in this chair, I become profoundly, overwhelmingly bored.

Eliot, the end of "Burnt Norton":

> *Ridiculous the waste sad time*
> *Stretching before and after*

Why do you consent to these sessions?

I'm in prison, and I'm cooperating with my jailors. It's the only sane thing to do under the circumstances, isn't it?

Have you considered rebellion?

Powell stood suddenly framed in the doorway, his stocky silhouette beckoning. My timely savior.

*　　*　　*

196

Clay was waiting for my answer.

No, I said (standing, sidling into Powell's orbit, awaiting his grip. My heart like Eliot's, *beating obedient to controlling hands*).

Why not, Clay asked.

Rebellion would be pointless. I can't move, can't act. You're holding me prisoner here.

Judith, he said, we're not. You're here because you can't conduct your life elsewhere.

LeRoi Jones:

> *I am inside someone*
> *who hates me*

December 11

Len and Carol brought me a couple of new albums. Coltrane, plus something Carol said she likes — bossa nova, with someone named Stan Getz on sax and several Brazilians accompanying him on drums and guitar.

Now *this* album swings, she said, and they're all such good players. It'll really cheer you up.

Did you bring the newspapers, I asked Len.

He handed me the stack, which I slid beneath the bed.

The Israelis are keeping up the good work, he said. Since Eichmann they've learned how to do things right. They know you can't mess around with the Germans.

He pointed under the bed. His hands looked bigger and older than I remembered them.

There's a story in one of those papers about some Egyptian-Swiss guy named Kamal, he said. The Israeli secret service blew up his plane a few months ago, but Kamal escaped. Ap-

197

parently he's been helping German factories build planes and rockets for the Egyptian army. I guess he thought he'd make himself some nice pocket change behind the scenes.

He lit a cigarette, handed it to me, and lit another for himself.

Not for long, he said, exhaling. This Kamal is dead meat.

It just goes to show you can never trust the Germans, said Carol.

Not only the Germans, I said.

They both looked at me. I picked up Carol's bossa nova album.

Who is this man Getz, I asked. An American? Why is he playing with Brazilians? Who are these Brazilians? If the Argentines could hide a Nazi for fifteen years, why shouldn't their neighbors do the same?

Carol shook her head. Her face puckered with consternation. Suddenly I could see her as a twenty-year-old, standing before the stranger who presented her with a body: mine: small, orphaned, needing her as no one did — as she did not need herself. I could hear her saying to the stranger, *yes of course we'll take her.* And to herself, *no I won't do away with her. But I'll never tell Len how much I haven't wanted a child. How relieved I've been that I haven't yet had one. How much better it seems not to replicate your own confusion.*

Carol spoke now, her voice feigning calm authority.

Judy, she said, Stan Getz is a New Yorker. I think he's even Jewish. He plays with those Brazilians because they're good musicians.

Try to keep things separate, said Len.

Have you been talking to Dr. Clay, I asked.

They didn't answer.

Don't worry, I said. Can you please go now?

1963

January 2

Matt showed up with roses. For you, for this new year, he said.

His eyes filmy with reluctance. He tries to be brave, but the only way he can do it is to tell us both lies.

New year, I said, what new year? Nothing's changed.

He put the roses on my desk.

Things change, he said. Things never stand still.

I picked up a rose.

You brought me here, I said. Don't worry, I won't try to escape. I have nowhere to go.

He was watching each of my movements. What are you doing, he said softly.

The thorns of the rose as they dragged across the underside of my forearm: proof that I'm still within the borders of something. Thin red welts of flesh like lines on a map, a kind of topography . . . At that moment I felt something so far beyond self-pity that I knew I was no longer even remotely the woman who'd married this man.

I haven't got a crown of thorns like Jesus, I said. These are just the usual lacerations.

He flinched. Stop it, Judith, he said. Stop.

I swung as he was turning away from me. My blood-streaked arm caught him full on the side of his face, leaving red lines across his cheekbone, earlobe, jaw.

His hand went up, fingers probing the wetness in disbelief.

It's for the new year, I said.

March 12

I have given the roses to Powell. They'd turned a deep red-brown; each petal was dry and papery, almost translucent, and the stems and thorns were stiff as wood but very light. It was like handing him a bunch of insect wings impaled on sticks.

Here, I said. Don't try to revive these. Just throw them into an unmarked grave.

He looked at me without sympathy or fear. You sure, he asked.

Oh yes, I'm sure.

May 19

Clay and I say the same things over and over. Theme and variations.

With Matt, I tell him, I move between two extremes. I'm either completely swallowed or completely separate. Either overwhelmed by the force of who he is, or absolutely isolated from him. There has never been a safe middle.

But you know he loves you, Clay says.

Yes. But that doesn't make me safe. I'm either eclipsed or alone — there's nothing in between.

A variation:

Are you saying, Clay asked me last week, that the love between you and Matt is dangerous?

No, I answered. But it isn't a bridge.

What is it then?

A very sad and unavailing truth, I said.

And again today, more variations:

Why did you and Matt decide not to have a child?

We didn't decide. We just didn't have one.

But you talked about it?

Now and then. Until after the war, and then we stopped talking about it. There was nothing more to say.

Clay, breaking the silence: The miscarriage — did that bring you and Matt closer together? What did he do when you actually lost the child? Was he with you when it happened?

Yes, I said. We'd just gone to bed. I started bleeding hard, and he wrapped me in a blanket and somehow carried me downstairs and put us in a cab and made the driver race to St. Vincent's. And during the examination he held my hand. When the doctor asked us questions, I answered them, and Matt said nothing. He couldn't talk. His face was the color of ash.

Then what?

Then we took another cab home and he still wasn't talking, and when we walked into the bedroom and he saw the blood on the sheets, he began crying. I'd never seen him do that before. He cried and cried like children do, easily, hard. And so I held his hand.

When he stopped crying, did you talk?

No. We changed the sheets. We had a drink. We smoked. It was very late. We had another drink, another cigarette. We slept. No — he slept. I stayed awake for the rest of the night because I was afraid.

Of your loss?

I couldn't feel it, I said.

Did Matt try to help you feel it? Later, maybe in a few weeks?

I don't know, I said. Maybe he did, maybe he didn't. All I know is it happened. Somewhere among all the other losses.

I leaned forward, looked directly into Clay's eyes.

I know how many children were murdered in Auschwitz. Do you?

What else do you know, Judith?

I know I lost a child I didn't even realize I was carrying. What is there to feel in that?

Matt felt a great deal. How did that affect you?

Matt feels everything, I said. But he does nothing. It's all in Christ's hands.

Have you always been at odds with Matt over this?

Over what?

Religion.

Please, I said, don't change the subject. We're not talking about religion.

What are we talking about?

About being either engulfed or isolated. Remember?

No, said Clay. We're talking about your resentment of Matt's faith as his way of coping with loss. We should explore this further.

Faith? I repeated.

He nodded.

I could feel something like a swarm of bees in my head. ˙

Listen to me, you fucking moron, I said. Matt doesn't know the meaning of the word. All he knows is that he's been promised redemption, and if that means he has to take his suffering and his desire in silence, then so be it. That's not faith, but I'm powerless against it.

We're talking in circles, said Clay. (This, I have learned, is as close to retaliating as he allows himself to get.)

202

You know what? You exhaust me, Clay.

My words are rocks bouncing off rock. Noisy, pointless variations.

Death, I said, we're talking about death.

July 31

We're on our way to a weekend in the Poconos, said Carol. Thank God! The city's like an oven. I couldn't wait to get the hell out of there.

A year's worth of Sunday Times. It took Len three trips to the car to get all the papers inside. He used the blue bag for each load. By the time he brought in the final stack, he was sweating hard.

Hope nobody's watching me going in and out like this, or they'll think I'm crazy, he said.

He bent over to slide the papers under my bed. The back of his shirt was soaked.

Don't worry, Lenny, said Carol. Nobody's watching — I'm keeping a lookout here at this window, and I don't see a soul.

They know who's crazy here, Len, I said. You don't qualify.

Len stood up. His face was shiny, flushed, scared.

Christ! he yelped (as if I had struck him, as if he were ashamed of defending himself). Sorry kiddo, really, wrong choice of words, don't take it the wrong way —

— oh I don't, I said. I don't take it any way at all.

That's the spirit, Carol said.

Her hand grazing my forearm for a second. Her fingers warm, sticky; her touch messy and unfocused.

We gotta go, she said. Sorry to make it short, but we want to get there before dark, you know. Len can't drive worth beans at night.

She's right, Len said. I'm hopeless.

He lit up two cigarettes at once and handed one to me.

Give me a cig too, Carol said.

And the three of us smoked. And they left, to go live happily ever after again.

I read in last Sunday's paper that Johnny Griffin has taken himself and his tenor sax to France. I know he'll see Bud Powell there. They'll get together, swap stories, drink, play *Now's the Time.*

They'll take care of each other, stay out of trouble. Stay away from this place. This America, safe haven; this lie.

November 27

First Powell, then Clay told me about the assassination; but I knew Matt would visit within a few days to make sure I'd heard. This much I can still predict about him. He can hardly bear to be near me, but he wouldn't want me not to know.

He arrived this morning, early; he must've gotten up at dawn to be here before seven. He came with a flask of coffee and a bag of rolls and a newspaper. He stood in the doorway, his breath steaming and the collar of his grey overcoat turned up at his pale throat. His eyes bloodshot.

I don't know what you know, he began, whether they've told you about what happened.

Yes, I said. They did.

Our president has been murdered. John Kennedy is dead.

I thought you might like to know how it happened. I brought you a paper, said Matt.

Come in, I said. It's cold.

He took off his coat. I put on my robe. We drank the coffee and ate the rolls while he told me details. Dallas, the open car, the shots. Ruby, Oswald.

It'd been several years since I'd heard Matt speak so many words.

I don't know what to think, he finished. I don't know *how* to think about this. It's too large, too unbelievable.

Since 1945 nothing's unbelievable, I said.

My mind goes blank each time I try to focus on this, he said. The only thing in my head is disbelief. Kennedy murdered. His alleged murderer assassinated. Everything over in a few seconds.

Nothing's over, I said. This is just the beginning.

He turned and looked at me, his red eyes scanning my face.

The beginning of what, he said.

Of all kinds of endings, I said. We're talking about death, aren't we?

He didn't respond; he can no longer respond to me. We sat without speaking for I don't know how long, and then Powell knocked.

Matt handed me the paper.

Keep it, he said. It's got the whole story of the assassination. They told me you're not supposed to have any news, but take this. I know it'll be easier for you if you can read the whole thing yourself.

Powell opened the door. Let's go, he crooned.

You're too late, I said to Matt. You think you'll make it up to me now? As if telling me now is compensation for throwing out my files? For destroying the evidence? For what I already know?

Powell stepped over to me. You're yelling, he murmured. You need to be quiet.

No, I said, no, don't make me be quiet (and I knew I was screaming but I couldn't stop), Jesus please, no please don't make me —

205

Matt's face, a retreating blur. Powell's body solid behind me, his hands locked around my elbows, pinning them at the small of my back. His words soft and clear as blues: *Don't move, you'll just hurt yourself. Don't even try. Just go on, cry now, go on, cry.*

December 23

They've put up a small tree again, in the lobby. The usual decorations: angels and horns.

My fifth Christmas here. This time I have no desire to burn the tree. Though I'm bothered by the star at its top, that presumption of light where there's none.

1964

February 20

What I exist for: my daily walks, reading, a bath each evening. Small oblivions.

I can't bear listening to vocalists anymore. The lyrics, those harmless-sounding agonies.

> *The way you haunt my dreams!*
> *No no, they can't take that away from me*

It's no longer possible for me to absorb such words. They throw me into darkness. I've given several records to Powell, who will get rid of them for me. He stays silent. He knows the futility of speech.

June 27

It's been almost a year but Len and Carol look exactly the same, as if nothing's happened to them. Carol in an orange checked shirt, brown skirt, sandals; Len with the blue bag, the sweat glinting on his forehead as he unloads it. The veins raised on the backs of his big hands.

That may be their secret: nothing happens to them.

I brought them glasses of water while Carol talked.

The daily grind, she said. Work's busy as hell for both of us. Seems like everybody's buying music. There's even a new piano store in the Village, for Christ's sake! Lenny's got his hands full.

Yep, things are swinging, said Len. Here, read this.

A short column in the Times: Earl Ruby claims his brother Jack shot Lee Harvey Oswald because Oswald had assassinated the first American president to actively support the Jewish people.

Till I saw this, said Len, I had no idea Ruby was Jewish. His brother said he was crazy about Kennedy. Went nuts when the president was shot. Had to get revenge.

Wait'll word gets round, Carol said. Kennedy's killer offed by a Jew. Won't do much for the rest of us, will it?

Len lit a cigarette and dropped the box of matches onto the stack of newspapers.

It wasn't a great move on Ruby's part, he said. He should've stayed out of it. Let the system do its thing. Let Oswald be brought to trial. This way we'll never really know why he did it. Or if he did it alone.

He didn't, I said. You don't kill the president of the United States by yourself.

Carol's fingers played with her limp curls, pushing them into shape.

Jack Ruby should've thought twice before popping Lee Harvey Oswald, she said. Now we'll never know the whole story.

We never would've known, I said. A trial wouldn't have explained anything. It would've been just like with Eichmann — for show.

Len's gaze: angry, incredulous.

What're you talking about, Judy? Didn't you read the fucking newspapers I gave you? Didn't you read how the whole world watched that trial, the whole world heard the evidence against Eichmann? Listen to me! Everyone knows now, everyone knows what happened to us.

Us: the impossible word sliding like a razor into me.

I picked up the matches. Len's gaze traveled to the little box in my hands.

Nothing happened to us, I said. We weren't killed. We didn't notice the missing, we never spoke about them. It was as if they'd never existed. Nothing happened to us.

I lit a match and lay it on the papers. The flame lapped at the top sheet. There was a small noise like an intake of air; then the flame pulsed and the fire took, its small orange tongues chattering.

It was Carol who put out the flames. She emptied her glass of water on them expertly, without fear or hesitation. Then she walked out, closing the door carefully behind her.

An inky smell of burnt newsprint.

You know you won't see her again, Len said. That's it. Just so you're clear on that.

I know, I said.

He lit a cigarette, held another to its tip, inhaled until it caught, and handed it to me. I saw his large hand trembling. He moved to the window.

You can't stop people from doing what they're going to do, he said. You can't protect them. If they've got their eyes open, they protect themselves. Otherwise there's nothing you can do.

Something unfamiliar in his voice. Not just the words but the pitch, pace, tone.

Are you talking about Lottie and Sam, I said.

He said nothing.

They didn't die on lower Broadway, did they?

No.

Or in a car.

No.

Or even in New York.

I waited. Len put out his cigarette, moved from the window to the bed, and sat down. It struck me that what was unfamiliar to me was the sound, in his voice, of the truth.

They died in southern Russia, he said. Byelorussia, actually. In 1918. They'd gone over there with several other Americans. To be part of the Revolution. They were socialists; this was what they were supposed to do with their lives.

You were six months old when they left New York. I told them they were crazy, but they both insisted on going. For them it wasn't a matter of choice. It was duty. Sam was a printer — you know that already, I've told you that before. They were going to help the Reds set up a printing press in some godforsaken village. And they were going to raise you somehow. In the middle of a fucking civil war, they were going to raise their kid.

He paused, shook his head. After all these years it's still unbelievable to me that they ever went there, he said. With a fucking infant.

Anyway. In the summer after they arrived, a troop of anti-Bolshevists came through the village. They were looking for Jews because Jews were the ones who'd started all the trouble — you know, the ones who were going to ruin Russia. The soldiers destroyed the press. Burned it to the ground. Then they shot Lottie and Sam. Along with several other Jews.

One of the other Americans managed to leave. He took you with him. He had our name and address scribbled on a piece of paper when he showed up at our door. I think this was about a month after Lottie and Sam were killed. He looked like a real bum. But as soon as he opened his mouth, before he'd said two words, I knew what he'd come to tell us. I asked him how he got you and himself out of Russia alive, but he wouldn't say. I've never met anyone so exhausted as this guy was. He told us what had happened to Lottie and Sam, and then he went out the door, and in an hour he came back and handed you over. Then he left. That was that. We never saw him again.

Len stood before me, as if to confront me with his physical self, the reality of his presence in my life, but did not let our eyes meet.

Carol and I talked it over before telling you about the car crash, he said. We decided it would be easier to keep it simple. It'd already been hard enough.

He moved toward the door, then stopped and turned again.

You see, something did happen to us, he said. Problem is, there wasn't a damn thing we could do about it. That's the bottom line. Don't fight what you can't beat.

In the doorway, Powell.

One of Len's blue-veined hands raised in unsteady farewell; then gone.

Powell advancing on the stack of burnt papers, a question in his eyes.

An accident, I said. Let's keep it between you and me.

July 6

At night, dreams: Len at my window, talking; Carol curled up like a fetus on my bed, talking; Clay in the chair opposite me, talking.

Matt, in the doorway, silent.

In the apartment on Grove Street, a little girl who is me and not me. Broadway, Byelorussia. Balanowka, Bar, Belzec, Bergen-Belsen, Buchenwald.

In the Times: *pianist Bud Powell will be returning to New*

York from France in August. Friends at Jimmy Ryan's club re-
port that after an extended stay abroad, Powell is ready to
come home.

If you know what's good for you, Powell, stay where you
are. Don't fight what you can't beat.

July 29

Hayden, my particular Hell. Each night a warm bath, my own
Lethe.

August 15

Powell no longer escorts me to my room. They must have
found out about the newspapers.

What have they done with him —

October 10

Yom Kippur.

Hadesh yameinu ke-kedem: Make our days new as of old.
Open for us the gates of repentance.

The scapegoat Azazel, bearing the sins of all Jews, was
thrown off the precipice on the Day of Atonement. Forgive us,
said the High Priest as he tossed Azazel over the edge. Forgive our iniquities, our transgressions. If we must be exiled,
may we be exiled to a place of Torah.

Some Kabbalists said Azazel was a fallen angel. Others
said Azazel was the first Satan.

All that Azazel knew, however, was that he was pitched off
the peak, and every bone in his body broke before he reached
the bottom.

November 18

I am sleeping two, maybe three hours a night.

I no longer talk to Clay.

It is only a matter of time before they authorize shock treatment.

December 2

Matt, directly in front of me.

You don't look well, he said. You need to sleep more, Judith. The doctors say you have to get more sleep. You're making yourself ill.

LeRoi Jones:

> *(What we had*
> *I cannot even say. Something*
> *like loathing*
> *covers your words.*

Where's Bud Powell, I said. Just tell me where he is.

I have no idea, Judith.

But he was supposed to come to New York.

He did. Len and Carol heard him play in August.

And since then?

Since then he seems to have disappeared.

What are you telling me, disappeared?

I'm telling you all I know about Bud Powell. That he came back to New York, and now he's gone again. He hasn't played anywhere in the city since September.

But where would he go?

I have no idea. Try not to think about him, Judith. It won't help you to think about him.

He's been murdered, I said. Like Lottie and Sam.

What are you talking about?

The Jew you call Christ, I said. The one you say redeemed you. They murdered him. Not because he was the son of God

213

but because he was gathering the pieces of light. Retrieving them.

It happened for a reason, Matt said. That death wasn't meaningless. It was a gift of grace. It's always in front of us.

> *You shimmer like words*
> *I barely hear. Your face*
> *twisted into words. "Love, Oh,*
> *Love me."*

Us, I said, there's no us.

Directly in front of me, the one I call husband: turning away as a stranger does, back to his life's recesses, those places I have not been and never will be invited.

A silhouette in my doorway. The sure slope of his shoulders, the taut lean torso. I've wanted only this man. This one who stands here inert, overcome by fear of me.

Only this man who will not look at what I've looked at, and take me hold me tell me *yes I see it, yes, but we do still have each other.*

The world terrifies, but it's me he fears.

You need to leave, I said. To leave me.

His is the only silence that has ever spoken to me. I hear it saying everything. All jumbled like the Torah — a welter of words spilling forth from Matt's silence like those first bursts of light, blinding and unbearable.

More than anything else, I hear his silence speak of his unendingly powerless love for me.

I nod, he nods. Our eyes meet for one literal and true and necessary instant.

He's seen me now, and he won't try to stop me.

1965

January 1

My books and poems are for my husband, Matthias Lane.

My records are for my uncle and aunt, Len and Carol Rubin.

This journal is for Dr. Harold Clay, on the understanding that it is to be burned after he has read it.

LeRoi Jones:

> *I cannot lie*
> *and say I think of you.*
> *& now*
> *I am sleeping*
> *& you will not be able*
> *to wake me.*

Three

THE LIBRARY GUARDIANS PROJECT was under way by the end of June. Edith saw to the details. Irritated though she was by the whole thing, she was unable to suppress her usual conscientiousness.

"It's all yours now," she said, dropping into a chair in my office one warm afternoon. She twirled a noisy key ring around her index finger. "The three students have been through a library orientation, and I've drafted their assignments for the six weeks they'll spend in the Mason Room. Matt, I hope you understand — the Board insisted I get this thing up and running. Darnton's already publicizing the Guardians Project as the library's newest triumph. Jesus! You'd think he's got absolutely nothing to do with his time."

"He may not," I said. "But we do. Look, this thing's just a dressed-up volunteer project. Let the Board milk it — who knows, maybe we'll actually get some new donations because of it. But just leave the three musketeers to me. All right?"

Edith smirked. "I like that," she said. "The three musketeers." She looked somewhat less tense, though she was still jiggling her keys.

"Well?" I allowed a little impatience into my voice, to spur her.

"OK," she said quickly, closing her fingers around the key ring. "Here's the scoop. They've each got their work cut out. I tried to create assignments that would require the least amount of supervision."

"Excellent. Who's doing what?"

"George is the historian. He'll look at a selection of the Roosevelt papers and do a very general article on them for the alumni quarterly. Just pick a decent sampling for him to read, and send him off to some corner. He's very serious and dull — you won't hear squeak from him all summer.

"Now, Yasuo — the Japanese computer scientist — he's another story. He wants to get his hands on the Harlem Renaissance photos. He's one of those foreigners who's fascinated by black American history. I told him he has to swear to wash his hands before he enters this archive. I made him a gift of some of that special soap you use. He looked at me like he thought I was joking. These computer types amaze me! They treat a diskette like it's made of gold, but they'd sit a cup of coffee on a rare book without a second thought. Five minutes after meeting me, Yasuo was proposing that we use some new scanner thing to convert the photographic images to digitals or pixels or whatnot. My eyes just glazed over. I told him all we want is a decently written description of the collection for the annual report. He looked extremely disappointed."

"What about the third student? Roberta Spire?"

"Ah, yes." Edith stood and walked over to the sideboard. She poured us both some coffee and leaned against the wall, cradling her mug in her hands.

"I decided to capitalize on Roberta's desire to see the Hale letters. Oh, don't get me wrong — you look alarmed! It was the envelopes she asked me about, and that's what she'll see. Here's my idea. When you catalogued the letters, you organized them by year, remember? So we know the date on which each letter was written, right? But what we don't have is a listing of when and where each one was mailed."

She walked back to her chair and sat down.

"You know," she said, "I've worked a lot with biographers, and this is the kind of thing they love — little details about the habits of a correspondent. Does he mail his letters immediately after writing them, or does he mull over them for a while and then send them? Biographers go nuts over those types of questions."

"It all sounds rather — what's the word? — niggling," I said.

"But we're not biographers! The thing is, we want to keep Roberta very busy for six weeks of this summer. So busy she won't bother you or anyone else. Right?"

I smiled. "That's thoughtful of you," I said. "Though I'm not worried about her getting in my way."

"No," Edith said, "I wouldn't think you are. You're exceptionally well defended."

"What on earth do you mean?" I asked, laughing.

"As a professional, I mean," she said. "You don't take any crap from anyone."

"Except you," I said. "But have no fear. Your orders will be carried out."

"Good," she said, standing. She held her keys and mug in one hand; with the other, she pointed in the general direction of the Board's administrative offices. "Let's hope they go on vacation soon. I just want to be left alone to do what I do."

I raised my own mug as if to make a toast.

"I feel," I said, "exactly the same way."

A S IT HAPPENED, I didn't see Roberta Spire for several more weeks. At the time of my meeting with Edith, I had a chest cold. A few days later, it flared into pneumonia. I seldom get sick, and the whole thing took me by surprise. The university's doctor ordered me home to bed after prescribing several medicines that I didn't take. Like my mother, I've never trusted doctors.

Edith, always solicitous, came over with a bag of grapefruit and some decent paperback mysteries. For two weeks I confined myself to bed. The experience was less trying than I'd expected. I slept, and I dreamed.

Several of my dreams were of apartments: the one in Washington Heights and the one on West 79th Street, which Judith and I had shared until she went to Hayden; the Rubins' place on Grove Street; my drafty, high-ceilinged apartment on Park Road just beyond the library; and an undistinguished apartment building that at first I couldn't place but finally — after awakening — understood to be Roberta's, as I'd seen it from my car the night I dropped her off.

My dreams of the West Side apartment were especially vivid. I moved through its spaces alone, slowly, as if recording everything on a video camera. There were no indications of Judith's presence. It was as if the place had been stripped of the small reminders I'd kept around me during her absence: her jewelry box on our dresser, her copies of Shakespeare and Milton, a pair of rubber-soled boots by our kitchen door.

During her stay at Hayden, while I lived alone in the apartment, I'd used those objects to help myself retain images of her: a tall, dark-haired woman, a woman with large hands and feet, who rose silently and swiftly from our bed each morning, reached for her robe, and went down the back stairs in her boots to fetch the copy of the *Times* that a neighbor always left for us at the base of the stairwell. The sound of her boots would mark her slow progress up the stairs; she would be scanning the front page of the paper as she ascended. Sometimes a story captured her so completely that she would remain outside the kitchen door for several minutes, reading. As I stood by the counter, waiting for her to open the door and kick off her boots, I would try to anticipate her reactions to the day's news. There'd be signs, small but visible: a slight furrowing of her brows, a pursing of her lips. When her gaze lifted from the paper and went to my face, I would see the effort it cost her to stop reading. And I feared that daily moment in which I wondered if she would be able to disengage, or if she would find the news more relevant than I was.

The moment always passed. Judith would put the paper on the counter, move into my arms, and sing *hello, love.* Always the same greeting, low and sweet.

But in my dreams, then as now, I pictured myself alone.

The pneumonia, which had not been severe, ran its course. My fever broke, my lungs cleared, and I began to grow hungry for something other than citrus fruit. I had some prepared foods delivered to me, and within a few more days I was ready to return to work. Although Edith fussed over me, I could tell she was glad I was back. The three guardians (she used the title with reluctant deliberateness) were taking up too much of her time.

"They have questions I just can't answer," she said during lunch on my first day back. "You're the only one who really knows how the Mason Room works. Thank God for that! I think you should schedule meetings with each of them separately — at your convenience, of course. I've told them to expect to hear from you."

I must have frowned. Edith quickly softened.

"Look, Matt, don't bother chasing after them — just leave a note in their mailboxes. Their schedules are byzantine, you know how it is with graduate students. But they'll meet you on your terms."

That evening, I typed notes to my three charges. I decided to deal with George and Yasuo together, the next afternoon. A fifteen-minute briefing would suffice. In my note to Roberta I asked her to meet me in the Mason Room the day after, at around four, for tea.

I'VE SELDOM ENJOYED surprises that aren't of my own making. Though I was waiting for Roberta, her actual appearance in the doorway of my office threw me.

"Long time," she said. "Several months, in fact."

We surveyed one another. She looked unwell. Her complexion was sallow, and her hair needed brushing. She wore a grey T-shirt tucked into navy blue sweatpants; across her shoulders was a black sweatshirt, its arms tied at her neck. She looked less like a woman en route to a gym than a normally stylish person who had ceased, for the time being, to care about her appearance.

"Have a seat," I said, pointing at the chair opposite my desk. "I've made tea."

Roberta poured us each a cup, then sat down. Her actions didn't appear to concentrate her. She stared into space as she drank the tea rapidly, her expression diffuse.

"How've you been?" I asked.

"I've been better," she said. "But then so've you, from what I hear. You don't strike me as the pneumonia type. Is it over?"

"Fully," I said. "And is yours over, whatever it was?"

"No, actually, it's not," she said. "My mother got very sick at the end of April. A heart attack. There have been complications."

"I got your note about her," I said. "I'm sorry to hear this. What sort of complications?"

"At the moment, the biggest problem is my father. It seems like he also needs to be sick. I think he's jealous of my mother."

I said nothing. Roberta put down her cup and quickly tugged the sweatshirt from her shoulders. Very small beads of perspiration had formed above her upper lip.

"It's the tea," she said. "A little strong, isn't it?"

I watched her. She seemed acutely uncomfortable, and I was riveted. The room shrank; Roberta filled it.

"I'm so tired," she said. She leaned back in her chair, closing her eyes. "I haven't been very productive lately. It's been hard to read or write anything. Or even to talk. You know how it is. Don't you? No, don't answer that. Just tell me why you're still listening to me."

Her eyes opened and focused on me: steady, unblinking, like a lens. I sat very still.

"You've had plenty of time to think about how to deal with me, you know. I'm sure you've got a plan — Edith Bearden recently shared some of the details with me, in fact. Something about sorting envelopes into neat piles. She *is* fussy, isn't she? But then so are you. And you're much better than Edith at putting me off. You have this way of pretending to hear me while actually maintaining a perfect deafness. It's effective — I mean, usually I know when I'm being put off, and for a while you tricked me good."

She leaned forward, her knees slightly spread.

"I think I get how it works. You keep talking with me, but from your perspective the conversation's over — in fact as far as you're concerned, it never really began in the first place. I raided your territory, and you're defending it. Masterfully, I'd say. You're quite practiced, aren't you?"

I felt something shift. The sensation of anxiety was very nearly physical — primitive and familiar. Roberta's eyes had closed again; she ran her fingertips across her damp brows and exhaled softly.

"You have a fever," I said. "You're ill."

"No," she said. "I told you. I'm exhausted."

She stood suddenly. Her knees buckled, and she folded. Before I could get up from my seat, she was on the floor. Her face went extremely pale. She lay on her side with her hands clasped at her thighs, like someone sleeping. I knelt next to her. Her breathing was almost undetectable. I put my hand on her shoulder, having no idea what else to do.

"Roberta," I said, shaking her several times. It was hard to believe that she'd fainted or even that she was sleeping; despite her paleness, her essential force had never seemed so evident to me. Her eyelids flickered, then lifted.

"Damn," she said quietly. "Did I just pass out?"

"Yes," I said. "Here. Sit up if you can." I took my hand off her shoulder.

"In a minute," she said.

"Has this ever happened before?"

"No," she said.

"It can be disconcerting," I said. "Don't let it alarm you."

"I haven't been sleeping much," she said. "Actually, not at all for the past two nights. The tea hit me wrong. Too much of a jolt."

She eased herself up onto one elbow. I backed away, still crouching, and watched her. Her color was somewhat restored. She didn't look at me as she stood, slowly, using one knee and then the chair for balance. Only after she sat down again did she return my stare.

"I'm not good at taking care of other people," she said. "I forget to take care of myself, and the whole thing backfires."

"I know what you mean," I said.

Her expression clouded. "Don't just hand everything back to me, Matt," she said. "It's like talking to a trained parrot."

Her tone roused me; I understood that I would risk losing her if I continued trying to keep her at bay.

"Roberta," I said. "You just blacked out. You *should* take care of yourself. I think you should go home and sleep. We can talk some other time."

I moved to her side, put a hand under her elbow, and gently pulled her up. She stood, not facing me: utterly near, utterly distant. As she walked to the door, I saw she was all right. There was no wobble in her step. In the doorway she shouldered her black bag.

"Yes," she said calmly. "But next time we talk, I'll be waiting for you to tell me something."

"What about?" I said.

"It doesn't matter," she said, "as long as it's true."

In her sneakers — hours later I remembered they were red leather, an incongruous detail — she made a silent departure.

W HEN DR. CLAY CALLED ME (I recognized his voice immediately, that peculiarly mixed tone of concern and impersonality), I was in the living room, reading. The chair in which I sat was next to a window overlooking West Seventy-ninth Street. I can remember little of the substance of the conversation, though I know that Clay began by telling me how and when Judith had died. At one point he said he would send me her "personal effects." I'd never heard that phrase spoken in real life, only in books or films.

Clay spoke about suicide, its meanings and consequences. Of all this I remember nothing except the unpleasant feel of the phone receiver in my hand — a bit gummy, I must've been perspiring — and the way the traffic in the street below gradually increased. Rush hour had started. I watched the cars and buses weaving their way slowly across town; the drivers heading west had their sun visors down to block the glare. In the left corner of my window, the sky turned salmon, then a deeper shade, the color of blood oranges. I remember identifying the color with the fruit and then feeling suddenly sick. Clay's voice was a drumbeat in my ear, soft and persistent but uncompelling; I heard but didn't listen. The idea of blood oranges took over. I told Clay I had to go, and after hanging up, I stood and immediately passed out.

When I came to, I was lying next to the chair. I pulled myself up and sat. Outside the sky had darkened fully. Seventy-ninth Street was a strip of blackness streaked by headlights. For hours I watched those paired dots of yellow light travel steadily back and forth. I suppose I was in shock, though that sounds more melodramatic than what I experienced. Perhaps it was something more like a necessary anesthesia, blunting any reality but that of the headlights illuminating the street below.

I've wondered, since, if this was all I could absorb — light and motion, nothing else — or if I took it in simply because it was the opposite of darkness and immobility.

I stayed in that chair for days. Eating, sleeping — these must have taken place, but I have no memory of them. Yet that, too, sounds full of bathos. I have no desire to invest this time with more meaning than it deserves. Suicide allows, after all, only a limited set of responses. Eventually one runs up against the futility of trying to imagine what the dead must have gone through to become dead.

Judith was the only fully awake person I'd ever known. She watched and listened; she paid attention. History was anything but abstract for her, and she couldn't defend herself against it. The war wasn't somewhere else, at some other time. It was irrevocably present for her. The terrible things that had been done, not randomly but under unimaginably well-organized circumstances — these were realities her psyche couldn't encompass or deflect. Europe's crisis set her adrift. It became impossible for her to distinguish between the world's darkness and her own.

By the end, her body reflected everything. She'd been for too long at too high a pitch. She could no longer modulate any of her emotions. In our last encounter she would hear nothing of solace or grace. My words were like fuel on flames, and I could say nothing that wouldn't injure her further.

My mother had embraced the defeat of her body as God's clearest gesture toward her, the most profound attention He could pay her. Her morbidity had had something of ecstasy in it, which now makes me shudder. But my wife was not morbid. She sought meaning in another arena, one into which I'd never ventured until meeting her.

Definitions of madness have never interested me. Clay and the others arrived at names for Judith's condition, but I never did. I saw she was in danger, and I told myself that my role was to remove the threat as I perceived it. I would protect Judith from news accounts, photographs, anecdotes — all the revelations she'd catalogued during those months after the camps were opened, when she became an archivist of evil. So that she could live her life safely, I would take control over its locus. I would separate us so she could make herself whole.

How completely I failed her.

Matt, please, don't hide from me! You think it's me you're protecting, but it's not me. Her hands, her lovely large hands, grasping mine.

She'd never wanted me to save her, only to love her as she was.

On the day I drove her to Hayden, I understood nothing of what lay in wait for her. I went back to the city that evening, numb with sadness, and prepared for a night of reading, to distract myself. The first thing I picked up was a new poetry journal that Judith had left on our bedside table. I opened it to a poem called "The Liar," written by LeRoi Jones. Judith had marked several of its passages. They return to me now with the force of a confession — not hers; my own.

231

What I thought was love
in me, I find a thousand instances
as fear.

       Where ever I go to claim
my flesh, there are entrances
of spirit. And even its comforts
are hideous uses I strain
to understand.

L EN SHOWED UP UNANNOUNCED one morning about a week after Judith's death. He brought along a thermos of strong coffee, several rolls, and two packs of cigarettes. Carol wasn't with him. I hadn't spoken to either of them since receiving Clay's call, and I found Len's sudden presence in the apartment very disconcerting.

"I thought I'd just come over," he said.

I led him to the kitchen. He found mugs and plates and an ashtray, and quickly fixed us breakfast. I ate; I was hungry. Len had some coffee and lit his first cigarette.

"You OK?" he asked.

I nodded. "You?"

"OK," he said.

He squinted at me as if trying to keep me in focus.

"I've been thinking about you," he said. "There are some things I need to tell you."

I watched him smoke. His face was long and angular. Fine creases fanned like spokes from his eyes and especially above his dark brows. His dense beard-growth was peppery grey like his hair, which he wore brushed back from his forehead. The same dark color as Judith's hair, I realized, but wavy. Hers had been straight, without any hint of grey.

"Such as," I said.

"I've been wondering what Judith told you about her real parents. My sister Lottie and her husband Sam. There's some things maybe you should know."

His words left me neutral. I felt no onrush of curiosity, though at the same time I didn't want him to stop talking. He paused, and when I said nothing, he continued.

"Lottie raised me," he said. "I mean, she literally brought me up. She was much older than me, twelve years older. When our mother died, I was five. Lottie dropped out of high school — she was in her last year. She got a job in a textile shop downtown. She stayed in that job and kept food on our table till I was fourteen. Then Sam showed up."

I poured us both more coffee, and Len lit another cigarette with the end of the one he'd just smoked.

"What about your father," I said. "Where was he?"

"In Russia," he answered.

"What was he doing there?"

He looked at me quizzically, and I realized that I knew less than he thought I did.

"He lived there," said Len. "Lottie and I were born there. My father sent my mother and Lottie and me to New York when I was a year old. He was supposed to join us as soon as he got more money together. The three of us stayed with some cousins of his in the Bronx and waited for him, but my mother never heard from him. She never found out if he'd died or been killed, or if he'd left her for somebody else. Of course I didn't know about any of this, but Lottie did. She remembered him. I can hardly even remember my mother. The only one in my family I really knew was Lottie.

"My sister did everything for me. Food, clothing, shelter — the works. She wasn't going to let either of us go under. Our mother basically died of exhaustion. I guess she was lost without a husband. But Lottie — she was very, very tough. Once she told

234

me, when I was about ten, to stop being a coward like our mother'd been. I remember that word so clearly: the humiliation of it. I'd never heard her talk like that. It made me furious — I still don't know why, I can barely remember our mother's face! I smacked Lottie, though. She grabbed me by the hair and slapped me in the face so hard I got a black eye. And then she said, 'You listen to me. You've only got one chance, so you better decide if you're taking it.' That's the kind of person she was."

Len paused. I hadn't been in human company for over a week, and I'd been living without speech. It was difficult for me to take in Len's words. I felt as if I were listening to someone reading aloud from the middle of a story.

"My sister ruled me, ruled my life, until Sam. Then things changed. Sam was the perfect man. He was tall and good-looking, he worked hard, he was Jewish. His parents were Russians too, and they spoke a little Hebrew. He and Lottie got married in 1911. I was seventeen; by that time I'd known Sam four years, plenty long enough to hate him. Right from the start, he'd taken over our life. Whenever he showed up, he'd move furniture around, lamps and chairs and whatnot, so the place was exactly how he wanted it. We lived on Elizabeth Street, in a small walk-up; Lottie kept it spotless, but Sam was always complaining about the bathtub being dirty, or how the kitchen cabinets were a mess. He'd throw things out that he figured we didn't need, like newspapers. Sometimes Lottie would get really mad — I mean, she could hold her own in a fight — but mostly she just caved in. I guess she needed someone like him, someone with that much power.

"Sam knew everything. He knew about Zionism, about socialism, about Europe, about Russia. He knew what was going on in the city. He told Lottie about Eugene Debs and dragged her off to all sorts of political meetings. They were quite the radicals, let me tell you.

"Sam was cocky. He didn't have even a touch of humor, and he liked to hear himself talk. Whatever peace there might've been between me and my sister went completely to hell with Sam around. Lottie couldn't take my side — she had to keep Sam at any cost. She was already close to thirty when she married him, and she'd done what she had to do for me. Lottie wasn't about to lose Sam, even if his way of dealing with me was to chew me up and spit me out. Who knows — maybe she thought I needed a little toughening."

"Did you get it?" I asked. The question sounded harsh to me, not what I really meant to ask.

"Yes," he answered. "I did." His brows raised slightly; the creases above them deepened. He was staring across the room. All at once his face seemed remarkably expressive, but I couldn't interpret what I was seeing. I closed my eyes and listened.

"Sam knew the streets," Len said. "Growing up where he did, downtown, he'd gotten into a lot of fights. And he had a temper. I remember one night, it was summertime, stinking hot, and we had to pick up Lottie at some friend's place. I was sixteen. We took a cab uptown and got out on Second Avenue and started walking east. Suddenly these two guys were in front of us — not too big but strong-looking. They said something in Italian that got Sam's attention. He said, 'You take the one on the left,' and then he swooped down and grabbed an empty bottle from the ground and cracked it open and lunged at the guy on the right — all in one move, like a dancer — and that guy had the side of his face split open before he even knew what hit him.

"The other guy came at me, and I couldn't move. I mean it: I was frozen. There wasn't any way I could do what I was supposed to do, which was to fight, because I didn't want to. It was really that simple. The whole thing seemed incredibly — I don't know — ugly, ridiculous. I knew I couldn't win; there was no point in trying, no point in aggravating the guy even more than he

236

was already. I stood my ground, if that's the way to put it, but I didn't fight back.

"His first punch took most of the air out of me, and I didn't straighten up again; I kept my arms over my head and let the blows come. They didn't come for long, because Sam had basically disabled the first guy, who wasn't the stronger of the pair as it turned out. Sam jumped the one who was pounding me — by this time I was getting kicked, mostly, because I was bent over — and they went at it for a few minutes. Then Sam laid him out with a couple of short punches.

"I heard those hits, but I didn't see them. I was still doubled over. It took me a little while to realize I wasn't getting beat up anymore. Naturally I was in pain, but more than that I was in some other world. It was as if I'd left the street and entered a kind of dream. Not a nightmare, just a dream where stupid pointless things happen over and over till you wake up.

"Sam started talking to me in a very loud, slow voice. He was enraged with me. He called me a shit-scared little coward, a worthless putz, and then he pulled me up to a standing position and screamed at me, 'Don't you know how to use your goddamn *hands?*' And when I didn't answer, he said, 'You go like this,' and he gave me a whack with the flat of his hand across the side of my head.

"It broke my eardrum. I guess they used to call it getting your ears boxed. I blacked out. When I came to, I was in a cab, and then in a few minutes Lottie was there, and Sam was saying something about how the Sicilians should stay in their own neighborhood. He must've told her some kind of story — I couldn't hear too well at that point — because she spoke to me later like she thought I'd fought the Italians, too. I think Sam presented it to her like it was my initiation into manhood.

"After that I made sure never to be alone with him, and I stayed away from the apartment as much as possible. Lottie spent a fair amount of time over at Sam's family's place, so I was on my own mostly. Which was fine. I needed to learn how to live by myself."

The morning sunlight cast sharply outlined shadows on the kitchen table: squares of windowpanes, the thin-lined geometry of a TV antenna. Plump blue veins stood out on the backs of Len's large hands. He was fiddling with a box of matches; any minute now he would light another cigarette. He'd gone through close to half a pack already. I got up and opened the back door, and a cold backdraft tugged at the smoke. When I sat down again, I knew what my question was.

"Carol," I said. "You haven't mentioned Carol."

He leaned back in his chair, his gaze drifting in what might have been reminiscence or anxiety; I couldn't tell.

"I met Carol the next year, when she moved here from Chicago. She was broke, but she knew how to get by — she's always been a hustler. I had no definite ideas about what I was going to do when I got out of high school. All I knew was I'd get a full-time job someplace. I'd already been working several years part-time, in a music store. Carol and I met in that store, actually. She was buying sheet music, and I noticed her. That same night we were eating lousy steaks in some uptown dive and talking about ragtime.

"It was Carol who came up with the plan of selling pianos. Being with her, I saw that Lottie had taken me over. I didn't really know how to do anything that wasn't Lottie's idea. With Carol it was different: she saw the person I really was. Not a fighter, not a radical, not even a first-class tradesman like Sam, who would show the world what a *bren* he was, how he was going to leave his mark.

"Carol knew exactly who Sam was, too. She didn't need explanations. 'He's mean,' she said to me once. 'He's the kind of man who would whip a kid for no reason.' At that point I hadn't

238

said a word about the scene on the East Side. A few weeks after we were married — that was in March of 1912, in a courthouse — I told her about the fight. She said nothing at first. We were both only eighteen. I think Carol couldn't help being scared of what it would mean to go up against Lottie and Sam. She had no family in the city — her people were still in Chicago, and she'd basically left home for good. In a sense my sister and her husband were all Carol had in the way of family.

"Of course they didn't think much of Carol. She wasn't serious enough for them. Sam was especially rough on her, always saying she wasn't well informed, didn't know what was going on in the world. He used to tease her about being an empty-headed blonde. Carol took it well. She's easygoing that way. Lottie and Sam both thought I'd married her too soon — in fact, Lottie thought I'd gotten Carol pregnant."

Len passed a hand over his eyes, pinching the bridge of his nose briefly between thumb and forefinger. He didn't look at me as he resumed.

"I should've guessed then, but I didn't. Something about the way Lottie said that to me, the harshness of it . . . I heard it, but I didn't know what it meant. Now it's obvious — Lottie's jealousy — but I didn't get it then. Not that it would've made any difference in what happened, ultimately. But it would've changed how we felt."

He stood, walked to the back door, and leaned against its frame. I didn't shift in my chair to look at him. Our bodies faced in opposite directions, yet he commanded my attention. His words sat at the center of my consciousness, pushing out all the rest: Hayden, Clay's voice, the color of blood oranges.

"A few months later," Len said, "things fell apart between us and them. Carol went over to their apartment one evening to visit Lottie. She was nervous. It was the first time she'd gone over on her own like that, spur of the moment, but I encouraged her. I thought it might be one of those things that would bring Lottie and her together.

"It turned out Lottie wasn't home, but Sam was. He told Carol to come in, and they had a glass of sherry. That particular detail always strikes me — I just can't imagine Sam drinking sherry, but it's what he offered her. They talked about Carol's job. At that time she was working in the same music store as me, in the back; the owner didn't like women on the floor of the shop. Carol was the bookkeeper, and she sat behind a closed door.

"Sam poured himself some more sherry and said a few things about how women weren't supposed to work with numbers, it wasn't what they were good at. Carol got understandably a little het up about that — I mean, she wasn't any suffragette but she's always known the value of work. She didn't like what Sam seemed to be saying, and she let him know it. She got up to leave. He stood in front of her, placed one palm on each of her collarbones, and gave her a quick, hard shove. Naturally she toppled backward, onto the sofa.

"Sam was on her, one hand clamped over her mouth and another under her skirt, when she shoved him, I guess pretty hard. He must've figured she'd fight, so he let go and made her stand up and compose herself. Those being his words, I should say."

Len shook his head. "Carol doesn't scare easily, but Sam scared her. She told him if he stepped any closer, she'd kill him with the thing she was holding in her hand — a silver letter opener that usually lay on the table by the sofa. I remember it — it was Lottie's. Actually, it had been our mother's. It was Russian, one of our only souvenirs.

"I guess Sam took her at her word. Carol's someone you'd believe in such a situation. But he barred the door and wouldn't let her go till he'd said a few more things. About what a tramp she was, how her hair was never combed, how she looked like some goyische blond out to snare good Jewish men and ruin their lives — wasn't that her plan for her husband, after all? What kind of Jewish girl leaves her family and moves to a place like New York by herself? She deserved whatever happened to her; no man should take her seriously. At least she hadn't propagated herself, he said. Those were his words. 'No babies from you,' he said, 'blessed be God.' And then he turned, opened the door, and added, 'or from Lottie, either. What kind of world is it when Jewish women can't have babies?'

"Carol walked out, still holding the letter opener, and took a cab home. She told me right then and there that she'd have no further contact with my sister or her husband. She wasn't crying or anything, and I was confused. When I asked her what she was talking about, she took the letter opener from her bag and threw it across the room. I remember how she did that, just like one of those knife-throwers in the circus — you know, the way they hold the blade between the thumb and forefinger and give it a little flick, and the thing travels straight and fast? It was an impressive toss, let me tell you. 'Don't pick it up,' she said. 'Let it lie there.' And then she told me what I just told you.

"The next morning, I found Lottie at home. She looked awful. Her face was grey. She told me she'd just got back from a friend's place where she'd been staying for the past few days, recuperating. 'From what?' I said. 'I had another miscarriage,' she said.

"I handed her the letter opener. 'Where'd you get this?' she asked, and I told her to ask Sam. She knew something was up. 'What's going on here?' she said, but I wouldn't answer her straight. I told her Carol had borrowed the thing from Sam the night before. Lottie didn't buy it, but I didn't have it in me to tell her the truth. I felt relieved to have a reason not to see her again."

Len sat down again and lit a cigarette. I took one from the pack and we smoked together, silently. The apartment resonated with Judith's presence. Her death felt suddenly and wholly real to me. Nothing I might say or do would make any difference.

"Did you see Lottie and Sam again?" I asked.

"Not for several years," Len said. "And then they just showed up one day, carrying a newborn. Carol heard a knock and opened the door. I knew from her silence who it was. Lottie looked the way women do right after childbirth, kind of shapeless but happy. Sam never spoke one word. Lottie had this expression on her face — I knew what it was saying: 'See, I've forgiven you.'

"Carol took one long look at the baby, said 'Mazel tov' to Lottie, and turned to Sam. 'Lucky man,' she said. It chilled me — it was like a curse.

"Lottie looked at me. In that moment her eyes were talking only to me; it was as if Sam and Carol weren't there. Her look wasn't a confession — it was so much sadder than that. She was saying something to me about how our life had been before Sam broke it up. But it was all happening too late. I felt completely empty. Even if we'd been alone, just Lottie and me, I wouldn't have known what to say.

"Carol took command at that point. 'We were just on our way out,' she lied. 'Some other time, maybe?' Everyone knew what was happening. The weeks went by; we didn't call on them, they didn't call on us.

"Carol and I didn't talk about them. We both knew it was better not to get into any of it; we wanted to put the whole thing behind us. I can tell you exactly how we felt: we finally had our lives to ourselves, and there was a scary kind of thrill in that. For both of us.

"Another year went by. Then one night some guy shows up at our door, carrying Judith."

It was nearly noon. The apartment's rooms were sun filled and utterly silent. I walked through them several times. On the kitchen counter were the remains of breakfast: near-empty coffee cups, half a roll, a full ashtray. The dining-room table was covered with stacks of unopened mail. Before he left, Len had helped me carry it up from the building's foyer, where it had been accumulating for a week. All of it — including several cartons bearing Hayden's return address and postmarked two days after Judith's death — was addressed to me.

The bed in the room I had shared with her was neatly made. Since Clay's call I had been sleeping in the chair by the living-room window, or on the sofa; the bed had ceased to exist. I looked around the bedroom, noting its details, remembering them. Judith's navy-blue robe hung on a hook next to mine in our closet, in the place it had occupied for six years; the closet door was open and I could see the robe resting there, its back to me.

I closed the door and returned to the living room. My chair beckoned me. Sitting, I realized that I was exhausted; my lower back ached, and my hands and legs felt swollen. I moved to the floor and lay on my back, straightening my knees and arms. Patches of sunlight bobbed on the white ceiling. I slept.

When I awoke, several hours later, my first thought was that Len was still in the kitchen; I could smell his cigarettes, the strong coffee. His voice, too, seemed to linger. I contemplated the people he had sketched for me. Their lives had crisscrossed Judith's life, enmeshing it.

Len had come over that morning to let me know what my wife had been caught up in. I suppose he wanted to give me a setting for her chaos, and at the same time to free himself from the fear that the chaos was mostly of his and Carol's making. But I mistook his rendition as a veiled plea for absolution. His motives were less simple than that. Len needed to confess, but he also needed to accuse, and his story was a preface to both acts.

At Len's suggestion, our next and final encounter took place a few weeks later, in a little bar on Eighteenth Street, just north of

243

Union Square. In those intervening weeks I managed to unpack the boxes from Hayden and sort out everything: clothing, albums, books. At the bottom of one box was a dark blue leather portfolio I had given Judith as an anniversary present, early in our marriage. I opened it, expecting to find some papers — poems, letters, notes — but it was empty. In another box I found a letter from Dr. Clay, taped onto a green looseleaf binder filled with typewritten pages. The letter stated that Clay was returning this notebook, which was Judith's journal, directly to me — *against her wishes*, he wrote, *as you'll see if you read these pages.* He had, he said, no other option. By law, Hayden must send the personal effects of deceased patients to their next of kin: me, in this case. Would I be so kind as to see that Mr. and Mrs. Rubin received their albums? If I wished to discuss the contents of my wife's journal with him, he would be more than willing to do so. The choice, of course, was mine. I should know, however, that he had not read the journal in its entirety — only the final entry, in fact. It was the practice of the psychiatric staff to search immediately for notes from suicides to their families; typically, those notes were found at the very end of a diary or journal. Such was the case, Clay explained, with Judith. In closing, he sent regards and condolences once more, and hoped I would stay in touch. A discreet footnote indicated that a final invoice would be forwarded to me within the month.

I took care of the rest of Judith's possessions before turning to her journal. Her clothing went to the Salvation Army, as my mother's had; this seemed the easiest solution. I distributed her jewelry evenly among her women friends, whose addresses I found in a little book we'd kept next to the telephone. Each woman wrote back to me — brief, kind letters of thanks and solicitude to which I didn't respond.

I gave most of Judith's books to the local branch of the public library. It was too jarring to see the entire familiar collection on

my shelves; I tried dispersing the books throughout the apartment, but that didn't work. In the end I kept for myself only a few
volumes of poetry and the Kabbalistic titles.

After everything else was disposed of, only a few days before
my meeting with Len, I read through Judith's journal twice. I
started reading at about ten o'clock one night and ended at
roughly the same time the next morning. When I finished, I put
the notebook in a padded envelope, sealed it, and placed it in the
blue portfolio. That afternoon, I took the portfolio to my office
and locked it in the bottom drawer of my desk: the safest place.

M Y MOTHER WAS THE CENSOR and revealer of experience. She opened and shut its doors. Librarians, too, are gatekeepers — not of actual experience, of course, but of its written accounts. My job is to safeguard those accounts. Not to judge them; simply to see to their proper dissemination.

As an archivist I have power over other people. I control access to materials they desire. Of course this power has limits. I can't arbitrarily bar from the library someone who is entitled to use it, nor can I prevent materials from entering the collection simply because I don't like their authors or content. Libraries have rules, which librarians follow so that readers can find what they seek. A good archivist serves the reader best by maintaining, throughout the search, a balance between empathy and distance. It is important, I've discovered, to be neither too close to nor too distant from a reader's desire.

These things I have learned through years of professional experience. But almost everything else I know, I've found in books. Reading has given me time to learn what I want to learn. Naturally, books contain confusions and ambiguities, but they arrive in a more easily assimilated form.

The most important things I learned about my marriage didn't derive from my experience of it; I was closed off from that, much of the time. No: I learned the most important things from my wife's journal. From its indictments of me, and its love, and its unreason.

Those lines from Eliot's "Little Gidding" . . .

And what the dead had no speech for, when living,
They can tell you, being dead: the communication
Of the dead is tongued with fire beyond the language of the living.

T HE BAR WHERE I MET LEN was musty and dark, with lots of booths in the back. When I arrived at a quarter to four, the place was empty. It was still early for the after-work crowd. I dragged the two boxes of records through the door and asked the bartender if I could stow them someplace. We stacked them neatly behind the bar, and he even produced some heavy twine for me to tie them together. I picked a stool at a distance from the TV and awaited Len.

The place was familiar to me, and completely unchanged. My father and I had met there several times to talk about matters un-related to ourselves; chiefly about the war. My father had done most of the talking. Sometimes, after we'd both had too much to drink, he would invoke my mother, and through him she would come to abrupt, disturbing life. When my father spoke of her, his words cut through the bar's noise. "Your mother" — that sudden vociferousness, how the two words could carve out a life! — "your mother went to her grave thinking that her prayers mat-tered. There it was, right in front of her — this was 1939, for God's sake! The absurdity of prayer in the face of all this . . . Any fool could've predicted the mess we're in. And there she was, praying for deliverance."

He was speaking of death, of course, and its imminence — not only, I now see, for the millions in Europe; also for himself.

Behind his boozy bitterness, which was all I could absorb then, was a cry of fear to which I would've had no response, had I been able to hear it. After my mother died, there was never any hope or question of a genuine dialogue between my father and me. For a little while, habit bound us with loose reins, a light harness. Then he too was gone.

Len was late. I was well into my first drink by the time he showed up.

"Sorry," he said, dropping onto the stool next to mine. "Got held up. A little tiff with Carol, in fact."

I smelled bourbon and cigarettes. Len wasn't looking at me, so I stared at him a little. He seemed somewhat the worse for wear.

"I was thinking Carol might be with you," I said.

He flagged the bartender. "Jack Daniels. Straight up, twist of lime. Water back." The bartender disappeared. Len turned to me.

"Actually, Carol's steamed at you," he said. "Wonders why you haven't phoned. Says you're never home when she calls. You answering your phone?"

"No," I said. "It doesn't ring much."

Len tilted his head back and swallowed the bourbon. He rolled the shotglass between the extended fingers of both hands.

"When the phone rings at your place," he said, "it's Carol."

"Tell her I'll be in touch one of these days," I said.

Someone opened the front door. A cool draft slipped around us; the door closed and the air settled. The place was empty except for us. The bartender stood in front of a small sink, washing glasses; steam hovered on the surface of the soapy water. Len was still staring at nothing.

"You're not getting it, are you," he said. "She's really mad at you."

"Why?"

"You owe her a call. She needs to say a few things to you. How come you're not answering your phone?"

His gaze swung toward me now: intent, pained, earnest.

I raised my glass in the direction of the bartender, who wiped his hands on his apron and brought over a bottle of whiskey.

"Another," I said to him.

He poured, left the bottle, and turned away from us. I wanted him to stay, to listen, to intervene; to shield me.

"I'm not interested in justifying what I'm doing," I said. "To Carol or you or anyone else. It's really not what I feel like doing at this point."

Len shook his head. "Nobody's said anything about that," he said loudly. "Nobody. Look. All I'm trying to tell you is you've got Carol pretty rattled. You haven't once spoken to her, Matt. Not once since Judy died. You haven't called, you haven't let her call you. You haven't dropped by. So of course she's upset. Why not?"

He paused. When he spoke again, the hectoring tone was gone, and I understood that he wasn't trying to persuade me. He was battling an irruptive despair.

"I mean, it's her loss, too," he finished.

He poured himself another drink. I took the bottle and slid it down the bar, out of reach. Len lit a cigarette. I felt him looking at me.

"I brought you the albums," I said. "Two boxes. Judith wanted you and Carol to have them. You can take them home — they're right over there. That's all I can do. You'll have to explain it to Carol. I can't talk to her now. I guess she just needs to accept that."

Len shifted his position on the stool, then turned to face me.

"Listen," he said. "There's something I need to ask you. It's a question from Carol and me both. What kind of treatment did they give Judy?"

250

"Treatment?" I asked.

"Yeah. Drugs and whatnot. Therapy."

His eyes interrogated me.

"She was given Miltown regularly. It's a tranquilizer, fairly common. As far as therapy goes, during the last couple of years she talked with Dr. Clay several times a week. Sometimes with other psychiatrists too, but mostly him."

"What about shock. Electric shock. Did you authorize it?"

"No," I said. "I didn't. Dr. Clay asked me to, but Judith didn't want it, so I refused."

Len's eyes held steady.

"Carol thinks you let them give Judy shock treatment," he said. "She's pretty much convinced you did."

I closed my eyes. Judith's image lunged into my consciousness. I sat immobile. Grief picked me up and threw me down. I fell into its hole, and the hole was covered over. In this hole was nothing but my loss; it was all I had.

"Matt," Len said. "Did you hear me?"

Out of nowhere came Eliot's ending to "Prufrock" — *Till human voices wake us, and we drown* . . . Panic rushed me, animal-like, insistent. Somehow, words found their way to my mouth.

"Len," I said. "I authorized nothing."

The expression he wore wasn't suspicious so much as frightened. He'd accused me of lying, and the accusation had unnerved him. He lit another cigarette.

"I never should've co-signed those admittance papers," he said. "She shouldn't have been there. They screwed her up. Those fucking doctors. Those sons of bitches." His large hands went to his face, covering it.

"Len," I said. "Blaming the doctors won't work. Blaming Hayden won't work. There's no point."

The face he showed me, as he took his hands off his eyes, was newly dark with pain or fury — both, I guessed.

"No. Too easy," he said. "Carol and I wanted Judy out of there, but we respected your judgment — and that doctor's — and you kept saying she should stay." His voice spiraled. "Like a prisoner! She couldn't even read the newspaper, for Christ's sake! So cut off — how could she keep from getting worse in a nuthouse like that?"

I was no longer fending off panic, and I no longer had access to my loss. Both were gone. I knew what I wanted to say.

"She had newspapers, Len. You and Carol brought her newspapers, even though the doctors told you not to. Has it occurred to you that maybe giving her newspapers wasn't such a good idea? That perhaps you confused an already dangerously confused person? Or that maybe you should've told Judith the truth about Lottie and Sam a long time ago?"

He looked at me with scorn. "I told her years ago," he said. "She knew about them."

"She didn't know everything."

"Listen to me. I told her all of it when she was a girl — eleven, twelve — you know that! I told her who they were, how she came to us, how they died in an accident —"

"— which accident, Len? The one on Broadway? Or the one in Russia?"

I had never seen him so thrown off guard.

"So she told you, then," he said. His tone was quiet, half-questioning; he wanted to find out exactly what I knew.

"Yes." My lie was a reward for enduring his lie. Len knew nothing of the well-typed pages, the notebook in the bottom drawer of my desk. I'd buried Judith's devastations, and I wasn't going to exhume them for Len. She hadn't intended that I become her archivist. Clay alone, whom she despised, was her intended reader.

I waved at the bartender, who returned with the bottle and poured us each a shot. I drank mine down.

"I saw no reason to tell her sooner," Len said. He was once again staring into space. "The whole thing was too complicated. It seemed like much more than a kid could handle. And then, once she got older, neither of us — Carol or me, I mean — could make ourselves do it. The real story just kind of emerged, sometime last year when we were visiting Judy. I said something, and she figured it out. I guess it wasn't all adding up right in her head, so she asked me a direct question. What could I do — lie to her face? Of course not."

He drank his shot.

"But I didn't think it was necessary to tell you. After she was gone, I mean. Before that — well, it was her call, Matt. Evidently she chose to tell you. I sure as hell wasn't going to."

It seemed to me that at last he was speaking the truth.

"Why not?" I asked.

"It was basically nobody else's business but Judy's."

In the silence that followed, I acknowledged to myself what I wanted: never to have to talk to Len Rubin again. I felt nothing like hatred toward him, only a profound sense of futility. He was a wall I chose not to scale. I would need to be very direct. Nothing in our twenty years of skirting one another had prepared us for this.

"Your albums are in those two boxes under the bar," I said, pointing. "I'm taking off now. I'm not going to say I'll be in touch, because I won't be. I'm leaving town in a few weeks, Len. I've got a job at a university library."

"You're serious."

"Yes."

"Where?"

"It doesn't matter. I just want to be gone from New York. I'm ready to leave, and I don't want to be in contact with anyone from here. It's not a question of starting over. I don't believe in that. I just want to be left to my own devices."

253

I paused, then found my way forward. "I'm hoping you'll be able to explain this to Carol. I can't, Len. I can't even face the idea of trying."

I stood, drew my wallet from my pocket, and put a twenty on the bar. Len was struggling to absorb my words. He watched me vacantly, as if I'd already vanished and he was looking at the place where I'd just been.

"Be well," I said. "OK?"

His eyes focused. I saw how alone he was. Even Carol hadn't been able to rescue him from the adolescence in which he lived still — the isolation of Lottie's kid brother, who longed for a father and instead got Sam. Judith's death had stripped everything away, leaving Len only the quiet anguish of the man who remains, the one for whom adulthood is no solace.

"I'll tell Carol," he said, so softly I barely heard him.

We shook hands. It was the briefest, saddest handshake imaginable.

A few weeks later I left the apartment and New York. When I arrived at the university, I felt ready for a reconfigured life. In a sense, that is exactly what I entered, but such renewals do not obliterate what precedes them.

I didn't see Carol again until Len's death in 1977. I read the notice in the *Times,* and I knew I had to go to his memorial service. This realization was one of those certainties that can't be questioned or fended off. I took a train to the city and walked from Penn Station to a funeral parlor on Madison Avenue, conscious of how many years I'd been gone.

There were a good many mourners present. I recognized no one but Carol. She found me and took me aside, after the service, to tell me that Len had died at peace. I remember her words: *He made a choice, to not go out miserable.* Her eyes were puffy, and her dry hair, flyaway as always, had turned the color of dirty sand. She was otherwise exactly as I remembered her. She thanked me for coming, and then she turned away from me. I saw she was habituated to her losses; she needed no condolences. I watched her circulate, her hands going out to the people around her, her high laugh occasionally lifting across the room's quiet thrum of voices. Her behavior aroused in me a strong envy, and I left feeling glad that I'd seen her, too, for the last time.

"IT MAY SEEM OBVIOUS," said Roberta, "but the way the world looks when you're Christian is significantly different from the way it looks when you're Jewish."

We were sitting at adjoining tables by a large window in the Mason Room, as we'd been doing for several weeks. No one else was in the room. Its late-morning light was extremely strong, and I had drawn the blinds to shade our work. Spread out across Roberta's table were piles of envelopes addressed, in T. S. Eliot's distinctive hand, to Emily Hale. Some were white, some blue; most were personal-size, though a few were business envelopes with the return address of Faber, the publishing house where Eliot had worked in London. Hale had used a letter opener, and the top of each envelope was expertly slit. Massed on the table, the envelopes made a curious impression: each was empty, but collectively they represented several volumes of letters.

Roberta had understood immediately that the envelopes mustn't receive direct sunlight — their ink might fade. In fact, she displayed a constant fastidiousness in dealing with the materials in her charge. I sat near her, organizing several drafts of a long H. L. Mencken essay that the Mason Room had recently acquired. Roberta's carefulness impressed me. She was implementing Edith's new cataloguing scheme — unenthusiastically, I could tell, though she didn't complain.

She was easy to work with. Our separate tasks weren't mindless, but they did involve a certain tedium, and I discovered that it was possible to talk with her and still make progress on the work at hand. That morning, we were carrying on about types of religious experience. I had just suggested that people make too much of the differences among faiths. The religious impulse was what mattered, I said. Its form was less relevant.

Roberta shook her head. "People stay in their own realms," she said. "They don't like to go beyond the walls of what they think they believe."

"Look at Eliot," I said. "'Four Quartets' is full of references to Eastern thought. So's 'The Waste Land.' Eliot saw how his religion related to other religions."

Roberta carefully set her pad and pencil to one side of the envelopes and put her elbows on the table.

"Some of them," she said. "You're talking about an anti-Semite, remember. Have you read 'Christianity and Culture'? Now *there's* a scary little book. Eliot was never fond of Jews. They offended his sense that civilization had to be Christian if it was going to be civilized."

She leaned back in her chair and folded her arms across her chest.

"You're oversimplifying, Roberta," I said.

Without looking at me, she smiled a little. "Maybe."

She stood and walked over to a pitcher of water we'd set up on another table. Pouring herself a glass, she moved to the window and drank. It was obvious that she was no longer in the mood for work. Making a note of where I'd left off with Mencken, I covered our materials with muslin cloth and then opened the blinds.

Warm light streamed in, bathing us. For the first time I noticed that Roberta's hair had coppery highlights; they glinted as her head moved. She returned to her chair and sat with her legs stretched out in my direction, her hands wedged in the front pockets of her black jeans. Her feet, exposed in flat sandals with thin leather straps, were long, like her hands. The toenails wore a muted polish, nearly flesh-toned — a paler shade than her fingernails, which were very well manicured, each week a new color.

The sun's glare was powerful. I angled my chair so I could see Roberta without squinting. When she spoke again, her tone was reflective.

"I was just remembering how Virginia Woolf once said Eliot was sordid and intense. Did you know that when he was still married to Vivienne, he occasionally wore face powder when they went to dinner parties? Can you imagine? I guess he couldn't resist the temptation to dramatize his suffering — God knows Vivienne wore *hers* on her sleeve. I read someplace that he once sent Conrad Aiken a page from an English journal of midwifery in which he'd underlined all the words describing vaginal discharge. No comment, no accompanying letter — just those underscored words. I mean, this is a world-famous poet with some very strange preoccupations, no?"

I opted for silence.

"But he did find a great place to escape, didn't he — the Church of England! I mean, he could say his prayers and confess his complete unworthiness and never have to deal with what Vivienne knew — that the two of them had created a waking nightmare for themselves. And that he'd abandoned her when it got out of control."

She gazed absently into space, absorbed in her narration.

"You know, after he and Vivienne's brother Maurice had her committed, Eliot never visited her. He paid the bills — that was it. Locked the door and threw away the key." Her laugh was short and hard. "A shining example of Christian charity."

"You're so dismissive of Eliot's faith," I said. "You have no way of knowing how it helped him — or what it showed him."

"No," she said, "I'm not dismissive. It's just that I find his belief highly questionable. I mean, what kind of faith allows a man to diagnose the spiritual illness of his culture so well, and at the same time view his wife as some kind of witch who needs to be walled in? Even if she *is* sick?"

She shook her head. "You know, there's something about Eliot's kind of belief that terrifies me. The way he could tell himself, oh yes, I'm unworthy, and let that be an excuse for such passive-aggressive behavior."

"You're being an amateur psychologist — the worst kind," I said. "You trivialize Eliot's spiritual pain. It's right there in the poems — his doubts, his torment. Not being able to act. The tendency to be heartless."

Her eyes drifted over the envelopes. "Heartless? I'd say spineless. If I'd been Emily Hale, I'd have dumped him. Who needs it — all that guilt, that resistance to being loved, everything gussied up as faith?"

It was time, I felt, to tone down our conversation. "We should either get back to work or stop for lunch," I said. "It's noon."

She stood and stretched her arms over her head. "So let's take a break. We can pick up sandwiches and sit on the quad."

"Too hot," I said. "I want to stay indoors. Air-conditioned indoors."

"Forget the campus cafeteria — you know the food's revolting. I feel like having a sandwich from that deli on Third Street — ever been there?"

I nodded. "But it's take-out only," I said.

She paused. "Does your apartment have air conditioning?" she asked.

The question, so casually asked, left me speechless. I sat silently before her; she stared at me, then burst out laughing. I'd never heard her laugh like that — loudly, carelessly. It was a provocation, a testing of my composure.

"Yes," I said. "But I've no desire to eat my lunch there. Two meals a day is enough."

She eyed me, then nodded. I'd passed the test. But her next sentence upturned everything.

"Well, my place has fans and a couple of beers; it'll do."

The first thing I noticed, as we entered the apartment, was a large canvas that dominated one wall of what appeared to be the living room. The canvas was actually a collage. On a background of paint thickly layered in shades of brown and grey, various photographs overlapped. Some were whole, some in torn or cut pieces; all were snapshots — color and black-and-white. The photos seemed to be scenes from a summer camp: girls and boys standing in a semi-circle next to low clapboard cabins; a girl by the side of a canoe (perhaps Roberta — impossible to tell); several children waving from a tree on whose wide trunk was a lively bull's-eye. One photo showed a cluster of children in the main hall of Grand Central Station. The children were waving and smiling at the camera, and their parents were gathered behind them. Everyone was pointing at a conductor who stood in the doorway of one of the platforms, holding a sign that read "LET'S GO TO CAMP!" Another snapshot, somewhat out of focus, showed what looked to be the same group of children emerging from a train. To one side was a small station-house, forest-green and predictably quaint, draped with a bright banner on which "You're Here!" had been painted in bright block letters.

Next to the photos (which filled much of the canvas's left side) were cut-out clippings. They were advertisements, I realized, for summer camps in the Berkshires, the Adirondacks, New England — various pine-sheltered places with pseudo-Indian names where (the ads said) children could learn archery and weave lanyards and sleep outdoors.

On the canvas's right side, painted in neat letters, was the word "CAMP." Beneath it was a list of definitions, also in blue and evidently taken directly from a dictionary: *a tent or cabin for temporary lodging, a place in the country for vacationers, a group of people supporting a common cause.*

The last two definitions stood out. One, printed in a brilliant orange, was nearly ugly against its grey backdrop: *banality, mediocrity, or ostentation so extreme as to amuse or have a perversely sophisticated appeal.* The other definition, painted in very small black letters, was harder to read, but I was able after some peering to make it out: *a place you're sent when we've had enough of you and are planning never to see you again.*

Roberta stood silently for several minutes as I looked at the collage. When I turned to her, she shrugged her shoulders.

"One of my few attempts," she said. "I'm not much of a visual artist, even though my parents are painters. Maybe I should say because of that. Whatever."

She pulled a pack of cigarettes from her bag and lit one, then held out the pack.

"Want one?"

I shook my head. "When did you do this?" I asked, nodding at the collage.

"When? Oh, I don't know — around the time I graduated."

She wasn't looking at the canvas as she continued talking. "I remember showing it to my mother. She hates anything too conceptual, so she had trouble praising this thing. I mean, she wanted to; she always praises anything I do. But with this, she was kind of stumped. I figured it hit a nerve, though of course at the time I didn't know which one."

Roberta's gaze moved back to the collage.

"So my mother restricted her comments to technique — 'nice how you placed the photos within the larger composition' and so on." Roberta snorted lightly, then smiled. "My father's reaction was more interesting. 'What'd you call it?' he asked. 'The Meaning of Camp,' I said. 'You might consider leaving it untitled,' he said — which is of course a perfectly defensible position. 'Why?' I asked, and he said, 'To let it speak for itself.' I suspect he really knew what I was doing. But then he took it all back, because he went on to say how strong the photos were, the composition, blah-blah. The usual pointlessness."

"You're not easy to please," I said.

She stubbed her cigarette. "Who likes obvious flattery?" she said. "Let's bring the sandwiches in here — it's cooler by the window."

I followed her to a large room with a table that apparently also served as a desk. Roberta hastily cleared it of books and papers and then produced plates, napkins, and beer from the adjoining kitchen.

"That should do it," she said.

An overhead fan and the open window kept the room pleasant; a soft crossdraft blew over us. We ate quickly — whether because of hunger or a certain awkwardness, I couldn't tell. Roberta pushed our plates to one side, but neither of us made a move to get up from our seats. The air and light generated a languor I found difficult to resist.

"You have a nice apartment," I said. "They're not easy to find."

Something I couldn't identify flitted across her face.

"I inherited it a few months ago," she said.

"Literally, you mean?"

Her smile was slow.

"Figuratively. It belonged to a man I lived with for a year. He moved out, and I took over his lease."

"Was he a graduate student?" I asked.

"No. He was an engineer. Not the train kind — the building kind. Also a writer, an essayist."

"How did you meet?"

She sipped her beer before answering. "I met him at a public lecture. On Martin Buber, of all things."

"So you and he shared an interest in philosophy," I said. My words sounded wooden to me, but the prompting worked. For a few moments, Roberta was silent. Then she lit a cigarette and began talking again.

"Theology, in fact. I'd just found out I was Jewish, and Peter had decided he wasn't."

"How do you mean?"

She slid a bottlecap across the table and tapped ash into it.

"He was raised a Protestant, like me, and when he was twenty-one he married a Jewish woman and converted — for her, basically. Her family wanted it, she wanted it, and so he went along. The marriage was lifeless. At the point when I met him, he'd begun extricating himself from it, though he was still living with his wife and children. And he was rethinking his entire relationship with Judaism. He ended up leaving everything — his family, his adopted faith. Me, too."

She paused, drumming the fingers of one hand on the table in a delicate yet aggressive rhythm. Her hair was pulled back by a clasp, exposing her neck. I could see the tendons tighten slightly as if in response to her moving fingers. The wide neckline of her white shirt revealed her collarbones and, between them, the dip of mauve-toned skin at the base of her throat. The shirt's fabric lay loosely over her breasts; its hem rested at the top of her hips and abdomen. Although her legs were hidden by the table, I knew from her body's angle that they were crossed: the left over the right.

"Peter was a brilliant man," she said. "He read constantly, and he was always taking in something new. It's hard to describe him without sounding hyperbolic. He had one of those minds that link things."

"Well," I said. "So do you."

"No. Not in the same way. Peter was someone with special powers. At times I felt completely daunted by him."

"That's natural," I said. "People with special powers are frightening to love. That's why Eliot and Vivienne were doomed, by the way — why their marriage was bound to fail. They terrified each other."

She looked at me, and a question crossed her face, but she said nothing. Then she leaned back in her chair, her hands folded in her lap. Her body was large and definite, and I felt as if in the silence I could hear not only her breathing but the interior sounds of her lungs working.

"Peter didn't terrify me," she said. "Although maybe he should have. Sometimes people like him become sociopaths and commit horrible crimes without blinking. But Peter wasn't violent or cruel. It's different — it's hard to describe. Peter's not plugged into the same switchboard as the rest of us. He's unassailable. Nobody lays claim to him."

She stopped, looking away. Her sudden silence disconcerted me.

"Well, it doesn't seem like you could've seen any of this coming," I said.

Roberta shook her head — whether in agreement or disagreement, I couldn't tell.

"I was totally blindsided," she said. "You know, I do have some sympathy for Vivienne Eliot, even though she was such a mess. I can imagine how she kind of got pushed over the edge. I mean, she took intimacy for granted — it seemed utterly natural to her. She and Eliot were both writers. He'd always shown her his work, and she was one of his first editors. Plus, he published some of her work. How could she possibly have anticipated that he'd ditch her? In his eyes, you know, Vivienne simply ceased to exist except as a symbol of his own fallen state. To be turned into an abstraction — that really must've been more than Vivienne could handle."

Her grey-green gaze pinned me for a few seconds. Then she closed her eyes and brought one hand to her neck, idly massaging it as she rolled her head gently from side to side. The tendons at her collarbones arched, and in that instant I wanted her without reservation. My eyes closed, and Judith rose before me. It was morning, and she was singing "Ev'ry Time We Say Goodbye" in her reedy, dense voice as she pulled on her blue robe and her boots and headed down the back stairs. My eyes opened, and Roberta was touching my wrist, saying, "Matt, you still here?"

Somehow the moment passed, the aperture closed. We were once again the man and woman who had entered the apartment an hour earlier, carrying white sandwich bags.

"Yes," I said. "I'm here."

Roberta went to the kitchen and returned with a glass of water, which she placed in front of me.

"Drink it," she said. "You look kind of flushed. It's warmer than I thought, even with the fan. We should head back — the library's nice and cool, you'll feel better there."

She gathered up the sandwich wrappers and beer bottles and took them into the kitchen. I followed with my empty glass, but she wouldn't let me enter.

"Out," she ordered. "It's not a pretty sight." She glanced at my face. "You're looking much better."

"I don't do well in hot weather," I said.

At the front door, she turned to me. "Are you up for the walk back? We can drive, you know. I have a car."

"No, no," I said. "I'm fine as long as we stroll. I walk everywhere. An old habit from when I lived in the city."

"New York, you mean — that's where you're from originally, right? I thought so."

We descended the stairs. Despite the heat, I was glad to be moving. Roberta's street was well shaded and quiet, with little traffic. We walked at a leisurely pace.

"I miss the city," Roberta said. "Do you?"

"Seldom," I answered. "I haven't been back in years."

"Why not?"

Her hair glinted again. A small exultant ache claimed me; then it passed.

"I have plenty to do here," I said.

"Any friends left in New York?" She threw me a glance as she spoke.

"No," I said. "Not anymore."

"Family?"

Several blocks down, the university's brick walls beckoned; I could just make them out.

"No. My parents died in the mid-forties. Neither my wife nor I had siblings."

"What part of the city did you live in?"

"I grew up in Washington Heights. My wife and I lived on the West Side."

"And when did you leave?"

"In 1965."

"You came straight here?"

"Yes."

Roberta frowned, calculating. "That wasn't long after the Hale letters arrived."

I could see the library now, its grey mass ringed by large rhododendrons. Its fixity calmed me.

"Just a few years after," I said.

"Who catalogued them — you or Edith?"

"I did."

This time she gave me a longer glance.

"Did you enjoy it?"

I laughed. "I'm not sure I'd put it that way. It was a hell of a lot of work. The correspondence was immense, you know. It took me several months to deal with everything."

"I'll bet it did." Her tone was superbly uninflected.

We had arrived at the library. The hallway to the Mason Room seemed exaggeratedly dark after the bright outdoors. I unlocked the door, and we entered the cool, familiar space. At my side, Roberta laughed softly.

"I just remembered the first time you let me in here," she said. "How I alarmed you."

"That's not the word I'd use," I said.

She turned and looked directly at me, and I felt a sudden rapid murmur of blood in my ears. A momentary flare; a cautionary signal.

"I never use the words you use." Her eyes performed a featherweight dance, a delicate scan of my face.

I turned away. She moved to her table, and I moved to mine. We worked the rest of the afternoon in a silence neither dangerous nor safe but provisional.

I BEGAN WORKING AT THE UNIVERSITY on April 3, 1965. About six months later, after thoroughly familiarizing myself with the Mason Room collection, I undertook the task of organizing Emily Hale's bequest. I knew it would be a huge job. The first thing I did was to assign responsibility for my more tedious duties to one of the junior librarians so I could closet myself with the sequestered materials. Then I moved a worktable into my office, shut and locked the door, and emptied the cardboard cartons onto the table.

The contents were completely disorganized. Many of the letters weren't in their envelopes, though I discovered (after several hours of what felt like a mix-and-match game) that each did in fact have one. A large portion of the airmail correspondence, written on pale blue onionskin, was wadded in a corner of the box. The rest was interspersed, without apparent logic, among letters written on plain but top-quality bond stationery. For some reason all the postcards were rubber-banded together, and I set them aside — they would be a separate cataloguing task.

To my surprise, nearly everything in the box was handwritten, although there were a few typed letters here and there. I also came across several pencil sketches, mostly of cats, with annotations. These didn't surprise me; since the publication of Eliot's *Old Possum's Book*, it was no secret that the great poet liked cats.

For most of the letters, Eliot had used the same fountain pen and the same ink color, a deep blue-black. The pen had evidently had a narrow nib. All the letters were drafted in a hand that was neither crabbed nor messy but quite compact, as if Eliot had wanted to cover as much of each page as possible.

I looked for consistencies, the usual physical details. Dates, salutations, and closings: these had to be recorded for every letter and postcard. Almost everything in the box was dated — day, month, year, with the month spelled out and the year given as two digits. The place of writing appeared routinely in the upper right corner of each letter. The salutations were remarkably similar: most letters opened with "Dearest Emily" or simply "Emily."

The closings, however, were another story. They were unusually varied. As I prepared my inventory (because of the sheer size of the correspondence, this process took several days), I came up with no less than forty different closings. Some were amusing wordplays and puns having to do with cats or Brits; others were merely silly, or lightly affectionate. A few, scrawled in apparent haste and clearly connected with travel plans, were neutral ("till the 20th — Tom"). The conventional (but always, in letters, ambiguous) "Love" closing, and the more intimate "Your" followed by "Tom" (or, sometimes, the initial T), showed up frequently. But there were others, and among them I read a few whose heat completely startled me.

It was those few closings that spurred my further reading. My inhibitions (so sturdy after years of maintaining an ethic which seemed utterly natural, and which I never dreamed I'd violate!) — my inhibitions were overcome by a handful of closings so strangely ardent that I was unable to stop myself from exploring what had prompted them. This breach was the only one in my career. Naturally, it made me very anxious. I knew what might happen if anyone suspected I was reading the Hale letters, and there were days when it seemed almost unbelievable to me that I was jeopardizing my professional life in so bald a fashion.

Yet I was in the grip of a compulsion that only grew as I kept reading the letters. I read early in the morning, before any of the library staff showed up, or in the evening, long after everyone had left — never during working hours, which I devoted to cataloguing the collection. I told the library's two security guards that I was working extra hours, and they inquired no further. To Edith Bearden I explained that I was taking my time with the Hale project. She had, of course, no objections.

In the space of about three months — during which I managed to catalogue Hale's entire bequest, choose and install a set of new cabinets to house the collection, and perform the physical acts of filing and storage — I read every letter and card. I did, however, draw one clear line for myself: I read none of the half-dozen drafts of poems that I found in the collection. Hale was a critic as well as an intimate of Eliot's, and he shared a great deal of his work with her. The two must have talked at length about his work when they were actually together; I found many allusions, in the letters, to writing-related conversations they'd had during her visits to England or his to America, in the thirties. It didn't actually surprise me, I must say, to run across this buried work; Hale would've been its logical reader. But it took away my breath to find those poems.

I thus have no idea if the six drafts I came across — all of them untitled and neatly dated at the bottom — were of poems that have already become part of the Eliot oeuvre, or if they are wholly new and undiscovered work. I suspect, however (and here I'm drawing on a few oblique statements in the letters) that those drafts deal with matters not directly addressed in the existing canon. Matters concerning Vivienne, and a crisis of belief.

I did what I was supposed to do with the drafts: I assigned each of them a number (which I penciled very lightly on its back), and I recorded the date and physical condition of each one in a separate log. When the doors to the bequest are formally opened, this portion of the poet's work will be read for the first time since Emily Hale delivered her treasure for safekeeping here.

In August of 1965, I made my report to the library's Board on the status of the Hale bequest. Edith was very impressed with the quality of my work, and the Board was pleased that it could finally announce, to the academic community and the public at large, that its enticing new acquisition had been archived. The letters, I reported, would safely sit out the next fifty-five years in a temperature-controlled environment until their ultimate unveiling.

The job had been done. I, however, would have to live with my transgression.

TOWARD THE END OF THE WAR, before meeting Judith, I attempted to go to church. My very brief reentry into organized religion was sparked less by the war than by the death of my parents. Newly alone (or perhaps I should say alone in a new way), I decided to see what church felt like, now that nobody would attack or defend me for going. One Sunday late in 1943, I returned to the church of my childhood, a little Presbyterian chapel in Washington Heights. I sat in the back as the liturgy, familiar and meaningless, floated over my head; and I thought of the way my mother had said grace at our Sunday dinners, making it sound not like an offering of thanks but a plea.

The next week I went to a church on the West Side, near Seventy-ninth Street; the week after, to one off Seventh Avenue near Sheridan Square. There were a few others, scattered around Manhattan. Each was decorated for Christmas, its altar hung with pine wreaths and poinsettia.

I didn't bother about denominations, and I didn't listen to the sermons. I went because I needed to tug on the invisible cord that bound me to the sacred. I wanted to feel the slack rope tighten in response to my tugging: that affirmative pull, like an undertow, which I hadn't felt in many years.

These visits offered none of the quiet luminosity of my earliest spiritual experiences. When I closed my eyes, I no longer saw the Cross as a tree to climb and then claim — my secret vantage. I knew that the physical spaces in which I sat, during those Sunday forays, were meant to serve as Christ's capacious, high-vaulted residence; yet I found myself transported instead to my first home, the low-ceilinged apartment in Washington Heights. I saw my father standing silently in his darkened study, heard my mother praying softly behind her bedroom's locked door; I smelled stale Pall Malls in the living room and the bittersweet, steaming cocoa my mother made me for breakfast. As each choir sang its hymns and each congregation knelt for communion, I drifted up and down the apartment's long central hallway, the narrow spine of my childhood. Eliot's lines from "Burnt Norton" returned to me:

> *Footfalls echo in the memory*
> *Down the passage which we did not take*
> *Towards the door we never opened . . .*

It didn't occur to me that Eliot might be mourning an actual intimacy, one he'd forfeited. The apartment in Washington Heights was the incarnation of loneliness, just as Christ was the incarnation of holiness. I harbored no belief that a living person could deliver me from one condition to the other. That, I told myself, was the task of faith.

Europe's undoing was well under way by the time I made the decision, sometime in the spring of 1944, to stop attending church. Instead, I would read the New Testament and stay alert to signals, clues to action. I accepted a certain inertia as the natural response of a thinking person faced with the vast moral and physical chaos that the war represented. Now and then my emptiness took on the aspect of a ubiquitous landscape — a sere flatness extending to all horizons — and I panicked and looked for a woman to take to bed; or else I drank, hard and purposefully, until the landscape blurred. Meanwhile the radio and papers blared the news of an unassimilable nightmare, and I read, among others, Eliot: *There is no end of it, the voiceless wailing.*

T HE DAY AFTER OUR LUNCH, Roberta called and left a message with the Mason Room receptionist. She wouldn't be coming in; her mother had had another heart attack and had been hospitalized.

I spent a restless morning with the Mencken materials and an even more restless afternoon performing tedious record-keeping tasks. A few students and professors showed up, and I helped them half-heartedly. At six o'clock, disgusted by how little I'd gotten done, I left the library and drove across town to a small pub I like, a quiet place with decent music and food and fewer preening intellectuals than the other nightspots near campus. I ate a light meal and read the newspaper, nursing a beer for a while, but my restlessness caught up with me. At about eight-thirty, I decided to go back to the Mason Room and finish off something, anything. My life seemed suddenly full of loose ends.

I entered the side door to my wing of the library and flicked on the light. The entrance hall blinked into brightness. The air conditioning, a relief after the evening's mugginess, whirred around me. I paused for a minute as my eyes adjusted to the fluorescent glare. Then, keys in hand, I walked down the hallway toward the Mason Room.

A few yards from the door, I stopped. The door was slightly ajar. There was no master key in the doorknob and no key in the second lock below the knob. The hallway was completely silent; I knew my approaching footsteps must've been audible to whoever was inside.

I stood to one side of the door, debating what to do. My instinct was to enter, so I did — although I had the presence of mind to pull on the door itself rather than the knob so as not to disturb any fingerprints.

I walked past the secretary's desk and through the door, also open, leading into the archive itself. A pair of reading lamps suspended over the long worktable had been turned on. The rest of the room lay in darkness. I approached the table.

Roberta was sitting at its head. A manila folder and a pad of paper lay in front of her. Scattered around the table were loose sheets of yellow paper, typed, with handwritten notes and cross-outs in colored ink. I took in all of this automatically and quickly; nothing seemed to me to be disturbed or out of place.

I moved closer so I could see Roberta's face more clearly. She stayed motionless in the soft light, making no effort to avert my stare. Her eyes were completely empty of defensiveness or apprehension. It almost seemed — except for a certain distractedness, something slightly unsettled in her expression — that she'd been expecting me. She said nothing.

"Would you tell me what you're doing here?" I asked.

"Working on some poems," she answered, leaning forward a little. She was wearing a silky, pale-gold shirt — sleeveless, with a scoop neck — which I hadn't seen before. It called attention to her bare arms.

I remained standing at the side of the table. "How did you get in here?" I said. My voice sounded strained to me, artificially neutral. Out of nowhere I remembered Prufrock's little aside, in the "Love Song," about women's arms — *But in the lamplight, downed with light brown hair!* — and the tension in my voice invaded the rest of me. I was suddenly perspiring, despite the coolness of the room.

"The security guard let me in." Roberta picked up a pencil

and twiddled it; the orange tip of its eraser bobbed up and down. "I told him I was assisting you on a project. He believed me. I gave him my ID card, and I said I'd leave the door open so he could check periodically. To make sure nobody else was here."

"Which guard?"

"The tall one. Thomas, maybe?"

"I know who he is," I said. "He's new. I'll have to speak to him. Nobody comes in here alone."

She frowned. Behind the frown was a kind of vacantness. She was attending to something unrelated to my words.

"I wanted to work on a couple of poems. It's so much quieter here than at home. When I'm working there with the windows open, I can hear everything on the street. Some nights even the passing of a car is more than I can take." She paused. "I needed the silence."

"There are other places," I said. "This is an archive, Roberta. Not a writer's room or a study hall. And it's not open at night. I'm actually stunned to find you here."

She looked at me almost as if I'd just entered the room.

"So what are you doing here?" she asked. The stress on the *you* was light but unmistakable.

I found myself unable to feel anger. Instead, all the muscles in my torso and shoulders tensed as in a fight-or-flight reflex.

"I don't have to answer that question, Roberta," I said. "But you do."

She stood up and began circling the table. Her pace was neither sauntering nor purposeful; she wasn't moving around to distract me but rather to release a stored-up energy. When she began to talk, I sat. It was obvious, though not for any reason I could consciously assign, that I needed to listen to her.

"My mother's sick again," she said. "The reprieve's over. It turns out she's got a serious heart condition. She's stabilized. This attack wasn't a bad one. In fact she's already back home. The hospital released her this morning. But if she has another heart attack in the near future, it'll probably kill her. The doctor says that's not inevitable, but the situation's unpredictable."

In the room's dim light her silk shirt looked like chamois cloth, supple and tawny. The shadows around her eyes were a soft taupe. I could see she hadn't slept the night before; the tiredness was there in her posture, in the way she was pausing now to lean against one of the book stacks.

"My parents seem to be handling it all right. It's not like they haven't dealt with it before — I mean, this is her second attack, and in a weird way it's less scary than the first one. Ever since leaving Holland, my mother has thought of each year as the extension of a deadline. That's how she sees things."

Roberta resumed her circling of the table. She walked with her hands in her skirt's pockets.

"You know, my parents never talk about their experience of the war — the dislocation, the hiding, the losses. Everything that happens in our family happens in relation to those events, but the war itself is invisible. Nobody ever mentions it."

She was standing before me now. She closed her eyes; I could see their full lashes, the tips turned delicately upward. I was conscious of her nearness as I'd never been before. Her low voice filled the space between us like water.

"There's something ridiculous in all this, I know," she said. "My divergence from my parents, our failure to communicate — it's inevitable, commonplace, it's what happens when you grow up. You spend a few years of adolescence feeling betrayed because your parents no longer understand who you are — if they ever did — and then you move on. None of this should be mattering to me, but it does. My mother will be gone soon, and I have this horrible sense that her death will be like a seal on me — like a key turning, locking me in. I should be able to budge, and I don't."

Her hands lightly covered her face. I heard a brief intake and exhalation of air; then she lowered her hands. I looked once more into the grey-green lambency of her eyes, and the Eliot lines she'd once read aloud returned to me:

> . . . *and I knew nothing,*
> *Looking into the heart of light, the silence.*

"I'm sure I haven't explained anything clearly. To you, I mean. I owe you some explanation for being here."

I stood suspended, her presence my only certainty.

"You know, all my mother wants from me is forgiveness. But I seem able to forgive only something I can understand — not something I can't fathom." She smiled a little. "Though that's exactly the kind of thing you're supposed to forgive, isn't it?"

She crossed her arms over her chest, one palm cupping each shoulder, her head lowered. The arms wrapped around the self: that frightened embrace which children give themselves when they are forced to confront, in their silent rooms at night, their perfect aloneness.

The moment held still. And then she moved, she was leaning into me; her arms still crossed, the intersecting forearms pressing on my heart, her bent head at my neck.

This one who stands here inert, overcome by fear.

My own self, motionless.

The buried sheaf of paper. *The only silence that has ever spoken to me.*

Somehow I found Roberta's wrists and pried them gently apart, and even more gently pulled her arms around me and then put mine around her, my wrists crossed at her waist; and we stood like this without speaking, until the guard called out Roberta's name.

"Spire. Roberta Spire. You still in here?"

THE SECURITY GUARD was easily dispatched. I explained to him that Roberta was assisting me with an upcoming photo exhibit for the main library, and he asked if she would need a pass for future evening work. I told him she wouldn't — conscious, as I answered him, of her eyes on me. We'd lock up, I said. He could go home if he wished. Looking grateful for the unexpected reward, the guard left. There was a heavy thump as the outer door closed.

"I'll be right back," I said to Roberta.

I walked into the receptionist's area and pulled a small bottle of brandy from a side cabinet. Roberta's brows rose in surprise as I reentered with the bottle. She was once again seated, her legs crossed, and her expression was composed but slightly tense.

"I didn't know you drank on the job." Her voice too was edged with tension. Its teasing note was forced.

"I don't," I said. "We sometimes have receptions here, so I always keep brandy around." I put the bottle on the table. "I think we could both do with a drink."

"Just a little. Please."

I found two teacups in the supply cabinet. "No snifters," I said. "Can you handle brandy in a cup?"

She smiled and took the cup. I sat down in a chair near her; we sipped in silence. The brandy's smooth warmth slid through me, cutting the sharper edges of my nervousness but leaving me alert.

Roberta glanced at me, then looked away as she spoke.

"You were kind," she said. "When I get tired like this, I'm not aware of exactly when I've crossed the line. Things sort of fill up and spill over. I'm sorry if I —"

"— don't," I interrupted.

"All right," she said quietly.

Within me a wave of anxiety swelled, crested, then broke. "This man you lived with," I said. "Peter. Tell me more about him. You started, the other day. But you didn't really finish."

One of her hands, resting on the table, twitched very slightly, the only sign of her emotion. We were sitting within the circle of light cast by the two lamps suspended overhead. Darkness lay pooled under the reading carrels, whose attached metal bookshelves and sides transformed them into small confessionals.

"I don't really know what else to say. I hardly ever talk about Peter. I tried to, after he left, but talking didn't clarify anything. There was nothing to clarify."

She gazed up at the ceiling. "What was he like? He had this vitality — it was like nothing I'd ever come across before. It was the vitality of a precocious child. You know — the kind who doesn't notice what the adults think because he's so much more aware of things than they are. Peter didn't walk around bragging about his mind. He just loved using it. Like a kid using his favorite plaything.

"He liked games. The mental kind, complex games like chess and Go, puzzles with intricate designs, acrostics and word games — anything you can lose yourself in, even when you're playing with or against another person. He loved mazes and labyrinths. I guess they appealed to the engineer side of him. He was a terrific storyteller, and he could invent characters and

281

scenes and dialogue on the spot, without any inhibitions. It was like putting up scaffolding, he said."

Her laugh was low, brief. "We used to make up little games of our own. Like, one of us would start a story, and every two minutes the other would pick up the narration, and we'd alternate like that until one of us ended the story somehow — usually me. Peter could keep the thread going forever. When we first began living together we used to play that game a lot. We'd lie in the dark and go back and forth, weaving the story . . ."

She hesitated as if unsure of her direction. When I spoke, my voice sounded unnaturally calm.

"Did he leave his family to be with you, or did he intend to leave anyway?"

"You're asking why we were together," she answered. "I'll never know the answer to that. All I can tell you is what I thought the answer was then."

"Tell me that," I said.

"His marriage was over. He was ready to leave it. We'd begun an affair, and I was tormented by it because I was already in love with him. So when he actually left his family, I thought the hard part was over."

Again her uncertain pause. She was slouching in her chair, her legs crossed. With one hand she perched the cup of brandy at mid-thigh. The forefinger of her other hand lightly traced the cup's rim.

I made myself speak again. "Did he blame you? For the breakup of his marriage?"

"No. It was nothing like that. When we first got the apartment, things were easy, like we'd been together a long time. I'd sometimes wake up in the middle of the night and sit up in bed and watch Peter sleeping. I'd think, this is home — ours! And it was a deeply interesting place to me. I don't know how else to put it."

She frowned. "I've always hated talking about relationships. Just the sound of that word — there's something ridiculous about it . . ."

"Keep going," I said. "Describe him."

Her finger stopped circling the cup's rim. "Peter wasn't living in the clouds. I mean, he'd had real experiences. The people and things that made up his life — like his kids, or his work, or our intimacy — all of it was comforting and real to him. But none of it was essential. He belonged to a special, small class of hugely gifted people — mostly philosophers, mathematicians, scientists — you know the types I mean. They're people who live for the experience of honing their abstractions. They refine their thinking until it becomes lustrous and elegant, like burnished gold. Everything else is secondary."

"What was his temperament?" I asked. "Was he ever aggressive?"

"No — which is partly what confused me. People who met him said he seemed balanced and tolerant — which on one level he was. His equanimity was one of the things I loved about him, in fact." She shook her head. "If I'd been able to *see* him, I would've seen how profoundly detached he was — and not because he was hiding some deep hurt. You know, before I met Peter, I thought that people who are incapable of intimacy have always suffered some early trauma or abuse, but that's not necessarily so. Peter had cut a deal with himself. He knew he couldn't pursue elegance and be engaged with the world at the same time — the two acts are antithetical. So he'd made a choice. You could call the choice emotional, or moral, or intellectual — I'd call it spiritual, if I had to call it anything. He'd set out to find the prime mover, the source of beauty and elegance, and pay his respects. Which in Peter's view is something you do by yourself. Not with other people. Other people muddy the waters."

She paused to sip some brandy.

"Why did he leave you when he did?" I asked. "Why not sooner, or later?"

Her brows arched momentarily: the reflex of memory.

"There's always some — what's the phrase — some precipitating event, isn't there? When something happens and everything suddenly looks different. Or maybe what I mean is, when suddenly everything can be seen differently. Peter and I had been living together for six months or so. I was happy, happier than I'd ever been, and he seemed happy, too, in his own way — which wasn't very verbal, as mine is. I didn't feel the slightest need to interrogate him about it, though. That was one of the pleasures of living with him.

"When we first met, he was beginning to get more interested in Christianity after years of sidestepping it. He'd started reading Augustine and Aquinas, exploring pieces of his Episcopalian upbringing — reading the Book of Common Prayer, the catechism questions. I remember a couple of long discussions in which Peter quoted all these theologians I hadn't read. He made several arguments for Christianity that I found a little bloodless. I chalked up my lack of responsiveness to my own doubts, which I didn't voice much to him or anyone else. I was sort of keeping the lid on that.

"Then came the incident with the photos, at my parents' house. I told Peter I'd discovered I was Jewish and that the discovery was enormously confusing and exciting. He wasn't able to conceal his disappointment. I was shocked — it'd never occurred to me that he'd be anything other than sympathetic. But by now he was through with his adopted religion. He said Judaism focused too narrowly on law and behavior, and not enough on suffering and evil. When I talked about feeling betrayed by my parents — all those years of lying and concealment — Peter became dismissive. None of that matters, he said. The only thing that counts is which religious system is more valid.

"At that point I knew something was very wrong. We weren't talking about what was actually going on. I'd just lost my parents as I'd always known them: as people who would never lie to me about anything important. And here was the man I loved, telling me that none of this mattered, that its painfulness was basically of no consequence.

"I burst into tears and started yelling at him. You aren't seeing what this means, I said. There's nothing to see, he said: what's happened doesn't *mean* anything. And in that instant I understood that he was completely disinterested in my experience — not scared or dismayed, simply bored by it. Emotion for him was like sex, or food, or faith: you entered these realms when you had need, and you satisfied your need — which in any case was always temporary — without taking anything that didn't already belong to you. And without leaving anything behind."

Her words and tone communicated something incontrovertible. I believed in the man Roberta had described to me. She'd delivered him whole, with the unintended force of accusation. Though I knew myself to be a different man, retreating had been as irresistible for me as it was for Peter.

I closed my eyes, and my wife's face came into sudden, shocking focus. It was pale, bloodless, and beautifully alert: I was seeing Judith at the moment of her death. For one instant, I was able to reciprocate her gaze without fear.

I opened my eyes. Roberta was staring at me.

"Where are you?" she asked.

"Here," I said. "With you."

"I can stop talking, you know. I think you get the basic —"

"— no, please," I said. "Don't stop. I want to hear the rest. When did you realize Peter was leaving?"

"I knew his leaving would only be a matter of time. So I decided not to wait for it: I asked him to go that same night. And he did. Peter was really not capable of behaving badly. He left me the apartment. It was leased in his name, but he had it signed over to me, and he paid the balance of his half of the rent."

"Do you know where he is now?"

"No, but I'm sure he's found someone to live with for a while. Then he'll leave again. He won't linger. He's learned how easy it is to separate from people, even from his kids. He doesn't have to struggle for disengagement. It's his natural state."

She looked directly at me now. "Can you tell what happened?" Her gaze lowered. "The problem with describing someone who lives abstractly is that the description itself sounds abstract. There's nothing to blame him for. This is who he is."

"I think I can tell what happened," I said. "It doesn't sound abstract to me."

"I'm always amazed when I think of him," she said softly. "And I miss that amazement. Despite what it cost me. Such a person enters your life only once."

I had to look away from her. Phrases from the letters were flooding me; I was sure Roberta could read them on my face.

Yet I continue living as if under a spell of immobility.
How can I make you see I have no choice?
Emily! — you're what I know, this clear truth is all I know. And still I can't have it.

Roberta's words came to me as if from a distant corner of the room. "I need to go," she said. "I'm exhausted."

"Do you need a lift?" I asked. The question sounded like someone else's. I couldn't recognize my own voice.

"Thanks," she said, "but I have my own car. I'll see you tomorrow. Sleep well."

Her fingers brushed my shoulder as she passed. Then I heard all the doors close.

The Mason Room was peaceful, as it always is at midnight. In a few minutes I heard the books' voices: a low, steady, unsuppressible hum. I'd heard it many times before. I've always had a finely tuned ear for a library's accumulations of echo and desire. Libraries are anything but hushed.

I listened, knowing I couldn't expect anything like concrete guidance, but hoping for some signal or prompt. At first I was edgy, but gradually I quieted. I sat and meditated, if that's the right word, on Roberta, Judith, and Emily; finally, on Eliot. I considered various conflicting imperatives. It took me a while, but finally I realized there was really only one thing to be done, and I might as well get started.

The archives were dark and still. I remembered my bedroom in Washington Heights — how it would fill with that same deep stillness, late at night. I would sit on the floor in the dark, next to my bookshelves, and all my storybooks would begin their susurration. Down the dark hallway, my mother lay awake next to my sound-asleep father. I knew she was listening to her Bible, mesmerized by its murmur — the bright promises, dark threats — and if I called out, suddenly afraid, she wouldn't be able to hear me.

T HE GREATEST RISK to paper is humidity; even excessive dryness isn't as destructive as damp air. The temperature in the Mason Room is controlled by a thermostat separate from the one regulating the rest of the library, and a combined humidifier-dehumidifier maintains a uniform level of moisture throughout the archive. A few very old manuscripts lie under Plexiglas in an even more precisely controlled cocoon of air. I remove them once a year, at most, to inspect them — an operation that requires special gloves and extremely careful handling.

I learned all the physical routines of archival work in graduate school. As a student I was taken to all the noteworthy public archives in New York, and to a few privately held collections as well. Their owners generously allowed student librarians to handle astonishing materials — chronicles and documents and notes whose existence none of us had even imagined. We sometimes found ourselves in a kind of archival heaven.

This was the aspect of my work that intrigued Judith when we first met. She was otherwise no more interested in what I did than I was in her secretarial job at the law firm. She accepted my need to be an archivist, and for the first few years of our marriage she found nothing in it to trouble her.

Gradually, though, my work assumed larger and more difficult proportions for her. One day in 1951, I came home from the library at Columbia, where I was working at the time, and told her that I'd taken a group of students to see the document collection at the Museum of the City of New York. I described its highlights to her: the marvelous essays of obscure borough-level politicians, whose written language was so inflected by their immigrant accents — Irish, Italian, Yiddish; a humorous and touching account by a courageous Brooklyn fireman; and the quietly riveting letters sent by a Civil War soldier to his parents as he made the long journey home through war-ravaged Virginia and Pennsylvania.

Judith was clearly moved by my description of the soldier's letters. They must have been so disturbing for the man's parents to read, she said — that revelation of a horror known only from a distance.

It was around this time that Judith began collecting news accounts of European survivors of the war, especially of Jews who had lived through the camps. One Sunday morning I found her sitting at the dining-room table with a small pile of clippings and several file folders. She was carefully affixing typed labels to the folders. I asked her what she was up to, and she said she was documenting what she called the realm of survival. She'd categorized her materials along very definite lines: children, adults, slave-labor and concentration camps, bombing, resistance, collaboration, heroism. From her office she'd brought home a sturdy carton into which she began putting her files.

The next day we had a short, somewhat tense discussion of her project. The whole thing seemed suspect. Something about the energy with which she approached this activity disturbed me. It wasn't simply her fixation on the dark details, which on some level I felt I understood, although it troubled me. My unease sprang more from the way in which she seemed to be casting herself in the role of witness, as if that were a duty. I knew she wasn't being self-righteous, but I wondered if she was perhaps taking things too far.

289

At one point she spoke of common themes she'd noticed in various accounts she'd been reading: the survivors' bittersweet relief, as she called it, and their guilt.

I asked about the guilt. Was it because they'd managed to live, and wondered why they deserved to?

No, she said, not that exactly. Guilt was what they felt when they realized they couldn't feel anything at all for the people who hadn't stayed alive — not grief or anger or pity; nothing. The survivors were numb, unable to respond to the scale and precision of the extermination that had passed them over.

She said other things I couldn't fully comprehend — something about the war as a manifestation of the initial divine crisis, and exile as humankind's mission. At this point my habits of skepticism began to assert themselves. I found her collecting of news accounts and personal stories depressing and needless; in fact, her entire stress on survival was problematic. And Judith's "remembrance" poems — she wrote a series on the Jews of Europe during this period — seemed heavy-handed to me, in danger of yielding to bathos or nostalgia.

Mostly I kept silent about my feelings. I did say to her, once, that evil can be trivialized by sensational renderings and that it might be better not to think so much about bearing witness. The future posed difficult challenges; it needed participants. The only way to repay victims of the past was to posit an entirely different future.

Her questions were unrelated to my comments, and unsettled me further.

What does Christ say to you, now that the war's over? How do you know what He wants you to do or feel?

He doesn't want me to do or feel anything in particular, I said.

I meant that Christ's teachings were never directly prescriptive, but Judith heard something different.

That's what I was afraid you'd say, she responded.

*　　*　　*

Her survivor files, as she called them, kept growing. In 1956 she began having trouble getting up and going to work. On several occasions she showed up at my office in the middle of the day, distraught, wanting me to read something. Once it was the story of a teenager who'd spent the war years alone in a barn. Another time it was a lengthy excerpt from a Frenchwoman's diary that chronicled a recurring dream of a single gunshot, its sound more terrifying to the diarist than the noise of bombs because it signalled an execution taking place on the street outside her darkened apartment. It was with difficulty that I persuaded Judith to allow me to wait until I got home to read these things.

She drank more and more heavily. One Saturday morning I found her in the kitchen, pouring whiskey into a bowl of oatmeal. She lost weight. Then, in 1957, the bouts of delirium began. For several horrific hours she would speak in a kind of babble in which the war, the accident on Broadway, and Bud Powell kept surfacing, interwoven with other disconnected themes. Then, as abruptly as it had departed, her lucidity would return. These intervals were agony for me, but in some ways I dreaded her depressions even more. They would last for weeks during which she was unable to talk about anything serious for more than a few minutes without crying. She couldn't sleep, she barely made it through a day's work, and she couldn't stand to be touched. The depressive periods too would lift suddenly, and in their place would often be a kind of brief arousal — usually to anger or laughter, seldom to sex. Then there would be a month or two of calm; our normal life would resume, and I would fall into thinking that she'd simply been under a great deal of pressure. She wasn't ill, I'd tell myself; she was a very sensitive woman who was going through a difficult period.

During these years we made love infrequently, and always at my uneasy instigation, until her condition worsened and I could no longer find the courage to encounter her. The fierce deliverance of our early lovemaking was gone. I was ashamed of the resentment I felt toward Judith, knowing that the impediments to intimacy weren't only of her making.

It had been Judith who took the chance, when we first met: breaking through to a place where I cowered, unable to express how much I needed her and too stunned to see how much she risked in reaching out to me. In the beginning all I knew was the unimaginable release of loving her: the moment of sourceless shuddering, when light seemed to spill from her body. I was awed by how unimpeded our lovemaking seemed. Awed, but also more deeply frightened than I'd ever been by anything in my life. The fear lay dormant, waiting for a chance to articulate itself.

Judith knew that certain tendencies were working their way up through us. From our parents, she said, we'd learned how to suppress attention. We were cut off from what we were feeling. Our own distraction was our greatest threat.

I thought she was too vigilant, and I told her the best thing we could do was to carry on with our shared life. I loved that life as I loved Judith, heedlessly, refusing to see what was falling apart.

Jesus knew God would never abandon His children, she said to me at Hayden. At the moment of death, Jesus had no doubts. But the rest of them, his supposed followers, took his name and twisted its meaning, jumbled the letters; and those letters could spell evil as clearly as they might spell good.

The son on the Cross spoke aloud, at the moment of death: *They know not what they do.* With this we comfort ourselves. But we always knew what they were doing, and how we might've stopped them.

I T S E E M S T O M E N O W that everything began unraveling after my discovery of Roberta in the Mason Room. Though perhaps unraveling isn't the right word; it connotes something of panic and chaos, and what I experienced was instead a necessary severance. But I'm getting ahead of myself.

Not long after my evening with Roberta, I came home to find a letter in my mailbox, postmarked New York City and addressed in a shaky hand I didn't recognize. Opening it, I saw it was from Carol, whom I'd thought never to see or hear from again. I was stunned. Almost ten years had passed since Len's funeral; on those rare occasions when thoughts of Carol actually broke the surface of my memory, I had assumed that she'd gone too — in her sleep, the same uncomplicated way. I counted decades: Carol had to be in her nineties. The letter lay lightly in my hand, two thin, pale yellow sheets.

The voice was unmistakably Carol's. *I have terminal cancer,* she wrote, *and I'll spare you the details but I can say it's no fun. I'm weak most of the time, sometimes in pain. Though God knows I've lived long enough, so it's not a huge problem, you know? Just a difficulty.*

When you're going soon, lots of things come up you might not wonder about, except now you have to. I've been thinking about Judith. I miss Len, but I don't need to think about him the way I do about her. And Matt, I have to tell you, it took some doing to find out where you are but I was determined because I have a question for you. And I won't be calm till I get an answer, and I expect truth.

All these years I've wondered. Did you tell those doctors they could give Judy shock treatment, and did they give it to her?

It just doesn't make sense, why she'd kill herself, unless they were doing that to her. It's the only reason.

Judy always took things so seriously. She didn't have such a gift for taking the long view like Lenny did.

You know, Lenny suffered things in his life too, he was a man with losses, but he kept the long view. Judy never gave him as much credit as he deserved. She was only a little infant when we got her, but I think maybe she already didn't trust the idea of a father. That would make sense because her real father was a real bastard, let me tell you. And maybe Lenny was in the same league in Judy's eyes. Who knows?

All I know is Judy adored you, Matt. She always did, right from the start and all the way through, and if you did this to her, if you told them they could give her shock, you have her death on your hands. I have to say this to you. Because all she ever wanted was to live a life with you. I can see it now so clear! You were the only one she trusted.

So now I'm asking you. Write me and just tell me this one thing, whether you told the doctors to go ahead. Yes or no — either way I'll sleep better knowing.

The envelope had a West Village return address. I mailed her a postcard with one word in its message portion: *No.* I signed my name; the truth deserved that much, I decided.

Seven weeks later, I received a postcard in return. It bore Carol's address but had been sent by her landlord, a Mr. John Kelly, who informed me of his tenant's death a month earlier. Mr. Kelly didn't indicate whether Carol herself had ever seen my card; this question is one I'll be left with, when my turn for sleeplessness comes.

ROBERTA'S BREACH OF THE MASON ROOM took place just before the start of the university's July Fourth recess — a long and very hot weekend, which I spent cloistered in my apartment.

Most holidays bore me. The ones I remember best are those I celebrated with Judith — especially our birthdays, which were two days apart and which we marked, on the day in between, by going to a concert or a jazz club and then to one of the nicer midtown hotels for a late, quiet supper. On that in-between birthday of ours, money ceased mattering to us; we dressed up and entertained ourselves. And the city was our ally on those celebratory nights, at least in the early years of our marriage.

Until one March evening in 1959: our birthday night. We'd each turned forty-one. At an elegant little downtown place where we were having dinner, Judith began giggling at a poor joke I'd made. Suddenly her laughter turned into hysterical weeping, and I had to get us both out of the restaurant and into a cab. Judith resisted. It was icy and wet outside. She slipped and fell against the open cab door; the calf of her right leg was cut, and blood fell on the sleet-covered sidewalk. I remember little dark red rivulets like lines of ruby ice; that, and Judith's panicky wailing.

The next day, at work, I did some research. I called Hayden in the afternoon and had a long discussion with Harold Clay, head of the psychiatric staff, who advised me to bring in my wife for what he called a consultation. I told him we'd be there that same weekend.

When I got home that night, I insisted that we see Dr. Clay. I think Judith sensed in me something larger than stubbornness, and she gave in. On that Saturday we drove up the Hudson River valley in silence. I remember my first look at Hayden's secluded greenness, its well-tended gardens and narrow gravel paths, the long drive to three brick buildings in a cluster of dark boxwoods. Tears ran from Judith's closed eyes. *Is it beautiful,* she asked, *I can't look — Matt, tell me!* And I answered her: *Yes.*

About a month later — a month filled with talks whose substance I've blocked, their anguish my only memory of that time — I persuaded Judith to stay at Hayden for a while.

How long is a while? she asked.

Till you're better.

How will we know when that is? she asked, and I had no answer.

On the Monday after the holiday, Edith and I met for lunch. She had a favor to ask me: would I take her place at a conference on new computer technologies for librarians? The conference would begin the next morning, in New York. I could take the train and stay in a decent hotel — would the Algonquin do?

I agreed to go. The break would do me good.

After lunch we walked over to the main library's staff lounge. We were sitting on one of the sofas, drinking coffee and discussing the details of the conference, when the door swung open. It was Roberta.

"I don't like to bother you," she said, "but I need to let you both know about a change in my plans."

For a few moments, no one said anything. In this brief lull, my hands remembered the small of Roberta's back, its firmness beneath the thin shirt she'd been wearing when I found her in the

leaning against the pedestal of one of the granite lions flanking the library's entrance. Its stony coolness refreshed me. I glanced at my watch: eight-thirty. My energy felt oddly concentrated, my entire body light.

By the time I'd walked a dozen or so blocks up Fifth, night had fallen. I turned east onto Fifty-fifth Street. On the block halfway between Madison and Park, two well-dressed men passed me. Their conversation sounded genial, as if they'd just signed a deal over a good dinner; their laughter lingered around them, then faded. The street stood still as I continued walking. At the corner of Lexington Avenue was a chocolate-brown building, vaguely Moorish in style. A low, wrought-iron railing ran along its side, and a set of wide steps led to its front doors. I rounded the corner so that I was standing directly in front of the building.

I knew where I was. Holding the banister of bronzed metal, I ascended the building's steps; they were steep, with a higher rise than I'd expected. A small plaque was affixed to the facade: *Central Synagogue, the oldest Jewish house of worship in continuous use in New York City. Built in 1870.*

Pivoting on the top step, I surveyed Lexington Avenue. Across the street I could make out the awnings of a shoe boutique and a men's clothier; they occupied two storefronts in an ugly apartment complex constructed of ersatz white brick. A seven-story red brick building — older, attractive — sat on the opposite corner. On the nearer corner, an old-fashioned street-lamp with a domed top stood next to a much taller traffic light. The streetlamp gave off a dull yellow, anachronistic glow in the humid darkness.

Judith, emerging from this synagogue, had descended these steps: a girl carrying a handful of mimeographed papers. *Look at these, Carol.* She hadn't called the woman *mother.* Even then, she'd had doubts about *mother* and *father.*

299

Can I take some of these?

Carol had scoffed. *This stuff? — propaganda! Ernst Thalmann's not even Jewish, for Christ's sake!*

But Carol had been unable to conceal her anxiety. Years later, in her journal, Judith had described Carol's edginess. *The world these days is not a safe place.*

For Carol, the past wasn't the problem. She'd learned how to extinguish memory. But the future scared her; it wasn't like the past, it couldn't be refused. Carol knew: its danger lay not in what it would bring but what it would take away.

When Lottie and Sam left New York, Carol had been thankful. She had everything she needed — Len, music, booze, work. Then came the child — the infant returned literally from the dead, speechless and wailing, needing a mother. Carol knew that the three of them — the three who remained — would become a family, but not like other families.

A family of orphans.

Carol also knew: this was just the beginning. *The world these days is not a safe place.*

My legs ached. I descended the synagogue's steps and turned down Lexington Avenue. At Fifty-fourth Street a granite and glass building sat at an angle in front of a much larger building, glistening in the dampness. I craned my neck and looked upward, then scanned downward.

The two structures were interestingly configured. From news photos I knew that the bigger one was the Citicorp Building. Crossing Lexington, I walked a few yards toward Fifty-third Street until I found a short passage, recessed but well-lit, which led into the smaller building. The door at the end of the passage was locked.

I knocked loudly, and after a few minutes a guard appeared. He was affable; I sensed he was also bored. Quickly answering his questions, I handed him my university ID. He inspected it, hesitated a moment, and opened the door.

I was inside St. Peter's Lutheran Church — the Jazz Church, the guard called it, explaining that weekly jazz concerts were held there. He flicked on some lights and took a closer look at me; then, apparently comfortable with my presence, he urged me to walk around. I listened politely as he gave a short but complete summary of the church's features. Then he led me to a small chapel filled with Louise Nevelson sculptures. In about twenty minutes, he said, he'd come find me. Shaking my head, I told him that I wished instead to see the main sanctuary. In a moment the guard had lit the large stairwell across from the chapel, and to my surprise I found myself descending rather than ascending its graceful curve.

I had never been in a below-ground church. The sensation was one of peaceful encasement. The design of the central space was spare and pleasing. Rows of modern-looking pews, their seats cushioned with brightly colored covers, faced an altar that was set at an angle, like the church itself. The blond wood of the pews stood out nicely against the granite floors and white walls. A huge organ rose up along one wall. Toward the back of the church was a raised platform with more pews; behind these, at the level of the floor above (where I had entered), several windows let in light from Lexington Avenue.

I sat in the front pew. The altar was utterly plain, a long, low table covered with a low-hanging white cloth. The cross behind it was draped with red fabric. I imagined touching this cloth — it would be supple, warm as its color. The wrought-iron cross put me off; I sensed, without touching it, its coldness. Two tall white candles flanked it on either side.

Traffic noises drifted vaguely from above. The silence of the church was itself a sound, low and steady, sheltering. I closed my eyes, not knowing what I wanted to hear or see or feel. It had been a long time since I'd felt so alert.

I waited. Words, phrases, then a few lines came to me, pieces of different poems Judith had recited. I was hearing her voice, reedy and dense, profoundly erotic and powerful: an instrument of connection and release. I put my head down and cupped my face in my hands, and I wept for her and for myself. I wept for my terror and my silence, for Judith's courage and her madness; for all our shared loss.

Somehow I heard the other voice. You gotta go now, the guard said.

A broad hand, a stranger's, settling on my shoulder. The grace of touch.

You OK now? It's time.

I SPENT THE BALANCE OF MY BRIEF stay in New York inside an icily air-conditioned conference room with several hundred other librarians, archivists, and computer buffs, most of whom were too techno-enthusiastic for my taste. When I returned to the university, I gave Edith a brief report. Then I sat down at my desk to tackle the three days' worth of mail that had accumulated in my absence.

Behind me, the door to the Mason Room opened. My entire body went tight with expectation.

"Hello," I said as I turned and faced Roberta.

She gave me a wan smile. "Hello," she replied quietly. I watched her swing her bag off her shoulder and hang it on the back of the chair next to my desk. She was wearing a white T-shirt and her black jeans; her body seemed lanky, as if she'd lost some weight.

"Talk to me," I said.

"Some tea first," she said, sitting down.

I made us a small pot of tea; she drank a cup, swallowing noisily.

"Much, much better," she said. Reaching into her bag, she pulled out a book and placed it on my desk.

"A going-away present. I thought you could use a fresh copy of the *Complete Poems*."

T. S. Eliot's elegant, anxious face stared at me from the book's cover.

Roberta slouched back into the chair. Her hair, falling loosely around her shoulders, was glossy and dark against the near-whiteness of her neck. Her eyes danced briefly over my face.

"I'm moving on Tuesday," she said. "In four more days. I've rented a studio in the city. A decent little place on a not-bad street in Tribeca. All I need now is a part-time job."

"Doing what?" My vocal cords felt tense and slightly tender, as if I had bruised them.

"Anything — waitressing, retail, it doesn't matter. I've got leads in a couple of bookstores. Something will turn up."

She was flexing the fingers of one hand; I heard the knuckles crack softly.

"Your mother," I said, "how is she?"

"Not good."

She stood and began one of her slow circle-walks, tracking the edges of the room. I followed her with my eyes. When she had moved behind me, out of sight, she stopped. My eyes were closed but I felt her standing in back of me, close by.

"Roberta," I said, releasing her name into the empty air.

In the room's utter stillness, all I heard was the rhythmic sibilance of her breathing.

"Tell me why you're going," I said.

She didn't answer me. I stood; she circled to my side, neither close nor far.

"I need to be back in the city."

"There's rather more to it than that," I said. "Isn't there?"

"I want the chance to talk with my mother and father," she said. "Before they're gone."

"You don't have to move to New York to do that."

"Yes, I do. I need to go back to where I was when something got interrupted. It's like I've been stuck on some kind of detour since I left."

"What do you want to talk with your parents about?"

She hesitated; I could feel her gathering the words.

"The whole thing. The full story. I want my mother and father to tell me every single thing that happened during the war — to them, to my grandparents, to their friends. All the details."

Something within me unlocked and swung open like a door. I turned, facing her.

"Listen to me, Roberta," I said. "You can't do that."

She stared at me.

"You're asking for something impossible," I said.

She had begun crying. I had never seen anyone weep with such quiet, almost austere dignity.

"I'm their daughter," she whispered. "Why didn't they tell me, for Christ's sake?"

"They probably thought it'd kill you," I said. "It'd be unbearable to hear about so much horror. A child shouldn't hear such things."

"But eventually I wasn't a child any more," she said. "And they'd survived. We were a family — we were safe here —"

"— yes," I broke in. "But they'd had to survive the knowledge that while they lived, their own parents perished. While they fled, saving themselves, their parents stayed and were doomed. And how could they tell you that? How?" I gestured toward Eliot's poems. "'After such knowledge, what forgiveness?'"

She was silent. I remembered Len at the bar, staring into space and speaking the truth: *Neither of us could make ourselves tell her.*

"Your parents kept quiet," I said, "to protect you. What else could you expect them to do?"

"Protect me less and tell me more! If they hadn't taken it upon themselves to choose for me who I should be —"

I broke in. "No. You still would've had to choose, Roberta. In Germany they had one life, and when that life was annihilated, they had the courage to choose another. Whether or not we condone the choices of others isn't really the question, is it?"

I reached out. Taking her jaw in my hand, I cradled the delicate border of her face, pressing lightly with my thumb and forefinger. As she met my gaze, I felt myself reentering a space that had emptied when Judith left it. The end of "Four Quartets" came to me:

> *We are born with the dead:*
> *See, they return, and bring us with them.*

"We're nearly strangers," I said to Roberta. "And yet there's this . . . this — what, rapport? Is that it? The right word eludes me. These things can sound ridiculous. But no matter."

Quick now, here, now, always.

"I know," she murmured, smiling slightly, as if to herself.

I was still holding her jaw. My hand began shaking slightly, the ordinary trembling of a wrist steadied in midair — a small banality of the body, but it forced the words from me.

"I'm not offering protection here," I said. "But I do have a suggestion: that you not leave." I released her jaw gently. "You could stay."

Roberta took a small but definite step backward. "Wait a second. Matt, please — for God's sake, don't be saying something weird right now." She had shut her eyes as if to fend off something dismaying. It was difficult for me not to reach for her hands, but somehow I kept my own at my sides.

"No. Hang on. It's not what you think. I'm saying, stay till you've finished what you're doing."

Roberta opened her eyes. She managed a skeptical glance in my direction but wouldn't look directly at me. "What I'm doing? Uh, let's see — what might that be? Well, I'm pretty good at eating a peach while wearing my trousers rolled . . . Actually, you know what? Most of the time I'm just sitting on my goddamn hands."

"Come on," I said, shaking my head. "Drop the self-pity. You know perfectly well what I'm talking about. You write poetry. Don't get sidetracked, Roberta."

"I can always write in the city." She was trying for an assured tone, but her voice, softer now, gave away her uncertainty.

"You can always write anywhere. But you might do it better if you stayed here. Where you'd be undisturbed."

Her eyes, encircled by dark, still-damp lashes: *where the grey light meets the green air.*

"Look," I continued. "Ultimately this isn't the place for you. I know that. You'll end up in New York — it's where you belong. And maybe, because of your mother's health, it makes sense for you to go now." I paused. "But I also know" — my ears were ringing, but I kept speaking — "that I've found it restorative, just asking you to stay here for a while. I feel tremendously good just making the case for it."

She was contemplating my words: their veracity, their implications.

"Matt," she said quietly, "isn't it time you played your cards?"

"Yes," I said. "It is." Without thinking, I reached for her hand. Her touch was cool and firm. Unhurriedly, her fingers surrounded and pressed mine.

"My wife was a poet," I began. "She shared your horror of concealment. Her parents were American Jews — socialists — who went to Russia during the Revolution. They were killed in a pogrom there. The people who raised her in New York, her uncle

307

and aunt, decided to hide that fact from her. After the war, when the truth began coming out about what had really happened in Europe, Judith started falling apart. She'd always sensed that she hadn't been told the whole story about her parents' death. And then, after she'd learned that most people had looked the other way during the war, everything came crashing down on her.

"She started having psychotic episodes. It was terrifying. Eventually she became — how do I describe it? — unreachable. I brought her to a psychiatric institution. At the time I thought it was the best thing for her. I didn't understand that what she really needed was to be doing her work in a safe place."

"What does that mean?"

"It means somewhere with people who would accept her as a poet, unreservedly, as I couldn't — because poetry seemed to me to be part of her illness. I discouraged her from writing, in fact. I thought it was making her condition worse. I was wrong; separation made it worse."

I paused, and Roberta let the silence stand for several long moments.

"What were her poems really like?" she asked at last.

"They were extraordinarily disturbing. And very powerful."

She nodded; I felt her fingers relax slightly around my hand. "And what was your wife really like?"

"The same."

"And she loved you?"

I didn't speak. Her hand jiggled mine, as if to awaken me. "Yes, she did," I said.

"What was that word you used before — ah, yes — 'unreservedly'?"

"Yes."

"And you loved her."

Roberta's fingers, their gentle cool tugging, retrieved me. For the first time in two decades, I found myself seeking actual speech. This desire, unfamiliar but urgent, left me shaky.

"Yes — no." I wobbled. "Insufficiently."

"Uh-uh," she said, lightly shaking my hand once more. "You can do better than that."

I began again, concentrating on the sensation of her fingers around mine: this, only this would deliver me.

"I mean — God, what do I mean? — I mean I was too afraid of her, of her fierceness — of everything she was capable of seeing and feeling — to love her sufficiently. In the way she loved me."

"Which was . . . Say more."

"She trusted me." The words were burning in my mouth; I wasn't crying, but I shed the words like tears. "She was very ill, and her illness made her terribly erratic and unpredictable. But fundamentally she was always constant. Toward me, I mean. Even when she realized I'd failed her, she kept trusting me."

"And you suspected you didn't warrant it."

"I didn't suspect it, Roberta — I knew it. I was like a paralyzed man. It's clearer to me now, what she needed from me. But I got it all wrong. I tried to shield her from the present, from the city, the daily stresses — as if any of that could stop her illness, or make it go away. I tried to hide everything from her — the war, all the horrors, without understanding that she'd already seen them. I did what her family had done, what most people did — what most people always do — I tried to conceal the terrifying things, to keep quiet about them. That's what got to her, more than anything else. She couldn't bear it. She couldn't bear that I, too, was silent. She'd always believed I'd resist silence — that I was capable of resistance. And I wasn't."

Roberta released my hand, then placed both of hers on my forearms. We had been standing for a long time. My legs ached.

As if she knew this, Roberta pushed me gently backward, walking me toward a chair. She made me sit, then she pulled up another chair opposite me.

We sat there for what felt like a very long time. Her gaze, which took in my entire face, was neither scrutinizing nor caressing, but like a reader's, as if she were carefully scanning a page.

Finally she spoke. "I think I get what you're telling me," she said. "Only there are a few pieces missing."

"There are," I said. "They concern you."

Her brows drew together in that frown I loved — a grimace like a child's, both serious and amusing. "You're not wanting to rewrite any scripts, are you? Because I —"

"— no, Roberta. I'll say it again: I'm not asking you to stay here with me. This isn't some kind of bizarre plea for rescue. I'm asking you to think about why you're leaving. I just don't believe you when you say you'll be writing. Sure, you'll work on your poems — but not wholeheartedly. Because you're distracted."

She shifted slightly in her chair — an attempt at demurral — but I kept going.

"You said it yourself: you want your parents to tell you everything. So somehow you can trust them again — isn't that right? But you don't really believe they'll come through for you; or even if they do, it won't matter — the damage will have been done. And it's not only Kurt and Trudy who're untrustworthy; it's Peter, it's everyone. You're thinking, if even the people closest to you can't be counted on, why bother? Why not simply disengage? At least you'll already be in a place where disengagement is easy. Another solitary New York poet — it's a venerable tradition . . ."

She had closed her eyes once more, but I knew she was listening. I plunged ahead.

"Trust involves truth, betrayal involves lies — isn't that your formula, Roberta? The problem is, it doesn't apply. Everything's tangled — we can't draw those neat lines we long for . . . Look, I know you understand this. You're scared — who isn't?"

I leaned forward, my elbows on my knees, my gaze full upon her. When her eyes opened, she didn't flinch.

"We're all terrified — of possession, connection, belonging to others. Eliot put his finger on it — 'Till human voices wake us . . .' But, Roberta, you know as well as I do that we can't just sit around worrying about drowning. We've got to wake up anyway. Even Eliot finally figured that out."

She sat entirely still.

"You're probably wondering why I'm rattling on like this. I'm an aging man, my dear, but not quite yet a foolish one. There are a few mistakes I'd like not to make again. When you're gone, I want to be able to look back at this particular moment and tell myself I wasn't shirking."

Roberta opened her eyes, then laughed softly. It felt to me as if everything between us, none of it utterable, was captured and contained in that full-throated laughter of hers.

"Shirking?" she said. "Now there's an odd verb. No, Matt. I don't believe shirking's your style."

"Don't be so sure," I said.

"Not at that level, anyway."

"No," I said, "not at that level."

Her mouth as I kissed her tasted very lightly of lime, with an underlay of something — rainwater. dew? — that kind of elusiveness.

"I'll remember this," I said. "And everything else."

Her smile was at once grave and amused. "That's quite a sum," she said, picking up her bag.

"Wait — I have something for you," I said. Unlocking the bottom drawer of my desk, I pulled out Judith's blue leather portfolio.

"What's this?" she asked as I handed it to her.

311

"The portfolio belonged to my wife. The contents belonged to Emily Hale."

Her mossy eyes widened. "No," she said disbelievingly, opening the portfolio and quickly thumbing its pages. "These are original letters?"

"No," I said. "Poems. Original poems. Six of them. Not the actuals, of course — I made you a set of photocopies. A little risky, because of the machine's heat and the bright light — it's not advisable, but I decided it was safer than scanning them. You know, the last time I ran a document through our scanner — my income taxes, in fact — the machine devoured it. Tore it to shreds. Taught me a useful lesson about betrayal."

Roberta took a breath and exhaled, softly and fully. Her color had risen a little, pinking her cheeks.

"Matt. These aren't, uh, little cat poems, are they?" she asked.

"I'd say not," I answered.

"You've read them?"

"No. I'm making an educated guess."

She squinted at me. "You're being rather elliptical," she said.

"It's necessary," I said. "It's my job."

Roberta looked at me for a long while. Neither before nor since have I felt so penetrated by a gaze. She was, I knew, contemplating her next question, which I awaited with an uncertainty approaching dread. I felt like a man on trial who is about to perjure himself. But when Roberta finally broke the silence, what she asked was something I could answer.

"This is about trust?"

I nodded. "It's about trust," I said.

Four

IN WASHINGTON HEIGHTS, solitude was my safest hiding place: the sanctuary from which I would never be evicted. When I left Washington Heights, the Second World War broke out. While everything that had seemed certain — the boundaries of nations, of decency and order — began caving in, I waited, immured in my solitude, believing in Eliot's truth:

> *Even among these rocks,*
> *Our peace in His will . . .*

I met Judith in 1945, and the war ended. We were safe. But Eliot had spoken another truth as well:

> *The memory throws up high and dry*
> *A crowd of twisted things*

Gradually, Judith dredged it all up; she wouldn't turn away from it. *Postwar collaborators,* she wrote in one of her remembrance poems:

> *we who say it couldn't have happened . . .*
> *Afterwards which is worse:*

the irrefutable facts
or the way we keep refusing them?

In 1959, just before going to Hayden, Judith wrote me a note asking me to safeguard her survivor files. I opened the file boxes soon after her departure. Along with the clippings, I discovered pages of handwritten annotations. I knew what those pages represented: they were the makings of poems. Yet this didn't matter to me. I believed that those pages, perhaps more than anything else, nourished Judith's illness. I told myself I had to act, to overcome my usual passivity. Judith could no longer cope. She desperately needed my help; our shared anguish had to end.

A few days after she left, I threw away all her files.

In 1965, I acted once again in defiance of Judith's wishes. She had wanted her journal to be read by one person — a man she deeply mistrusted but also needed — and then destroyed. Instead I saved it, hiding it as if it were my own secret life.

But it wasn't; it was Judith's. And I've only just begun understanding what it meant for her to record that life.

B EFORE THE WAR, strange, sad stories circulated about
T. S. Eliot and his wife. Their marriage had fallen apart,
and Vivienne was acting oddly. After Eliot moved out of
their apartment, Vivienne had searched for him everywhere; she
had gone to his office at Faber, called all their friends, even tried
to place an ad in a London paper: *Mr TS Eliot: Would you please
contact your wife at home as soon as possible.* One evening in the
winter of 1935, having found out that he would be addressing a
public audience, she showed up at a large hall packed with Eliot
supporters. Her arrival coincided with the end of his speech. She
was dressed dramatically, in a dark velvet cape, dark hat, dark
dress; her face was powdered white. With her was their dog, who
even after two years' separation immediately recognized his master and bounded to the podium.

Vivienne clambered up onto the stage, calling her husband's
name repeatedly, her arms extended toward him. Eliot was em-
barrassed and flustered, and deeply ashamed. This was precisely
the sort of spectacle he loathed. He thrust the dog at her. *Why
hello, Vivienne,* he said. Somehow he managed to direct his wife
and dog off the stage. Quickly, other admirers thronged around
him, edging Vivienne further away, out of the picture.

In one of his letters to Emily Hale, Eliot described that
scene — the torment of it, his inability to act. *Will it always be*

like this? he wrote in anguish. Yet he refused to visit Vivienne while she was in Northumberland House. To Emily, who must've asked why he hadn't done so, he wrote that seeing Vivienne there would be excruciating and unavailing for both of them.

He may well have been right. Who can tell another person what to endure — how much, and for how long? During the last year of Judith's life, I went to Hayden less frequently; I could no longer make my weekly forays there. My own powerlessness overwhelmed me. But I cannot imagine not having gone at all.

I'VE CONTRACTED PNEUMONIA AGAIN — a somewhat more virulent case this time. It appears that my lungs will be my undoing. Each of us has a weak spot, an organ or system within the body where death gains access. For my father, it was the liver; for my mother, the heart; for Judith, the nervous system and its intricate, treacherous circuitry. This isn't mordant romanticism, it's merely fact.

Kafka said of Milena's tuberculosis, when he learned about it, that it wasn't his lover's illness that scared him so much as the thought of what preceded its onset. I think I understand him. We resist ourselves — who we've been, who we've become; and the tension of this resistance enters our bodies and is incorporated within us. No wonder we finally tire.

As a child I would sometimes hold my breath, to prove I could control it. But always, against my will, the old air would force its way out and new air would flood in as my temples throbbed, my chest heaved; and I'd say to myself *it's here then, no matter what.*

I trust death will be no different.

I T HAS ALWAYS SEEMED miraculous to me that words actually do communicate meanings. That's not to say, of course, that they're reliable. T. S. Eliot knew precisely how language fails us. *The knowledge imposes a pattern, and falsifies . . .*

But I have always trusted words.

The creation of something new, said Eliot, alters everything that has gone before it. Each time he wrote to Emily Hale, Eliot wrought a small but real transformation in the whole of their relationship. What had begun in lightheartedness deepened into the most mature intimacy he'd ever experienced.

But the correspondence also led him inexorably to the past. After writing Emily over a thousand letters, he was forced to confront not her but Vivienne — still his wife, his incarcerated nightmare — and to reckon with an overwhelming guilt. Her death in 1947 turned everything upside down. Eliot's dramatic repudiation of Emily was a failed gesture, a capitulation to his own cowardice. He could — and did — refuse to see her again. But words had let him out, and there was no going back in.

In the late 1950s, Emily sent Eliot a note about her planned bequest to the university. Eliot wrote back, asking her to destroy all his letters to her. He was utterly explicit about this. *They're for you only,* he wrote — *no one else must see them. Emily,* he pleaded, *do this for me. Destroy them.*

He was silent, however, on the subject of the poems he had sent her. The fate of those drafts was left in Emily's hands. In this regard, it seems, he had always trusted her implicitly.

Emily Hale followed the dictates of her conscience. To my predecessor in the Mason Room she said simply, *I'm doing what must be done.* I can picture the scene: a handsome, conservatively dressed woman in her seventies arrives at the library one warm spring afternoon. She asks to speak with the archivist about several cardboard boxes of letters piled in the trunk of her car: a lifetime's treasure. By training, this woman is an actress. Her face shows nothing of her pain, only her determination.

As she hands over the boxes, she recalls the closing passage of "The Waste Land." *These,* she thinks, *my own fragments . . .*

AN ARCHIVIST SERVES the reader's desire. Yet what of the writer's — is it of no consequence?

After reading T. S. Eliot's letters to Emily Hale, I found myself reflecting long and hard on this question. My own training, of course, had taught me to privilege the reader's curiosity over all other considerations. Wasn't the writer's hunger for privacy always less compelling than the reader's appetite — voracious, insatiable — for more words? Eliot is already dead, I reminded myself. And by the time the bequest is opened, everyone who'd ever been close to him will also be dead. So whom could the letters possibly hurt?

It was the thought of my wife's journal, lying in the bottom drawer of my desk, that tipped the scales for me.

Judith had wanted her files saved, but I discarded them. She'd asked that her journal be destroyed; I kept it. Afraid and uncertain, I had sought her departure, insisting on our separation as necessary for her sake; and eventually, she was unable to return — to me, or to herself.

> *I that was near your heart was removed therefrom*
> *To lose beauty in terror*

On the evening Roberta entered the Mason Room, I realized it was time (late, perhaps, yet not too late) to cease living a life governed by fear; to make a different choice. Eliot's letters to Emily were not, I knew, his bequest. We were never meant to read them: only she was, and she relinquished them.

Poetry was what he left us. It was all that mattered. *The rest is not our business.*

Very late that night, I served Eliot's wish. It took several hours. I unlocked the cabinet and, after some hunting, located the letter in which Eliot had begged Emily to destroy the correspondence. I put this letter and all the cat sketches in an envelope and affixed it to the inside door of the cabinet.

Then I loaded every letter and card — everything but the poems, which I placed, safe in their protective wrappers of acid-free paper, on the top shelf of the cabinet — into two large plastic bags. I packed them tightly so I could carry them both at once. When I finished up, at around one in the morning, I hauled the bags to the trunk of my car; they were very heavy, but I managed in one go. After locking the archive's doors and setting the alarm, I drove home and parked my car in the little lot behind my building.

The lid of the large trash bin at the rear of the lot was completely closed, which signaled that it was already full. A different container would be required. From my apartment I retrieved a sturdy metal trash can, a small footstool, a book of matches, and some bottled water. Then I installed myself behind the bin.

No lights were on in any of the rear apartments, nor in the parking lot; the night sky was overcast and free of stars. I was alone. I sat on the footstool, put the trash can between my knees and the plastic bags at my side, lit a match, and began burning paper. I did this in very small batches — just a few letters at a time, to minimize visibility and to avoid fueling a fire I wouldn't be able to put out. Partway through, as I watched the flaring, ebbing flames, I remembered Judith's description, in her journal, of that dusk when she burned the Christmas tree at Hayden. She

323

too had been alone, in some remote, invisible corner of the property. The little tree, its branches dry, had gone up easily, and the flames' rhythms had reminded her of Thelonius Monk's music — how had she put it? — *those lovely staccato jabs at the notes* . . .

After the last letter and postcard were gone — sometime around four o'clock — I emptied the ashes into the bin and sprinkled water on them, to be safe. Then I went inside and drafted a memo to Edith Bearden, in which I suggested that the Mason Room could use some upgrading of its physical security. Our sequestered collections had lately been subjected to rather more wear and tear than was warranted. After the student internships were over, wouldn't it perhaps be a good idea to change the locks on all the cabinets containing sequestered materials, and to prohibit access to them — even by librarians — until they became available to the public? We had all gotten perhaps a little careless, probably because we were short on storage space. Even I, for example, had taken to storing open materials in the same cabinet as the Mencken papers. This was sheer sloppiness. Dust, light, and moisture were being introduced via repeated openings and closings of the cabinet doors.

My proposal was straightforward. The Mason Room could order some new cabinets for the public-domain material (there was, I reminded Edith, plenty of money in the budget for this), and we would then change the locks on the sequestered cabinets. The keys — and, for good measure, copies of all the bequests and their dates of release — would go to the university bursar for proper safekeeping in the administration's main vault.

I would be happy, I concluded, to spare Edith the implementation of this plan. There was no need for her to muck around with the literal nuts and bolts. The university locksmith could be retained; he'd do a fine job. Then all of us would rest easier —

including Eliot, Mencken, and the rest of the dead! — knowing that things were as they should be.

And so it was done.

When the great unveiling takes place, it'll naturally come as a shock to everyone to find that the Hale bequest consists not of letters but of poems. I am confident that no false accusations will be leveled at Edith Bearden or at my successor, whoever he or she may be. No one but Edith will have any reason to recall a graduate student named Roberta Spire, let alone accuse her of anything. And Roberta is in any case amply capable of defending herself, should the need arise, though I cannot imagine it will. Innocent individuals will not have to pay for what I did; eventually, it will become apparent that I'm the only one who could've done it.

Roberta, though, will figure it out before anyone else does. I can only hope she'll condone an act of destruction that will appall everybody else. And I believe (a little desperately, I'll admit: have I not gone out on a very long limb?) that she will. After all, she and I did more than talk about other people's poetry. We entrusted one another with our own discoveries: what might have been, and why it was not. When I'm no longer around for questioning, I hope she'll remember our mutual unburdening of sorrow and shame; and of love.

> *Teach us to care and not to care*
> *Teach us to sit still*

As for those unseen poems, sequestered in the Mason Room — they await their readers! And I suspect they'll change how people think about everything else Eliot wrote.

It is my large misfortune not to be able to count myself among those who will be the initial viewers, in the year 2020, of a half-dozen newly released poems composed by one of the twentieth century's foremost writers.

I'd place a great deal, however, on a bet that Roberta Spire will be first in line. Even knowing what she already knows. She'll want to see for herself. She's bold — a desirable quality in a reader. It's one of the things I liked about her. One of many.